TEA AT THE GRAND TAZI

Maia is leaving London to paint in the exotic setting of Morocco. Working as an assistant to a once-famous Historian, she is lured in by the freedom promised by her new surroundings. In the final days of summer, a sense of boredom and unease pervades the city. Maia is unwillingly drawn into the ways in which the clientele of the Grand Tazi pass their evenings. As the intense heat wears down her resistance, Maia succumbs to vice, and the freedom she once sought becomes eclipsed by shadowy dealings. Can she take back control of her life — and, more importantly, does she even want to?

Originally from Manchester, Alexandra Singer travelled the world before settling in the UK to study law, working for an international corporate law firm. In 2008, aged just 25, Alexandra was diagnosed with a near-fatal neurological illness, and spent three months in a coma. Remarkably, she is on the road to recovery and when not writing, teaches languages and literature. *Tea at the Grand Tazi* is Alexandra's debut novel.

You can discover more about the author at www.alexandrasinger.co.uk

ALEXANDRA SINGER

◆

TEA AT THE GRAND TAZI

Complete and Unabridged

ULVERSCROFT
Leicester

First published in Great Britain in 2012 by
Legend Press Ltd.
London

First Large Print Edition
published 2015
by arrangement with
Legend Press Ltd.
London

A catalogue record for this book is available
from the British Library.

ISBN 978–1–4448–2331–8

Published by
F. A. Thorpe (Publishing)
Anstey, Leicestershire

Set by Words & Graphics Ltd.
Anstey, Leicestershire
Printed and bound in Great Britain by
T. J. International Ltd., Padstow, Cornwall

This book is printed on acid-free paper

C46020393$

For my wonderful family; Theo, Diane, Michaela, Joshua and Poupée, and for all those who have helped me along the way.

1

Following completion of the act of love, many men had disappointed Maia by conducting their own battle in the war against Venus. Rigidly controlling their inner selves, she sensed that these men felt compelled to prove to her that they had stolen from her the very thing she had given so freely. They had taken from her something so precious, and spat it back at her, twisted and used. She resolved to free herself from their chains, from the fixed image they had created of her, and made her arrival in an ancient and eastern city. Here, Maia hoped to find a new light in which she might renew herself, after the desert had bleached her clean.

The driver was already busy creating his own image of her, locked in his own private battle against femininity. His eyes expertly grazed her body and succeeded in penetrating the long sleeves she wore in an attempt to shield herself from the prying eyes of men. Every so often, the driver managed to adjust the mirror so that he could catch her eye. He watched her and grinned widely, the yellowing teeth hanging askew from the corners of his mouth like the rotten keys of an old piano. Each time he succeeded in meeting her eyes, Maia smiled disdainfully and looked away, while he shifted in his seat and appeared to swell with pride. Maia watched the skin bulging at the back of his neck, and shuddered.

From the old, partly disused station at the desert's edge, they passed through long stretches of flat and barren land. This was a city at the crossroads, and that was the desert from which the slave caravans had once emerged. Towards the city walls, unfinished buildings decked in rags might have revealed signs of new development, if Maia had not been certain that such squalor had always existed there. In the early hours of the morning, red mountains rose up behind them.

'*Maktoub, maktoub!*' the driver shouted, pointing violently at a minaret hovering in the dawn. The mosque, thought Maia, yet her basic Arabic made her realise that he may not have been referring to the mosque. She nodded her head in agreement at whatever he might be telling her, but he simply laughed, bemused. It was a chuckle that came from deep within his throat, and she knew that he was mocking her. *Maktoub . . . maktoub?* She was sure she knew the meaning of the word, but for the moment it eluded her. Perhaps as a tourist he imagined she might be interested in the architecture of the mosque. But that was not her reason for being here. Something sparked in her mind and she grasped the meaning of the words: 'It is written'. Whatever could he mean? Maia glanced at the driver again only to find that he was still staring at her. She flicked her eyes down and gazed at the city ahead, wondering at the prospects where a thousand new lives might be offered up before her.

She opened her mouth to the night air and gulped down the taste of lost memory. The heat possessed the dry flavour of the desert and it rose upon her tongue. She savoured the sensation of unfolding into the early morning air; its deep, oppressive breath upon her face. The presence of the encroaching city, even the eyes of the driver roaming her body; she felt unshakable.

'For how long you stay here? You married? You alone?'

Here it seemed that a woman might have to account for every movement, flirtation, or flicker of the eye. A beautiful face, the shape of a leg; everything about a woman was deemed relevant for judgement. Only art permitted movement. Only in art did Maia feel that the vision of femininity might be subjective.

3

As the car approached the walls she saw that they would soon have to stop, and she recalled the Historian's instructions. 'Turn right here, please.'

The driver ignored her, but stared in the mirror almost as if he was challenging her to disagree.

'*A droit!*'

This time he obliged. The taxi now faced a labyrinth, far too narrow for cars to pass through. With immense relief, Maia felt here was a good place to stop. As she counted out her money he grinned at her, and the man's unbearable smugness forced Maia to swallow the urge to reach out and smack the teeth out of his grotesquely gaping mouth.

The taxi drove away and as the lights retreated, Maia was left standing alone trying to remember the rest of the Historian's directions. The tall buildings of the alley obstructed nearly every shred of faint light and Maia shuffled along in the gloom. For a moment she wondered which way to turn and realised she stood on the edge of the medina. As she edged along the side of another anonymous building with only dim light to show her the way, Maia saw that the Historian's house was approached by an alley leading off the main street. As she drew closer Maia was able to see that the house stood at the entrance to a second alleyway, even narrower than the first. Piles of rubbish lined the walls of the house and the foul stench was overpowering. Maia was taken aback; she had heard that the Historian was a particularly fastidious man, more accustomed to luxury than squalor. He was revered for his meticulous research, for which he had achieved numerous accolades, although he rarely bothered to collect them. It was said that a personal appearance or sighting of the Historian was a rare and much-revered event in academic circles. Maia wasn't sure what she had imagined his home to be like; but certainly not this. Then there came the sound of scurrying, something moving away. Turning, Maia saw a woman watching her from the doorway. She had not even heard the door open.

'How long have you been standing there?' she asked the woman, who was looking at her with a steady gaze from eyes which stared out disconcertingly from a crumpled face.

'Only long enough to watch you find your way.'

'Thank you for helping me,' Maia said. But the woman didn't seem to pick up on the sarcasm. Or maybe she did, and chose to ignore it.

'You are welcome.'

'Then I might ask why you didn't call out, if you were expecting me?' said Maia, hoping that her words would emit a tone of defiance.

The woman shrugged. 'The Historian has given you his instructions. Who am I to intervene?'

Maia looked at the woman, wondering at her odd character. Her skin was strangely mottled, with patches of dark, grey skin. The woman saw Maia looking at her and she turned away, her dark hair swaying with the sudden movement.

'So, you are Maia, the Historian's new assistant.'

'Of course.'

'My name is Ina.' The woman stepped towards Maia. 'You will come this way.' Her face was inscrutable, a perfect portrait of blankness, like the buildings surrounding them. As Maia stepped into the house, the door shut heavily behind her.

If the outside of the house had been all waste and refuse, peeling paint and shuttered buildings, inside the house was very different. Marble lined the interior as Maia was led through the outer hall, trailing her hand along the pleasant coolness of the wall. Ina looked at her silently, with a reproachful glance, and continued to lead Maia through the house into the courtyard. Maia took in the orange tree growing around the courtyard and the shallow pool lying in its centre, open to the sky.

Ina took her up two flights of stairs, and on touching the walls Maia found that everything was cold. Inside the house the air was fresh and sweet, no longer rotten and heavy from the stench of human waste, but gentle from the sweet smell of oranges. As Ina pushed open the door to Maia's new room, she smiled for the first time. Noiselessly she handed over the keys and shuffled away into the darkness. Maia turned to thank her, but Ina was already gone. As the door of the room closed behind her, Maia suddenly felt lonely, a sense of panic starting to prick.

The high ceilings of the room ought to have allowed for spaciousness and air, but it was strangely different from the rest of the house. Instead, the room felt stifling and oppressive, despite the exhausted fan silently stirring the warm air. The room was filled with dark wood and smelling as though it hadn't been used for many months. In the corner stood a small kitchen, the dust settling upon every available surface. Maia went to the windows, on which huge iron grills were fastened. She expected to see down into the alley below, but instead the room looked onto the courtyard and the tops of orange trees. It ought to have been pleasant, but the knowledge that she was unable to see outside the house only increased her sense of restlessness. Maia lay down on the bare bed in the centre of the room and slept.

Only a few hours later the cry from the mosque was sounding out the call to prayer. Already the day had begun. In the light of a new day, Maia now noticed a small spiral staircase in the corner of her room. Pulling herself from the bed, and drawn by curiosity, Maia went up the stairs anticipating only another dark and dusty room. Fumbling with the keys, she eventually found one that fit and the door swung open into the pale light of daybreak. Standing there on the rooftop, Maia watched the last of the night slip away as the sky came alive.

The thought of George entered Maia's mind, and she wondered if she had been right to leave him for this.

She lay back down on the bed, and enclosed within the four dark walls, thought of her time with George. As she drifted in and out of consciousness, Maia recalled being back with him and the abrupt ending of their four years of togetherness, love and hate in one short afternoon.

'This is the best thing we can do,' he insisted, confusing her further as he pressed her tenderly against his chest. 'This will all be over, all our arguments and lies.'

'My lies, not yours.' She looked up at him.

'Let's not argue again.'

They were his lies, reflected Maia calmly; the deceptions were only his. At the time, she thought that she was behaving calmly and accepting, watching him walk away. She thought that she could see a limpid truth in his eyes.

Maia was well aware of the weaknesses of which George was so fond, and she had long ceased to worry about them. They made no impact on her. It was his emotional infidelity which was her greatest concern. Things between them had changed subtly, then slightly more noticeably, until it was finally impossible to ignore the chasm between them. The rumours that surrounded George had suited her image. She preferred they discuss her in hushed and horrified tones than pity her.

It was rare that Maia felt threatened. So secure she had been in her own image, with her dark hair and pale skin. At an exhibition by a Milanese artist, an effusive gallery owner had informed her, 'You look like a fragile Russian doll.'

'Why? Do you suppose that you may unwrap me, only to continue to find smaller and smaller versions of me?'

'That would be delightful!' he said loudly, and then in lowered tones, 'I would certainly like to unwrap you.' As he leaned towards her, Maia smelt his stinking breath.

A quick exit left Maia ensconced inside a cubicle, finally able to enjoy a break from the incessant socialising which now consumed most of her evenings. She was, however, unfortunate to hear herself being discussed by Claudia, an acquaintance of George.

'She thinks she's an artist,' Claudia said, and the other girl, who earlier had been questioning Maia all about her own work, acquiesced all too easily. Claudia's face was a perfect heart shape, with delicate features, lips that flushed naturally and dark-rimmed eyes. Her long, ruffled straw-like hair was expensively coloured. When Maia had first encountered George and Claudia together, she had been amused by the way in which they maintained a strange distance for the rest of the evening. Yet on shaking one another's perfectly manicured hands, and looking into one another's kohl-swept eyes, Maia scrutinised the revelations of their body language. At first, Maia had tried hard to look past the initially beautiful face. The inane giggle which emitted from Claudia and her habit of subtly demeaning Maia's work

10

irritated her. Outside the cubicle the conversation before the mirrors continued:

'I saw an article on her in the paper yesterday; it said her work was ghastly. Obsessed with colour, to detract from her inability with technique, confusing, utterly self-obsessed.'

There came a hushed, mutual snigger, perhaps with hands draped elegantly over painted mouths as the heavy door shut quietly.

When Maia slipped out of the cubicle, and returned to the table, she began to look upon Claudia with a considerably less benevolent gaze. Later that night, as she examined herself in the mirror, Maia wondered if men really did see her as fragile. It was not how she viewed herself. With her child-like size and coquettish airs she was able to observe the gigantic egos with unhindered ease. The things she saw! These people held a great fascination for Maia, with their houses, their money and their marvellous, marvellous complexes. Life no longer held any aspirations for them. So tired they were, so jaded, that they searched in vain for new sensations with which to amuse themselves, in the interminable periods between this holiday and the next. They had everything and they had nothing.

On a separate occasion, Claudia had once explained to Maia her own private philosophy of the milieu of people in which she found herself.

'Being rich is wonderful, because it gives you the freedom to go anywhere and do anything.' Only in theory, thought Maia, was this true. In practice, once you leave the protective bubble, and enter the real world, you find it simply to be an expansion of the same familiar world, with the same familiar people as before. But Claudia would simply have laughed at this. She never had any trouble.

It was George who introduced Maia to this world, but by observing the people and their values, she became tainted by them. The eroding of her former self happened slowly and unconsciously.

Maia knew she had adopted the prejudices of George and her new circle. Maia's old friends now no longer recognised her. Sometimes, she found herself no longer acknowledging them.

Maia discovered that in her time with George, her life had become a comical miniaturisation. Her work had become as mediocre as her environment, and people began rejecting her paintings, when at one point they had been so in demand. Her preferred art school told her that they were short of places; the financial backing she had been promised by acquaintances dwindled, and then disappeared. Tarred with the brush of even temporary failure, her social circle diminished. This too was the time that while George was holding her close he was searching wildly for an escape route. Maia watched his boredom and she knew. For a while, the situation was indefinable, but then there came the sneers, which were as difficult to catch as butterflies, but there just the same. She began to suffer the sinking feeling of a woman who knows her time is up, and towards their parting, his deceit emitted a scent so pungent it lingered about him.

Maia no longer felt the excitement that she had experienced when she had first come to London. The city's allure quickly palled until it held no interest for her, and without interest, London was pointless. All she could see were the bundled-up people, trailing onto the buses, going home alone to their bedsits and shared flats, eking out an empty existence only to meet the extortionate rates that the city demanded of its inhabitants merely for the privilege of living in the capital. In the mornings she watched how the people shoved themselves out of bed onto the underground trains, day after day, for the sheer pleasure of the body odour emitted by their fellow passengers and the newspapers so rudely flicked in their faces.

When she received the Historian's unexpected offer, she accepted immediately.

But she was not due to arrive before the summer, and in the meantime she found that she was unable to relinquish George completely. Occasionally she encountered him at some place they had once frequented together, but he was elusive and refused to be engaged in conversation. Maia fled to Paris, where several weeks later George decided to follow her. She let him into her tiny apartment and he stayed for a week.

'I can't pretend I am not pleased to see you, but I don't understand why you are here.'

No answer came, just emotionless eyes blinking at her in the dark.

On their last afternoon together, she felt that she was making love with a demon; he bit her so hard he drew blood. He was unusually energetic, as he pushed her down onto the bed. Maia drew back from him in an instinctive act of self-preservation, but then in a surge of pure hatred threw herself towards him. The late June heat glared through the shuttered windows into the apartment, so that she imagined herself free from George's hold of her. She blinked away her tears of disappointment.

They parted on the corner just as dusk was falling. From an old, misplaced duty, he accompanied her to the Metro. Maia thought that she imagined the old companionship was still there; their arms brushed together, but he then became conscious of it and suddenly uncomfortable.

'Good luck with everything,' said George.

'Good luck? What do you mean? What an odd thing to say.'

He looked at her and he knew that this was not what she had been expecting. But with those words he conveniently and effortlessly closed the shutters on their relationship.

Now when she saw the distance between them, Maia could barely believe how they had passed the afternoon. Maia watched George retreat; the last reminder of a false idealism now on his way to his own form of normality, through the flashing lights and the advertisements for cheap and perverse sex. He never looked back, and eventually, Maia turned and walked away. At Pigalle, two hard-faced policemen were frisking an African at the entrance to the Metro. His carved wooden animals were scattered forlornly over the pavement. As she went underground, her Carte Orange irritated her by sticking in the barrier.

She hoped that she could forget about

15

George. Maia was astonished at how the years of involvement with one man might be destroyed in one amicable afternoon. Now, in the heat of a foreign city, his face came up again and again before her in the darkness. She was ashamed at how she had crumbled before him; now she wished that she might have been able to salvage at least some dignity. But there was no point. He had been successfully making a fool of her for years.

Now she wanted to be out of touch, and Morocco was the perfect place to go. For her it was a sort of revenge; a revenge for always being kept waiting, a symptom of an underlying, deeper dissatisfaction. Under the pretext of needing space to paint, Maia's plan was to become unobtainable.

In the bed, she wept, why she wept she didn't know. She sensed the light change in the room, telling her that outside it was moving seamlessly from morning to dusk. As she settled back down into the shadows, the day slipped on and the sun sank ever lower over the city. In between her bouts of unconsciousness and wakeful lucidity, her dreams were still rotten. In the courtyard below the maggots fell from the orange trees and dropped into the shallow pool as outside the people teemed into the city streets and came awake for the night.

2

The moment Maia stepped outside the house, the hassle in the narrow streets was tremendous. So overwhelming was the noise that she was barely able to think, barely able to understand where she was going. From the labyrinthine alleys the Arabs seethed into the streets, and above the wailing of the muezzin a relentless drumming could be heard which seemed to take her by the hips and shake her. Everywhere she turned, men were there blocking her way, hands grabbing and faces sneering at her. She composed herself; surely it was better to appear impassive and resolute, but somehow the men perceived her as ever more provocative. They intercepted her as she walked, and one man stuck out his foot before her and defiantly met her eyes as she stopped suddenly short before it. The crowd pulled her in one direction, pushed her in another, towards their shops, to a café, to meet their brothers, to help her find her way, caving in upon her as she desperately pushed her way through.

'Gazelle, gazelle, come with me! I am Berber, real Berber!'

The young man who was shouting at her stepped out from his position at the entrance to a store, its windows so heaped with spices that it was impossible to see inside. As she continued to force her way up the street his mocking shouts followed her for a few paces, and then he seemed to give up. She allowed herself to look back and saw him give his waiting friends a pathetic little shrug. Maia moved on quickly, past the men decaying in the smoke of their hazy enclaves, and the dirt that seemed to be everywhere. The heat rose from the earth and crackled along the pavements as the people and the buildings surrounding her emerged as if through a fog, moving towards her like phantoms. Her legs shook and her head spun. Maia sat down upon a low step in an attempt to regain some control. A few moments later, she felt calmer and rose up to meet the narrow streets. Now she walked at random through the twisting maze, the heavy aroma of spices, of sumac and cinnamon drifting from the stalls. As she walked, her mind continued to wander and she sank back down so deep into the heat that the city was warped once more before her eyes. Men were hawking ill-formed packages in the streets as shrill women beckoned and children ran wildly through the crowd. A young woman was sitting on the ground, scrabbling at dust, as a wizened man crawled on by. Swathed only from the waist down in his filthy rags, his skin missing and one leg curling beneath him, no-one in the crowd noticed him in his shame. Donkeys brushed past Maia, burdened down with their packages and Berber women sat cross-legged upon woven, multi-coloured rugs.

Car horns blared and strangers shouted to one another, in friendship and in hate, in old enemies and new acquaintances. Men were indolently standing outside their shops to talk; selling handcrafted items, intricately decorated bags, huge wrought iron lamps and furniture, Arabesque art, complexly patterned wall hangings, the variety of colour throughout the woven material. In large baskets, vegetables were being sold next to foreign electronics and stolen goods. Maia stumbled upon a courtyard, lit by a bright beam of sunlight, and in a moment the air filled with the scent of sweet perfume. A heavy door opened, offering a glimpse of the house within, before slamming shut behind the entering visitor. As she walked on and entered the pulsating heart of the city, the streets narrowed and wound more tightly around one another.

Through the climbing alleyways she walked in perpetual night, passing dank squares where she found only dead ends. Behind these commercial streets there lay small, private courtyards where water fountains coursed into small pools, and cool silences pervaded. But now Maia retreated through an uninterrupted darkness amongst beggars who stretched out to her their gnarled hands, moaning in the dirt as they eked out their lives. A hunched man sat on the ground, almost prostrated, and Maia shuddered at his right eye, protruding lazily from its socket. The city mirrored the discarded geography of her mind, and it unfolded itself to her like a story without structure, a sinister repetitive tale with neither beginning nor end.

Maia began to suspect she was being followed, but when she turned to look, no-one was there. She passed corners where no light penetrated, and she feared to wonder what was lying there in the gloom. Only an occasional ruin allowed light and space and the odd glimpse of foliage. She could not understand where she might be, not expecting such difficulty in understanding the city's layout. Slums replicated themselves in every area. Hearing voices behind her, Maia turned suddenly on the small Arab boys who were following her so incessantly. She approached them and their small faces looked up at her with hopeful eyes. She smiled at them. 'Do you know the Grand Tazi Hotel?'

The boys began to chatter unintelligibly. She stood there, in the centre of the street, uneasy and stiff. The smallest child held out his hand to her. Maia went to take it, but she felt another hand brush the side of her leg. She whirled round and met the eyes of another boy.

'I'm too fast for you!' Excitedly they began to chatter to one another again in Arabic. She realised that even if she were able to understand them, they would undoubtedly be giving her the wrong directions. When she looked at them again, they cackled hysterically and ran away. She continued walking, feeling hopeless, and as the alleyways sloped down towards the woodworking area, she stopped and watched men carving furniture.

High-pitched voices were trailing her and now the boys were once again behind her. They knew they could get money from foreigners by their sheer persistence. A cloying scent streamed into Maia's nostrils; the fetid stench of the unwashed inhabitants of this part of the city, of the spices and the people crammed in so closely together. Heaped before shops lay raw meat, and spices spilling over in the sacks. The scent of turmeric, cinnamon, cumin coming together in one single, heady fragrance. By the spices

21

lay cartons of oranges and lemons, the dismembered parts of slaughtered animals accompanied by swarms of enormous black flies, as grossly enthusiastic as the gate-crashers at a wedding feast.

As always there was the dust and the dirt, as inescapable as the faces which stared at her so curiously, even the hordes of covered women, who threw at her their strange, knowing looks. Some women jeered at her; she was uncovered and white. A woman came out of nowhere and gleefully thrust a tortoise into Maia's face, forcing her to rush away, stumbling. A woman beside Maia hissed and she swung around to meet her eyes. For a single moment they both stood entirely still, locked in an intensely pleasurable moment of hatred. Then the world intruded as the crowd surged along and the catcalls started up once more, the men blowing kisses and shouting to one another in a guttural language, which followed her through the streets.

Maia sensed only a sort of interested hostility that might take little to burst into open aggression. At a junction she almost walked directly into the head of a camel which had been stuck upright on the edge of a stick, a sickly sneer on its face. In horror she jumped back from the eyes looking at her. In the deep eye sockets, tiny maggots were wriggling frantically. At the entrance to the shop beside the camel's head a small, bent man watched her. The meager skin that covered his bones was dark and translucent, and he smiled at her sardonically. She began to wonder why she had come to this medieval place. A heavy wave of nausea gripped her and she shuddered away into the crowd.

One of the small boys was back. His huge grey eyes watched Maia, his tiny hand gripped at her sleeve. '*Bisous, mademoiselle, bisous!*' He was running alongside her. He could not, she thought, have been more than eight years old. Then she felt another hand on her, pinching her from behind, and then yet another child stood beside her. Suddenly they darted off laughing to sit with more boys who were perched upon rusting bicycles. The men in the café opposite were consumed with laughter at the scene.

'Let them laugh at me,' Maia muttered to herself as she walked along. Down here, marginalised by their grinding poverty, all that the boys could do was to scrape by in competition with the other urchins, forcing an acquaintance with whoever they found susceptible.

She found herself disturbed by yet another man with jagged, filthy teeth tinged the colour of strong tea. He reached out and clutched her arm tightly. He was disturbingly cheerful. 'I am student. You come for tea with myself and friend!'

He waved to a boy with greased black hair, so wet it shone, who waved back at them enthusiastically from the rooftop of a café. In huge black lettering, its name announced, 'Café Nadoor.' From a distance, although the man on the roof was attractive, Maia could sense that there was something repulsive about him. Their enthusiasm appalled her and she wrenched her arm away from the man.

'I am with a friend!'

'I see no-one.' He looked about him in mock confusion. He jumped backwards, and as she was trying to rush away, he grabbed hold of her again. 'Oh, there you are! What is your name? Come with me!'

He had her about the waist and was attempting to pull her closer still. Maia was engorged with fury, and her panic made her strong. Successfully she pushed him away.

'*Va t'en!*' she shouted at him. 'Go away!'

He followed her for a few moments but she managed to lose him when she entered another alley. Here the streets began to narrow even further, the houses were no longer so tall and narrow, and the streets were lined with overflowing bougainvillea and

24

obscenely young prostitutes. The girls gazed surreptitiously at her, nonchalantly leaning against the foliage and creeping along by the side of the walls.

As she walked on searching for the Grand Tazi hotel, the crowd eventually fell away and she found herself standing on the edge of a small square. It was twilight and the light danced upon the buildings of ochre and sandstone playing upon the faces of the men milling there as if they too had been carved in stone, but by a sculptor who had left them unfinished.

She came across men bowing upon the ground in their eternal rendition of sub-servience. Maia pitied them. She despised religion. To her, it was merely a social construction, the need of mankind to constantly prostrate himself before a higher being and to relinquish all individual control. She considered that religion's sole benefit was to offer people the opportunity to eradicate all personal responsibility. Too often, she noted how many people so adored being told what to do. Maia preferred freedom without encumbrances, but there were always people who wanted to tie her in. She must have stood for a while in a daze, for as she looked again, it seemed as if almost in the same moment the lowering sun was forming long shadows over the square, and acrobats, young men made up to look like women, their already strong features now grossly exaggerated, began to jump. Recalling the Historian's instructions, she crossed the square and made for the walls, keeping her eyes to the ground, hoping not to attract any further unwelcome attention and still despising herself for her feigned subservience.

On the very edge of the old part of the city, as Maia followed the twisting street to its conclusion, she found the hotel. Standing just outside the walls, large lettering in a faded bronze announced the hotel's name: Grand Tazi. The building appeared neglected, like a disused film set.

Next to the hotel was a small clothing stall where the extras thronged, a swarm of women swooning over the dingy fabric. As Maia stepped over the threshold into the hotel, she saw how simple it was to pass from utter poverty to comfort. Inside the hotel the foyer was arranged with deceptive precision, betrayed only by a perspiring queue of tourists who stood waiting for the only receptionist on the desk to allocate them their rooms. The floor was laid with the sort of marble coating which might have once lent the place a lavish air, but now it was covered in a thin film of filth, its decades of glory long

26

since past. In the stifling heat of the foyer the ambushed male receptionist was smiling nervously as he desperately searched through his book for the reservations list. In the background the telephone rang shrilly, but the receptionist ignored its incessant nagging; in any case, nobody else was there to answer it.

Maia watched him as he tried to placate the tourists, who appeared to be Nordic. They attempted to speak to him in English, but it seemed that other than Arabic he spoke only French, so all that he was able to say in reply was 'Sorry, sorry,' in English, which he kept repeating in a strange sort of rolling way. He did not look at all sorry, and in fact he continued to mutter angrily to himself even as he stood being assaulted by the torrent of demands. Indeed, the size of his apologetic grin increased as the confusion over the reservations and names mounted.

Maia busied herself in studying the hotel's faded interior. The ceiling was high and airy, decorated by a mosaic of minuscule, emerald tiles, but the desks and pieces of furniture which lay scattered around the foyer had all seen better days. The place did hold a certain louche charm. In one far corner of the room, a sign which enthusiastically advertised, 'Tourists: A Night of Psychic Phenomena!'

had fallen on its side, while across the way, a crudely drawn arrow pointed up the stairs next to a handwritten sign which proclaimed itself, 'Restaurant Gastromonique'.

As the group of tourists inched forward and then finally dispersed, Maia found herself at the front of the queue, but by that time the receptionist had fled. She rang the old-fashioned bell on the desk and waited. Eventually he reappeared, flustered.

'Hello,' she said, clawing on her knowledge of French.

'I am sorry, I in break now,' he said with unflinching finality.

'I thought you were the receptionist. Or is that your brother?' smiled Maia. She was brittle, speaking with a confidence she did not feel.

'No. I do all. Same, same. Sorry.'

'You are not really sorry at all, are you?'

He grinned at her and she saw how deeply his face was pitted with the scars of a greasy-skinned youth. He stretched out his clammy hand to her.

'I am Tariq,' he said, with great self-importance, and her hand slipped from his. 'Now I in break.'

'Wait — I don't need a room. I'm here to meet somebody.'

'Who are you?' Tariq's eyes narrowed.

'My name is Maia. I'm staying at Mihai Farcu's house.' She wondered at his questioning. Did everyone receive this treatment? It was an unusual vetting from an inept receptionist. Tariq was visibily delighted.

'Ah, the Historian. Welcome, welcome to the Grand Tazi, my friend! You are welcome guest.' Tariq came out from behind the desk to grasp her hand again. *'Par ici, mademoiselle.'* He ran his eyes over her. 'You go there.' He pointed to a spiraling iron staircase and she followed it up until she arrived at the restaurant on the rooftop terrace, over which a blue and white striped canopy was fluttering tawdrily in the early evening breeze.

The place was busy, but only with other Europeans and Americans who were well rehearsed in making this transition to comfort. Maia breathed out a sigh of relief at having entered a place where women left their hair uncovered and men did not look at her as if she were a curious object placed down in front of them. Her eyes were drawn across the room where she saw who she presumed to be the Historian. He was flaunting a plum silk scarf which was wound twice around his neck and then flung nonchalantly over the back of his chair where he had left it to trail pitifully on the floor.

He was attempting to get some point across

to the very large man who was sitting opposite him, listening intently. On first sight, together the men formed a compelling contrast. The first, elegantly tall and slender, his face looking as if it had been deliberately chiseled, and the second, reclining heavily and almost overflowing from his low seat. There she stood, poised on the verge of the personal fiefdom that the Historian had carved out for himself in his years of self-imposed exile. He was smoking a pipe, and the only disparity between the Historian in the flesh and the publicity photograph on the jacket of his first book was that he now appeared a little more aged. The book had been last year's success in historical academia; a relentless history of the Almoravids in which he had left no stone unturned. After a long banishment, there had been a triumphant return. But still he had not returned to the universities of the West, and there was a pervading silence as to the reason. At the pinnacle of the enthusiasm generated by his work, he even made it onto the cover of a respected Parisian broadsheet. After an extended period where he had been excluded by the small academic community, he had then been afforded a long-denied recognition and respect. All this, thought Maia, must have conspired to make him the envy of his intellectual peers.

She lingered a few moments longer, still reluctant to approach him. The job offer was satisfactory; a recommendation was put forward to the Historian by a former, rather lecherous university Professor she had encountered browsing in a London bookshop. Maia had chattered on inanely about her art and financial struggles, until suddenly he tired of her. But before he left, he told her of an old Romanian friend's opening for an assistant.

'Well, not a friend, exactly,' he had said, shifting from one foot to another. 'He was a colleague. It isn't permanent, you see. You'll be back soon enough.' He grinned, widely.

'How long will I be working for him?'

'About four months? You'll have to agree all that with him. Free place to stay though. Lots of room for painting. Fabulous people. You can do whatever you like. Plus — you'd be doing me a huge favour, get me out of a bit of a situation. He's a Romanian, but doesn't have many friends left in Europe. I said I'd find someone for him.'

His tone was pleading. Maia received the distinct impression that he was begging her to release him from this burden. Her curiosity was piqued; from all accounts this Historian was academically renowned, but now he was alone in a foreign country, imposing on his old colleagues to send him an assistant. It was all fabulously odd, and Maia decided to take the job offer at once.

'Don't worry,' she said softly. 'You've sold me.' The offer had come just at the right time.

'Wonderful! Very hot. You'll come back all tanned,' he leered, and placed his plump hand firmly upon her shoulder.

She agreed to go for a coffee with him, just to take the Historian's details, but fortunately she had been saved by the Professor's sudden recollection of an appointment at the university, and she was left to contemplate her new obligation. She had nothing to leave behind, and so suffered no doubts.

Now in the hotel bar, the belly of the Historian's companion was bulging over the arm of his chair. They were so closely engrossed in conversation only in kissing could their heads be any closer. The man's voice boomed, and his small hands flailed in the air as he made rapid, excitable gestures. He seemed to fill the space all around the Historian's table with his very presence, and Maia was unsure if she ought to disturb them. The Historian turned round, and seeing her standing there, beckoned her over.

'Hello, Maia,' said the Historian's companion, as he gestured to the empty chair next to him. 'We saw you loitering there!'

'Loitering?' asked Maia.

'Yes, loitering. Like a scared fawn! We suspected you were the new assistant,' he said, moving his arms around expansively.

'You are just on time.'

'For what?' asked Maia.

'For more mint tea, of course!'

As if on cue, a waiter brought a pot of mint tea, which he poured into three small, clear glasses.

'*Salut!*' he almost shouted at her, holding up his glass.

'This is mint tea?' asked Maia.

'Mint tea, of course! I drink it with everything. This even has a tiny drop of vodka in it. You don't mind, do you? Of course you don't! I drink it with everything. Everything!' He took a huge gulp, and his throat moved as he swallowed. 'Washes it all down!' He leaned conspiratorially towards her so that she assumed he was about to tell her something important. He lowered his voice. 'The Grand Tazi serves the best mint tea. The best. The very best! No-one else makes tea like it.'

'I see,' said Maia, not really seeing at all. Rather disconcerted by the man, she asked, 'To what are we toasting?' She held up her glass, and the Historian silently held up his own glass.

'To you, and of course to Mihai for taking

on a new assistant. The last one . . . ' He made a snorting sound. The Historian looked on at him with a bemused silence. 'Well, the last one . . . oh, don't be perturbed,' he said, noticing Maia's startled expression. 'It was insignificant . . . I do hear she was intolerable to work with. Not very compliant.'

'Did you meet her?' Maia wondered what he meant. Compliant was a strange word to choose.

'Of course! Well, only briefly.' He slapped the Historian's thigh with undisguised affection. Maia looked at the man. He seemed pleasant enough, but upon closer inspection, she thought that his eyes revealed something harsh.

Maia drank, and shuddered at the drink's strength. 'I'm glad you told me about the vodka.'

'Ha ha! I thought you would appreciate it!' he said, laughing heartily. Maia stared, at him, confused.

'This girl you have here, she has good sense of humour, no? Dry. I like it, I like it.'

'Hello Maia, please meet Mahmoud,' said the Historian, finally opening his mouth to speak. The languidness of his manner suggested that by speaking he was bestowing an honour upon them. 'He owns the Grand Tazi.'

He gestured extravagantly with his hands as if to indicate a vast expanse, but his movements were slow. Maia had no idea how old the Historian was, but the age spots littered his white hands, with fingers abnormally long and graceful. As Maia looked around, and reading the sceptical expression upon her face, the Historian softly admonished her, 'There is much you have not seen. Moroccans are very discrete,' he said quietly, but his face was wreathed in smiles. He was cordial enough, thought Maia, but a reflective man. His friend was openly welcoming; she assumed that this reticence was the Historian's nature.

'Welcome, my friend, many welcomes,' bawled Mahmoud, vigorously shaking her small hand. Maia felt that her first impression of him had been correct. The man was jovial enough on the surface, but something about the way in which the flesh folded over his small black eyes repelled her.

The Historian gazed at her reflectively. His eyes were a pale green, and they made her afraid to look into them for too long. His pupils were small, like two black dots keeping themselves afloat in the centre of a cold sea.

'Call me Mihai,' said the Historian, and stretched out his hand, his mouth forming a smile that did not match his eyes. 'I really am so pleased to finally meet you.' Maia returned

35

his smile, but she felt that calling him by his first name would be too familiar. He was detached, well known for his tendency to reclusiveness, and she sensed that he liked to keep others at a distance. She felt the detachment between them undefined, yet there all the same. In contrast to the bulbous Mahmoud, the Historian was tall and aged, still remarkably handsome, with clear white skin and grey eyebrows that formed a unifying frown across his forehead.

'I must leave you now. I have that appointment.' Mahmoud winked extravagantly at Maia, making her wince.

'We have known one another for years. He has a big personality,' the Historian remarked. It was more of a statement than a judgment. Maia nodded in agreement, wondering what sort of friendship this strange pair might share.

For a few moments they sat together in silence. When he finally spoke, the Historian's voice was soft and low, and peculiarly sad, as if radiating despair.

'It's been a very long time since I saw him,' said the Historian.

'You mean — '

'Yes,' he said abruptly. He was talking about the academic who had recommended the Historian. He tilted his head contemptuously. 'Feels guilty, does he?'

Maia wondered what the academic had to feel guilty about. 'He was very helpful.'

'Yes,' said the Historian. 'I am surprised he was so helpful. They don't think so highly of me in London.'

'Oh no, I believe you are very respected.'

'Oh yes, respected academically, perhaps, but not liked. They'll never like me again. Not enough to have me back.'

'I see,' Maia said, not knowing what she could say. 'I didn't know.'

'No, of course you didn't know. A young girl like you. Why would you know? Why would you know anything at all?' and he began to mumble something under his breath. As she watched his mouth form the words, she understood that he was swearing in French with a coarseness that surprised her, making obscene, bizarre accusations against his former colleagues. Maia began to understand why the Historian had been so ostracised, why he had never returned to London. He had a temperament that made others feel uncomfortable.

'Don't worry,' he said. 'I am not cracked in the head. Not yet, anyway. Memories of the past, they make me angry. Do you know what it is like to be pushed out of your position?'

'No.'

'Of course not. So tell me, how is that

lecherous little Napoleon? What I could tell you about him. Flourishing, I suppose?'

'I don't know,' said Maia, which was the truth.

'So, you have had time to explore?' he asked.

'Not so much. I didn't set my alarm to wake today. After all the travelling I've done in the past few weeks.'

'Of course, I know just how it is,' said the Historian, in a manner that suggested he had little sympathy with her.

Maia had felt justified in having slept away most of the day. All the travel and the emotional exhaustion had caught up with her. The endurance of the fact that four years had gone up in smoke and humiliation. Maia decided that if she wanted to sleep all day, she would.

'I only eventually woke because of the call to prayer.'

'Have you eaten nothing?'

'Not much.'

He called over the waiter and said something unintelligible in a throaty, gurgling accent.

Maia was taken aback. 'You speak Arabic?' He had lived here long enough, but she had not expected such fluency.

'I've been studying for years.'

38

Maia's late breakfast arrived: rolls of bread with butter and jam, sweet black coffee and squeezed orange juice with bottled water. Maia devoured it as the sun continued to set, turning the city's sandstone a deeper shade of pink.

At the next table along, a large woman was laughing, her head thrown far back. She must have been in her early fifties at least, and her voice made a low, rasping sound. Her head was uncovered, her skin pitted and her hands rough, and she was talking to her much younger male companion with all the innocent flirtatiousness of a school girl. But when she laughed, she laughed loudly, with the voice of a savage. Maia was enthralled by the woman's plumpness, her great femininity.

The Historian watched Maia so distracted, looking at the woman. 'You mustn't be so surprised, Maia. This is one of the very last decadent outposts of Europe. Africa begins here!'

'I'm afraid you haven't been to Europe recently then.'

'Ah, a quiet humour. My favourite type. But Mahmoud maintains that it is always the quiet ones one must watch.' He looked at her anew, and she shivered.

'Watch? What do you mean?'

The Historian ignored her question and

already he was gathering his thoughts. 'A few years ago, there were only a handful of foreigners living within the city walls. But now we are everywhere! This is a historic walled city, a veneer of Western influence contrasting ever more starkly with its Islamic core.'

'You sound just like a guidebook.'

'Ah ha! Already you have managed to catch me out. Clever girl. I did write a guidebook to the country. That was several decades ago.' He sounded nostalgic. 'It is true, what I am saying. When I first arrived here, there was only a small colony of expatriates, not so many of us. It was a place to hide, not the place to see and be seen, as it has become now. It has changed.'

'Not for the better, I take it?'

'No, certainly not,' said the Historian glumly. 'Rather significantly, I would say, for the worse.' He looked more closely at the woman across the room. 'That woman you are watching. She is very interesting to you, isn't she? She seems completely unaware of how she appears to others. But the persona she portrays is forced. She is not at all natural. You will soon learn about Moroccan ways.'

Together they continued watching her.

'Tell me, how are you getting on with your

painting? Have you managed to find that inspiration you were looking for?' asked the Historian.

'To be honest, I haven't done any painting since I arrived here,' she confessed. 'I have been moving around a lot. Tangiers, Essaouira. There were . . . complications.' Maia stopped and listened to herself speak for a moment, and she despised the tone of self-justification in her own voice.

But the Historian did not look surprised at all.

'You will find much more to interest you here. There will be distractions, of course. This is a very distracting city. But you will have all the time and space you need to observe and paint, and you will of course carry out any tasks I require, such as research.'

'What tasks do you require exactly?'

'In the morning, you will organise the library, perform research and carry out all my correspondence, of which there is a great deal, and which I find extraordinarily time-consuming. A lot of silly people to deal with. It is a little tedious, but it has to be done. They, after all, control the purse strings. I really do not know why so many people are interested in me and my life. Surely they should care only about my work! But always, you see, they want to know about me. It is unbearable, intrusive. These people, I detest them! The more I hide from them, the more they run after me. I have had photographers trying to capture me, even an intruder once, in the riad.'

'An intruder?'

'Yes, exactly. Do not worry. There will be no more. Now.'

'Is photography not allowed here, Professor?'

'Call me Mihai. No, no photography at the Grand Tazi. That is exactly what I said. You must listen to me carefully. I am an old man. I do not care to repeat everything I say.'

'You mean to tell me that absolutely no photography at all is ever permitted within the city walls?'

'And on the walls where the storks line their nests . . . ' He began to sing. His voice was surprisingly sweet. Suddenly he grabbed her hand so tightly that it was almost painful. She tried to pull it away. 'You must never harm a stork, Maia.' He looked at her intensely and she tried to break his gaze.

'Why would I ever wish to harm a stork, or any animal for that matter?'

'People here have ways of making you do things. To be malicious. For magic.'

'Surely you don't believe in such things, a man like you?' She looked at him, but couldn't tell if he was being serious. His eyes penetrated her. She had the strange sense that he was putting on a sort of private show for her, a character act. She decided to play along. She too would take a role, if life really was the stuff of reinvention.

'There are many things here that cannot be explained,' he continued, 'but I will tell you that some people here believe that storks are transformed humans, and you will receive a three-month prison sentence merely for disturbing one.' His eyes flicked over her. 'I can assure you that a girl like you would not last long in there. In any case, such a scandal would reflect badly on me.'

As Maia inspected him more closely, she now looked at him with a new admiration and could only wonder at his past. She began to suspect that the Historian enjoyed playing upon his advanced age; how it suited him to play the demented old man. From nowhere the image came to her of the Shakespearean fool, but the Historian was no servant. He was sharp, that much was certain. As she was talking to him, she sensed the Historian's insincerity, that for some unknown reason he was attempting to dupe her into believing he was confused. But she was able to see through him, and his mind was still just as sharp as it always had been. She watched him appraising her critically with his small reptile eyes, the enlarged pupils firmly fixed on her. She did not believe him about being forbidden to photograph. What he really meant was that he did not wish her to record any images of him.

'What is that song you were just singing?'

'Oh yes, that is just a song we used to play on the piano. Several years ago. At the bar!'

'Which bar?'

'You know! Mahmoud's bar. The downstairs bar at the Grand Tazi. It used to be much more exciting than it is now. I am afraid that Mahmoud has let standards fall. He seems to let just anyone in these days. Once upon a time oh yes, once . . .'

Maia looked at him, long and hard, and she wondered what sort of act the Historian was trying to put on for her, that of a cantankerous old man whose mind might occasionally wander. She did not know of any bar here. But she knew that the Historian was in complete possession of all his faculties. If he imagined that she could be taken in by his act, he was wrong.

'So I cannot take photographs at all? But it is essential to my work.'

'Your work here, I can assure you, is to work for me.'

'But not all the time. I am a painter; that

44

was our agreement.' She had feared that this may happen.

He looked at her disparagingly. 'You are receiving a good deal here. Try not to forget it.'

'As you wish,' said Maia. She allowed him a gesture of submission.

He relented, and smiled gently. 'If you insist you may photograph what you wish. But please be discrete as you go about it. As you may imagine, it is not pleasant for the locals when foreigners follow them going about their business, incessantly click click clicking without even bothering to ask for their permission. Remember, you may never photograph here, at the Grand Tazi.'

'Whyever not?'

'Because, my dear, this is a refuge, a paradise. The last remnant of exclusivity. It must be preserved.'

'A paradise? It is a restaurant. A lovely restaurant, but nevertheless, a restaurant. I'm afraid it doesn't resemble paradise to me.'

The Historian's condescending manner made her both desire his approval and urge her to question him.

The Historian sighed. 'So young, so naive, so very ignorant. For those who continue to live here, it is indeed a paradise of sorts. It is a refuge for people who require one. You will have to realise that you must not be so direct here. The Grand Tazi has become my second home, and Mahmoud is a great friend of mine. He has always been loyal to me. I will not have him insulted.'

'I wasn't insulting him.'

The Historian held up his hand in a gesture of finality.

'I'm very sorry,' said Maia, although she was not at all sorry, but only even more intrigued.

'In the afternoons and evenings you will have your own time, free to paint, sleep, whatever you wish. Yes, I do not spend a great deal of time here. I have often to be away. But, it is an excellent arrangement, don't you agree?'

Maia nodded. She was hardly in a position to complain, the arrangement was perfect. But now that she had met him, she wondered what lay behind his generosity. What might he expect, or even demand, in return? The Historian struck her as a little strange, but she dismissed it as his eccentricity. She did not have to pay rent, the job itself was not arduous, and it would be complete freedom from all those London acquaintances who had such high, exhausting expectations of her. It could, as it had been for the Historian, be a refuge for her. After all, her acquaintances believed that she was still travelling in North Africa.

'Who else lives in the house? I have already met Ina. She is not very talkative.'

'She has had a difficult life. There is only us. And my brother, when he is at home. Tell me,' said the Historian, in an attempt to feign interest, 'why do you like painting so much?'

'Because sometimes I like to paint the red city blue, and the sea yellow. Simply because.' She knew this was not an answer that the Historian would accept. He required an analytical reply to everything.

'You like to observe.'

'That is why I am here. When I paint, I observe. I see empty space and light. For most people, empty space is just that, empty.'

'But you, I suppose, do not see that. You are special.'

'Of course not!' she snapped a little too hastily. Maia was unsure if his lips were curving at the sides. He wanted to elicit some reaction from her. She tried to explain. 'Here, the blue sea is black at night, turquoise at midday. Painting makes one observe everything carefully. All the colours are intensified. Life can be intensified. You can observe the land as it stretches, curved onto the horizon. Look at the bright colours, the whitewashed houses. I like Islamic art, the intricate patterns. Look at the urban landscape or a remote village. Sometimes it dominates the

47

people, makes them invisible. Especially the women. They are the ones I want to paint.'

'Islam does not permit representation of the human form.'

'And I, Professor, am not a Muslim.'

'Even so, perhaps you will find it difficult to find a woman who is willing to sit for you. What makes you think that you will succeed, where so many have failed?'

She bridled at his doubt, trying to detect bemusement in his voice but finding none. She wondered why he was so hostile to her desire to paint women. 'Have you become a Muslim, Professor?'

'Certainly not. It has appealed, but it conflicts with certain aspects of my life. But could it be, do you suppose, that there is a profusion of messages in the West? Messages that diminish the value of everything and erode them deliberately? Here they understand that to represent a woman would be to devalue her. There is a lack of dignity and privacy in the West. That is why I left England — that lack.'

Without realising it, this was the moment Maia made an instinctive and important decision. She had found that life could often throw up some interesting opportunities, if one was able to remain sufficiently open to them. In that moment, Maia resolved not to block anyone or anything out. She would remain utterly open to all people, all experiences. She imagined herself as a sort of creative sieve, with the world passing through. The thought pleased her. In her imagination she saw vivid colours intermingling; azo yellow, earth green, purples and violets, crimson, ochre, and cadmium red.

The Historian was watching her as she looked around, taking in the scene around her. 'You do have a passion for it. I see that.'

'Art affects us just as light does. I found no light in London. I am interested in the light and air, the colours, and women, in particular the women in a closed society.'

'Just like Matisse. How very original you are.'

Maia discerned boredom, and for a moment she felt resentful. But the feeling passed quickly. She was unable to understand it, but there was something about the Historian that made her want to impress him.

'Matisse managed to change how we see the female figure in art. From depicting women as primitive, sexual beings in a supposedly enlightened society, he saw them first as individual characters, full of personality. You must admit, that given the attitude to non-western cultures at the time, that could be considered quite exceptional.'

'I have never liked Matisse. And I admit nothing. But what sort of women are you really interested in painting? Matisse had contact only with prostitutes. I think that even now you may encounter similar problems. Access is not so easy.'

'I thought as a woman, it may be easier.'

'On the contrary, it will be harder.'

'Then I will photograph them first, if I must. It seems that here even a covered woman may not walk down the street without being hassled. I want to paint all women. Veiled women, dark women, white women, upper-class women, poor women, beautiful women, ugly women. Particularly ugly women. The character in their faces is fascinating. Beautiful women can be so symmetrical, and . . . '

'Boring?'

'Exactly,' said Maia, distinctly. She would not be cowed by this man. She might quaver on many subjects, but never on this. 'The modest woman and the whore do interest me, I admit. That dichotomy never disappears. I think that must be very confusing for men.'

'And, you, Maia, are you the Madonna, or the whore?' A sleaziness lay behind his gentlemanly manners, and she was taken aback by his capacity for vulgarity. 'Yes, I have seen your work. But why this obsession with women? You do not prefer them?' He asked her this with a barely indiscernible smile, the lip slightly curled. Maia had no doubt which sex it was which he preferred.

'I really do not. But I do often think that if I could somehow change, it might make my life easier,' she said, laughing.

The Historian scowled.

'Believe me, Maia, it does not.'

'I don't know why I like to paint women so much. But it is even more intriguing to explore here, where women try to be invisible, and the men stare so much. Sometimes, it seems as if men here hate us.'

'Ah, a feminist is what you are. I sensed it in you immediately. Now I warn you, don't try to fight things here. You will never succeed. And I have friends here. I really would not appreciate attention to be drawn to myself by a troublesome assistant. Do you not consider that by depicting women so obsessively in your paintings, you will actually be submitting them even further to the gluttonous eyes of men that so worry you?'

'I have considered that. But the pictures are not only for men. It is a fact that women are enthralled by other women. We cannot deny it. We compare ourselves, all the time. And perhaps if men see women as people, living, doing things, not sitting for the pleasure of men, they will not be so scared of us.'

'Ha! You imagine that men are scared of you?'

'Yes. I can't understand any other reason for their behaviour.'

'It is not simply the religion, you know. It is complicated.'

'Do you find it difficult here?'

He peered at her. 'How do you mean?'

'I meant as a Jew?'

'Yes. I do not practice, of course. But the history is fascinating.' Then he slapped his thigh and raised his voice, as he peered down at her in an attempt at self-parody. 'A Jew? Of course I am! A Jewish intellectual, whatever did you expect? I know how they see me. But I abandoned all attempts to acquiesce to all those archaic expectations of me many years ago.' He noticed her smiling. 'Why are you laughing, girl? It is not a laughing matter. I might have left a long time ago. But I was never religious. Other things were always far more important to me.'

Maia had an inkling of what those might have been.

'Can painting be learned, do you suppose?'

Maia considered this. 'I think that technique can be learned, if somebody is willing to teach. One can learn how to see. But not talent. Never talent.'

'I hope you are correct, Maia . . . ' Abruptly

he stood up. 'Enjoy the city. I have much to do this evening. And now I must give you a chance to finish your breakfast. I have some people to meet. Look around the house at your leisure. Perhaps if I am at home sometime I may show you.'

As the Historian stood up to leave, the woman they had both been watching furiously threw her glass of tea and it smashed as it hit the floor. Shards of glass fell by Maia's feet, and the entire restaurant turned in shock, watching as the voices of the woman and her younger companion rose until the woman's voice was a high-pitched shriek that filled the room. The man stood up and the shouting stopped for a moment, while the other patrons fell back into murmurs. As the man left and the woman was alone, Maia watched as plump tears slowly rolled their way down the woman's moonface and smudged the black kohl onto her cheeks. Maia wanted to reach out to her, but the look on the Historian's face made her stop herself.

'You do understand she smashed the glass because it is exactly how she would want to be treated.'

'How do you explain that? Just a moment ago they were laughing together. Why would a woman wish to be treated like that?'

'Oh you would be surprised.' Then he coldly looked her over. 'Or, perhaps you would not.'

'I don't agree.' Maia was infuriated. 'If the man had smashed his glass, you would not have commented like this. You might have imagined him to simply have been angry.'

'True. This is how it works. But I am sorry to say that I really do find hysterical women very irritating.'

'Surely you do not find a woman irritating because she dares to express her anger? Perhaps the man she is with has done something? I suppose women should be seen, and not heard. And sometimes it might be better for them if they were not seen at all.'

'Maia, we must not argue. You have not spent much time here. Your arguments are indeed pertinent, but I fear that our views may be irreconcilable. Surely, you of all people must realise how others are so visual. Men look at women and how they behave before deciding how to treat them. You should know that. You, after all, are the artist. Now, I really must leave. I will try to find some time to show you around the house, but I may have to go away for a while. When I do, make sure you complete all the typing I need. My publishers are always pushing me.'

Yes, thought Maia. It was evidently

54

dreadful to be so respected and in demand. Yet the conciliatory tone of the Historian's voice made Maia suspect that she had misjudged him. His superior knowledge intrigued her. The Historian represented the closed-off and exclusive world of academia, of intellectuals and art. He knew people who might be able to help her, and she found that she longed to be accepted by him. He belonged to that world, and she was desperate to be part of it.

Yet Maia now saw his prejudices far clearer than he saw them himself, and she experienced a dangerous flash of superiority.

'And,' he went on kindly, 'you can still do your painting.'

He made it sound like a pleasant pastime for her. The unfairness of his judgement stung her. The presence of the man was harmless, dependent only upon the promise of power which he embodied. It was physical, or sexual, or economic. But the presence of the loud woman was entirely different: her promise was expressed in her own attitude to herself, expressing what may or may not be done to her. But then, perhaps the gesture had been handed to the woman? She tried to consider it from another angle. The woman's presence was manifested in her voice, her gestures, and her expressions. Instantly she had been scrutinised and condemned by both Maia and the Historian. Maia knew very well how a woman, any woman, was constantly accompanied by the image of herself. From her earliest years every woman is taught to survey herself.

In the streets below, the light was diminishing. Sitting alone on the rooftop of the Grand Tazi hotel, listening to the sound of Arabic catching in the back of the throats, and the background whispering of various European languages, Maia felt again all the uncertainty of a girl alone in a foreign country. This was no longer Europe, she was in Africa. From the way both men and women regarded her, from the café waiters to the man selling cigarettes on the street, to the woman at the next table eyeing her with unchecked, unabashed curiosity, to the resentment she sensed directed towards her as a Westerner, everything she encountered here was alien. She had the strange feeling that this unspoken antipathy was the product of a strange relationship. Greedily they eyed her, and at the same time they hated her for it.

3

Maia dutifully executed the tasks set for her by the Historian. She grew aware of the displeasure of his editors in Paris and London at the work that he had produced for them in recent years. Maia began to wonder what had changed. She took out the letters and read them. 'Not your usual style,' they read; 'Not sufficiently thorough.' She raced through more letters complaining of his lack of focus, the lack of research, and then more recently the recriminations couched in vague, diplomatic language, until she found, crumpled at the back of a drawer, the demand for the return of the advances he had already received. She could not confront him, and simply left the letter where she had found it. The administrative tasks numbed her mind and required such a huge amount of time that she barely reflected upon her past anymore. Her curiosity grew as she became aware of how the Historian was slowly destroying his academic reputation. He had no interest in hiding it; that was clear. She was here to organise his affairs, and that was the alleged reason for her presence. But now it appeared that he had not been performing his writing and research, the basis of his work as a historian.

Passing the hours trawling through his documents, her life was becoming one of isolation. The Historian was exceptionally secretive about his movements, and Maia felt she didn't know him enough to enquire. She knew when he was in the house, because she could feel his presence there, quiet yet imposing and not completely benign. On his part, he settled himself in his rooms and left her instructions in notes. She grew accustomed to their situation. Rarely did she venture out into the streets, dreading the persistent attention and the suffocating heat, and instead went up on the roof to sit in the sun as it rose higher in the sky and then sank down in the evenings over the city. She painted the mountains, the rooftops at sundown, and for a while she believed she was content.

Almost daily Ina crossed Maia's path, but the housekeeper barely acknowledged the Historian's assistant. The two women barely spoke. As the days passed, Maia was determined to force recognition from Ina. One morning as they passed, Maia blocked her way. 'Good morning, Ina.'

The woman barely looked at her, emitting only a noise that sounded more like a grunt, and neatly sidestepped Maia. She had worked for the Historian for many years, and lived close by with her elderly husband. Maia wondered at the unspoken animosity towards her, unable to understand. On a simmering afternoon, Maia retired to her room on the third storey, exhausted in the heat. After a few moments of peace, the Historian burst suddenly into her room. 'My dear, I must give you a tour of the house!'

'Now?'

'I know, I know, it really is rather impromptu. But I'm afraid I simply haven't had the time.'

Maia was unsure about the truth of this. The correspondence she completed for him never requested his presence in Europe. She could only guess at his movements, and now she wondered what he wanted from her.

'I must show you around. I have been so rude.'

Maia was shocked by his sudden enthusiasm.

Suddenly his face fell and he looked around him with distaste. 'Disgusting,' he muttered, 'disgusting,' and then he appeared to remember her presence and smiled. 'I have collected these . . . things,' he said, waving his hand disparagingly over the assorted furniture, eclectic and mismatched, 'from every corner of the country, and further still.' Hand-painted and carved, the cedar tables and cabinets and the Moorish benches were gathered around, stacked up in corners and gathering dust. 'This,' said the Historian, stroking a small round table, 'is a Nedhima Table. Very rare. It cost me little, but I shall sell it on for thousands. Those gullible tourists, flocking here for their taste of exoticism . . . ' He gave a short, grunting laugh of contempt. He recollected himself, and came towards her. 'Now for the tour!'

'Are you sure? I am quite tired; you have given me so much to do. And I have the impression that Ina would not approve. She doesn't like me.'

The Historian's presence unsettled her, and she wasn't sure to believe his friendliness. But even her sobriety did not quell his enthusiasm.

'Ignore her. I always do!' He paused, as if searching for the appropriate words. But he saw how questioningly she was looking at him. He sighed. 'Ina is a strict Muslim. She does not approve of women like you.'

'Women like me?'

He laughed, cynically. 'Liberated women, one must suppose. And she is old. It is now many years that she has worked for me. She is a good worker. But a little possessive of the house. And of me. She forgets that I am the master!' He began to laugh uproariously. It was very unusual behaviour. Abruptly, he became calm and looked at her. 'Do not offend her.'

'I have done nothing to offend her,' Maia said, bemused.

He smiled. 'I do know that. Now, follow me.'

The Historian's permission to explore the house pleased Maia; she now felt that she might be free of Ina's critical gaze. Through low arched doorways they passed into a room of the house that was cool, alien from the stifling heat outside.

'When did you leave London?'

'Many moons ago.' The Historian was intolerably vague, and he looked distracted.

'Please, do not play with me. I came here; I deserve an answer.'

'And why not, when it is so amusing to play with so earnest a girl?'

Maia was surprised. The Historian was almost debonair. He had made himself into a recluse. She had assumed that this had been the cultivation of his image, but now she began to wonder if he was hiding out here because, academically at least, he no longer had anything interesting to say. There were rumours about him. It was said that he had stolen money; that he procured girls, that he

61

was intolerably self-indulgent. But Maia never believed rumours about anyone; and in this case there were academic jealousies to consider. She was inclined to believe the best of people. Sometimes she thought that it took too much energy to consider the worst.

As they walked together through the house, the Historian bounding slightly ahead, he pointed out to her objects of interest.

'This is an Al-Khazar armoire,' he said, pointing to a small cabinet carved in mahogany. 'This is a marabou dining set.' And rushing ahead, he stopped at six carved wood and leather chairs, placed around a long, rectangular table. 'And this is a Tuareg Buffet.' Lovingly he stroked the leather. 'This will sell at auction, for a very high sum. And this! And this!' He pointed wildly around him.

Maia was surprised to see him almost hysterical in his excitement; his behaviour seemed so out of character. She realised he exuded only a hint of warmth when he was displaying his accumulated possessions. He had carved out a niche for himself here, and somehow he was both guarding it and showing it off to her. She wondered if perhaps he wanted her to return home and talk about him, to gossip about his success to his former colleagues.

'I knew the man who made this,' he said, pointing out a cabinet, which he assured her was made by the Ashanti tribe deep in West Africa. 'I stayed with him for several weeks . . . but now he is dead.'

'Why have you never returned to London?' she asked, hoping he might share some of his past while he was so relaxed. 'Surely you must miss it. You were such a fixture there.' Maia tried to sound casual.

'Yes, I was.' He was thoughtful.

'You know, I don't believe it about you, those rumours — '

'One has to live, no?' he said, almost nonchalantly, and carried on down the passageway.

At that moment, as she saw his face darkening, she knew that she had made a mistake.

He whirled on her. 'If you wish to stay here, never talk to me again about the past.'

She said nothing. He disappeared upstairs, then seemed to regret it, and he returned. But already she was sorry; she pitied him in his exile.

'I know I can be sharp,' he said, 'but I am so used to being alone here.'

Maia was silent.

'Come and see.'

The house was tall and narrow on the

upper floors, several storeys high. Rubble lay scattered on the ground.

'I began all of this restoration several years ago, but I never do seem to get round to finishing the work. Or even simply to stay here to see the whole thing completed.' He waved his hand with an excessive flourish of his long, tapered fingers, as if they might brush away the rubble.

'Can you not trust somebody to check on the work, and pay the builders?'

'I trust nobody!' said the Historian vehemently.

His complaints were incessant. The people here were unreliable, useless. The builders were lazy and corrupt.

'I am always deceived,' he said, bowing his head ruefully.

Maia almost believed him, but in his self-pity he was almost comical.

'I have exact plans for this place.'

Despite his relentless criticisms, Maia was convinced of his devotion to his place here. She smelled the scent of the oranges hanging succulently from the trees; saw the tiled blue fountain in the courtyard where he often spent the evenings, smoking incessantly.

He saw her looking at it. 'Why do you never come down here in the evenings? I do hope you are not scared of me.'

Now that he was behaving so hospitably, she hardly felt able to tell him that he had failed to make her feel welcome. 'I thought you would like to be alone.'

'Of course you may come down,' he said, and clapped her lightly on the back.

Maia was only able to speculate at his sudden turnaround. She wondered how he coped with his resentment, his self-imposed exile, the ostracism and critical treatment from his fellow academics, but he didn't mention it again.

When they stopped in the corridor leading to the front of the house from the courtyard, Maia was able to see that the corridor was turned at such an angle that nobody from the street was able to see directly into the house. The house was well protected, with long, twisting passages, offering her security, protected from the loud intrusion of the people outside. The Historian led her through a delicately tiled arch into his reception room. Both the floor and the low, round tables had been constructed from dark cedar wood and the walls were painted a deep, dark green evoking the cool enclosure of a forest. Stuccoed, geometrical designs flitted across the side of the far wall and in high alcoves the bookcases spilled over with huge tomes on subjects ranging from the esoteric and the philosophical to psychology and mathematics. Strangely, Maia noticed, there were no historical books. Ceramic tiles lay placed in symmetrical patterns across the floor.

He saw her looking at them. 'Zellige, my dear.'

The vividly coloured, terracotta tiles had been placed into geometrical shapes, spreading over the entire far wall. The Historian strode nimbly over to the wall and stroked the tiles. Carpets dyed in reds and purples lay across a raised stone platform, and the windows opened with shutters of latticed wood onto the courtyard outside. Maia understood why this misanthropic man might want to come in here and never emerge. She was warming to him. So far, she had found that the Historian's misanthropic contempt for human nature was so strong that he wished to have as little contact with the world as he was able.

'When I am in here, I do ask you not to disturb me . . . '

The intimacy of earlier was all gone. Maia was discomfited. Why had he wished to display this sumptuous room to her, and then forbid her from ever visiting it? Maia dismissed this strangeness merely as one of the Historian's many foibles.

Following the spontaneous tour of his abode, the Historian disappeared again without leaving word of his whereabouts. Occasionally she felt the urge to enquire about his travelling, but she knew that she would never ask. She had already witnessed a hint of the wrath that lay dormant in the Historian, and did not desire to witness it again. Somehow he succeeded in making her feel as if she judged him too harshly. She pitied the old man, living out the remainder of his life in isolation.

In the Historian's absence, Maia pushed on with the work that he had left for her and she continued to paint. Although Maia passed Ina in the corridor, the two women still never spoke, and Maia no longer made any attempt to elicit any civility from the woman.

Maia saw that the door of the riad was the main external feature against the blankness of the house, and savoured the privacy she found once inside. She often sat in the courtyard and worked in a room downstairs where two sofa beds sat, and rugs were laid out across the stone floor. In the corner, a wooden platform had been constructed for the desk, where at night, she ate alone with fresh produce she had bought in the day. She began to enjoy her solitude.

Maia did as the Historian asked her. She executed his correspondence with the various publishers and newspaper editors from Paris to New York, she translated articles for him and the articles which he had written upon varying medieval religious topics from French into English, and she transcribed his indecipherable notes onto his ancient computer. She could sit for hours, her hands poised over the keys, desperately trying to understand the illegibility of the Historian's handwriting, or looking abstractedly at the letters before her eyes, without really seeing them at all.

One evening she was distracted and failed to save his work on time before there was a disastrous power cut. She swore loudly, and as she looked up she saw Ina was staring straight at her. Their eyes met and Maia refused to take her gaze away. After a few moments, the old woman withdrew, leaving Maia with an unpleasant sensation of having been spied upon.

She looked into the shadows moving in the courtyard, at a bit of inky sky, and at the other side of the house, which was turning black in the darkness. Through the shutters she could almost smell the heat smouldering in the night and then somewhere, not far off, she could hear the rising tremolo of a lute. Maia began to ache again for excitement. She knew that out there in the streets below there was a party and fascinating, entertaining people, but she didn't know how she would find it and in any case she was tied in here now. In the isolation of her self-sufficiency, her longing for privacy and retirement from life was now morphing into loneliness.

With no-one to amuse her, Maia painted. The houses, the city itself from different angles and those inhabitants whom she was able to persuade to sit for her. She soon found the courage to enter cafés and introduce herself to the regulars, to explain that she was a painter who needed models she could paint in public, in all the mundane situations of daily life. But the men were all inappropriately keen, and disillusion showed on their faces when once they had agreed she began to take out her pens and paints, rather than inviting them to pose privately.

Inevitably, the men would begin to make salacious advances towards her, but they were always in public and as soon as this began, Maia made clear her lack of interest. She passed the afternoons with an interchange-able series of men in cafés, with passing tourists and people doing up their riads in the old medina, and soon she had amassed a small number of acquaintances. But the people she met were always on the cusp of leaving, and the lack of women in the midst of the crowds of local men began to concern her.

Too often, she saw that women were neither seen nor heard, and her curiosity about them grew. She saw that here women were allowed to exist only on the periphery of life, and only in the roles allocated to them, and even those she saw in the streets were often silent and covered, or hovering on the rooftops of the uniformly plain stone houses which lined the labyrinthine alleys.

Maia prepared her canvas in white, so that the material glowed through with the illusion of dazzling sunlight, and the light and colours splintered the surface and created an uneven perception for the viewer, in an imitation of the real life of the city. Her use of colour was so imaginative and exuberant that she lost hours in experimentation at sunset exploring all the shades of red and pink, vivid hues of terracotta, salmon and red earthstone. When she went out onto the roof to paint, Maia tried to forget the objects which stood before her, and she saw only shapes, lines and curves, rather than houses, trees, the small, drab black-clad figure of a woman. As she painted she increased her sense of perspective and an understanding of at least the architecture of the city. But it was a true appreciation of the character of the inhabitants of the city, which still eluded her.

Maia wanted to grasp the true character of

the inhabitants. She watched the women, waiting for an opportunity to see behind their doors into their lives. Sometimes she brushed past a woman in the street; she smelt her scent, looked at the worries etched upon her face, but Maia knew that she would never know her. She was aware that while the women were hidden from her, the city would not reveal its secrets, however hard she tried to immerse herself.

4

Maia was sitting at the Historian's dark wooden desk, translating a lengthy correspondence between his French agent and London publisher, when the telephone rang shrilly and knocked her out of concentration. The Historian hardly ever received telephone calls.

'*Bonjour, ma petite!*' bellowed the man at the end of the line. Immediately Maia realised it was Mahmoud. His voice was even more robust than at their first meeting at the Grand Tazi.

'Hello, Mahmoud. I'm afraid that the Historian is away in Europe.'

'Really? Do you imagine that I am not aware of where Mihai is, child? I know all his movements. I also know that you have nobody here and I hate to think of you sitting there all alone in the house and well . . . all cold and lonely.'

'I am not cold, Mahmoud.'

'Yes, yes, so you say. That is by the bye. Still, too much time alone for a young lady. Come back to my hotel and you can meet all my regulars. You come at once! Straight away!

I give you very nice time.' Then he thought for a moment. 'No — there is another place. A bar. Ask at the desk.'

'I have a lot to do for the Historian before he returns, Mahmoud.'

'Mihai won't mind.'

'I think, in fact, that he will. He is expecting this work to be finished.'

'But you must have some enjoyment too, my dear. That is what you come for, no, a new life?'

For a moment, Maia remained silent. 'Well, not only that.'

'You are too alone. It is never good for a young girl to be too alone.'

'I am happy.'

'As you say, my dear, as you say. Come this afternoon, this evening, whenever you wish. Consider this an invite, and you know, one must be invited to visit the bar at the Grand Tazi,' said Mahmoud proudly, with an unmistakable tinge of snobbery.

'I'm not sure . . . ' She was nervous to meet new people, and beginning to enjoy her reclusive lifestyle.

'But of course you will come!' It was clear that Mahmoud was of a persistent nature.

'I will come this evening,' said Maia, accepting her fate. There was to be no escape, no more revelling in her self-imposed loneliness.

73

'You need to see people,' said Mahmoud in a softer voice.

She could almost imagine him saying he had her best interests at heart. He was so convincing that for a moment Maia forgot that the man barely knew her.

'Well, that is settled then! Make sure that you bring a bathing suit,' said Mahmoud, and the click on the line signalled the call was over.

Maia decided to take the least revealing bathing suit she could find. She didn't know that the Grand Tazi possessed a private pool, but then, thought Maia, why should she? The Historian had not mentioned it to her. A thought struck her; perhaps the Historian would not be pleased if she were to visit the Grand Tazi. He might consider it an intrusion into the life that he had built for himself, a life about which he was so secretive. Maia decided to ignore these doubts. She was beginning to resent the Historian; surely in his absence she could visit the Grand Tazi, if she had been invited. The Historian had left her here, with piles of his work, leaving all of his affairs in disarray, publishers hounding him to return advances, and she, alone in the city. A sudden fury overtook her; she began to forget how she had arrived here searching for peace and a tranquility in which to concentrate upon her art; she now resolved to immerse herself again in the world.

Going down into the street, Maia found herself intrigued by Mahmoud's invitation. She was apprehensive at the prospect of entering his private bar and meeting his 'regulars'. Weaving her way through the crowds, all that she was able to hear were the angry voices of shouting men and women and the wail of an ambulance. She could see a mass of people peering round several police cars, with a camel at the centre of the chaos. Resisting any fruitless attempt at seeing anything further, Maia tore herself from the growing crowd, and continued on her way to the Grand Tazi.

Arriving at the hotel, Maia went through the empty foyer until she heard a voice frenetically calling her back. A woman was standing at the desk sporting a visibly black moustache that lined her upper lip. Maia was unable to tear her eyes away; the thing wriggled. The woman appraised her from top to bottom.

'I have been invited by Mahmoud. He knows I am coming. Where is the pool and bar?' Past events had disposed Maia to take a harsh position towards other women.

'It is a long, long way away,' the woman said mysteriously. She then spoilt the effect by smirking widely.

'Your boss has invited me.' Maia felt herself go pale with hostility. The woman relented, and she bowed low, with a false sycophancy.

'*Par ici, mademoiselle,*' she said, pointing to a half-open door in the corner of the foyer.

Maia crouched slightly and passed through the windowless, smoky corridor. Crumbling and peculiarly low, the few feet she took seemed endless, until she emerged into the sun.

A gloomy sight greeted Maia: a dried-up old courtyard filled with weeds, a wall at the far end peeling with paint, and a small, square-shaped pool with sea monsters carved of stone malevolently peering down into the water. The tangled snake hair of Medusa trailed along the ground, dripping into the pool and twisting round the sides. The statue's nostrils flared angrily at the guests. By the other side of the courtyard, only a few metres away from the pool, the bar curved softly, quietly admonishing the ostentation of the sea monsters. Beside the small pool there lay scattered small tables and cushions. Over the bar towered an enormous fig tree providing shade in the heat, and the pool itself was immaculately tiled with a pale blue, which lent the water an alluring glow in the fading light. The place had a certain louche charm, but the weeds beside the pool were overgrown and had begun to fall into it, so that shards of green leaves fluttered across the water's surface.

Maia saw that upon coming out into the open she had almost walked into two large Arabs who lay sprawled upon the threadbare chairs placed on the stone steps leading down to the bar, their square grooved faces leathery and as contented as baboons in the afternoon shade. The two men scrutinised her as she began to step down, but they let her go. Two gargoyles at the entrance, thought Maia, to add to Mahmoud's collection.

Maia took no notice of the men. It was obvious how used they were to staring so openly at the women who passed through the doors. The longer Maia spent in that city, the easier she was finding the constant scrutiny.

At the bar, Maia saw Tariq, the receptionist from the previous day, dressed only in a pair of voluminous swimming trunks. He was standing there looking around with a vague expression on his pitted face. The bar itself was an exhibition of Mahmoud's appetite for outlandish decoration, with swaths of ragged curtains surrounding the curved marble bar, tinged with a grey residue.

A male guest, stretching back his tawny limbs in the sun, looked at her and laughed, raising his half-empty glass in a sarcastic gesture. The man appeared to be the companion of a bulbous couple; the woman sat humming tunelessly, and the man with extraordinarily pasty skin, his hand placed over his forehead in a dramatic gesture of fainting. He exuded a fat feminine air, and immediately Maia could tell they were all British.

Tariq interrupted her thoughts. 'May I offer you a drink, Maia?'

'You know my name?'

'Of course I know your name! It is my job. Mahmoud has been expecting you.'

'No drink yet, thank you. Are you not working on reception tonight?'

'I do all here,' he said proudly. 'I am Tariq.'

'Everything?'

'Yes. All, all. All you need, I get you.' Unnecessarily, he bowed. It was embarrassing. The group across the pool was watching her intently.

'Just for the moment, Tariq, I think I'll take a dip.'

All afternoon the city had been sweating and it was still unbearably hot, despite the breeze that was starting up. The promise of cool water was alluring. Maia went over and undressed. A young, slim man of Latin origin was sitting at the centre of a small trio, regarding her attentively. Glancing over at the group by the bar, she saw that they were all now sitting up, looking directly at her.

The effeminate young man waved at her, and then he stretched back in his chair and yawned horribly, more like a lizard than a man. From the corner of her eye, Maia saw Mahmoud come out to sit at the bar, but he did not approach her. He waved his hand in greeting and fell into conversation with a nearby group.

Maia sat perched on the edge of the pool, dangling her legs. As the sun descended she lowered herself in and sank beneath the water. Above her head, she watched bubbles ripple and rise to the surface where, as if in slow motion, shadowy figures were moving about. When she emerged, Maia opened her eyes to find Mahmoud staring down at her, offering a towel.

She hoisted herself out of the pool and took the towel from him, looking around at the people by the bar.

'You are still in a trance, my dear,' smiled Mahmoud indulgently.

'The water was lovely. Thank you for inviting me.' He must have taken that as encouragement, for he took the towel from her, and began to wrap it around her shoulders. 'No, no Mahmoud. Please don't.'

He stroked her wet hair off her face and Maia masked the shudder she felt at his touch.

He frowned at her, then beamed. He took a step back. 'Do not fear me, Maia. I will show you where you can change.' He steered her with his large hand firm upon her shoulders. More guests had begun to congregate at the bar, and they muttered amongst themselves in different languages. Iron wrought lanterns had been lit and candles flickered. The bar warped and swelled with sparkling voices, the loosening of inhibitions, the sharp clink of ice in glasses, and the subtle, trembling rhythm of the guitars.

As Maia walked past the bar, she felt glaring eyes upon her. As she moved forward, her path was blocked by a tall man.

'Please, move for this lady,' smiled Mahmoud, muttering something unintelligible under his breath.

'Of course Mahmoud,' the man said, and allowed her through. In the moments he stood before her she saw that the man's features were at once virile and weak, and in his eyes, which were a pale light blue, she saw instantly that here was a man capable of great deception. But that failed to stop her being drawn to him; his eyes were searching, his skin was bronzed and his hair, an intense dark brown, swept about his eyes in an elegantly long fringe that he wore utterly without irony. His chin was hard and strong and two creases grooved into both sides of his mouth. He was tall and lean, wore an expensive dark shirt and trousers, without adornments. He looked as if he might be going anywhere in the world, from one second to the next. Maia was drawn to this man, while at the same time repelled by him.

Sardonically bowing his head, he let her past, and when he was out of earshot, she turned to Mahmoud. 'Who is he?'

'Someone you must learn to ignore.'

Maia looked up at him, but Mahmoud was no longer smiling. 'But — '

'No!' He lifted his hand, and Maia feared he was going to strike her, again doubting his friendly exterior. But then his hand fell, and he placed it upon her shoulder in a firmly paternal manner, and seemed to relent a little. 'His name is Armand. He is French. He likes to visit the bar. He is little, insignificant. No need for you to bother with him, no need at all. You only like the big fish, no?'

But Maia already felt the warning had come a little late. Armand had given her a shock. His expression was set firmly in stone; his eyes almost photographic. For reasons she could not yet comprehend she sensed that

Mahmoud suffered from a jealousy of Armand. Mahmoud's warning served only to pique Maia's curiosity.

'You will soon learn not to ask questions. This is a haven! Don't forget how lucky you are to have me here! I will protect you!'

As Maia returned from getting changed, Mahmoud dragged her around the bar area. 'Make her a drink, Tariq.' And the rest of the night passed in a haze.

Armand and Maia did not speak, and she purposely avoided him. She tried hard not to be struck by curiosity as to his behaviour, but she was aware of his enigmatic presence drawing her in. When he glanced only once in her direction, she found herself promising herself to him with an acquiescent smile. Mahmoud was relishing his role as the friendly, welcoming host and he succeeded in his quest to introduce her to many people, other inebriated foreigners, whose names she instantly forgot.

When with his offensive bulk Mahmoud pressed her towards the British group, he whispered, 'You're not going to like these people.'

'And how have you decided that?'

'I already know you. You will see.'

The group turned and looked at her as she approached, as if studying some new and strange animal.

'Who is this specimen you have brought us now, Mahmoud?' said the bored-looking tanned man Maia noticed earlier.

'Maia is working for Mihai Farcu. She is an artist, and his new assistant, isn't it.'

'Isn't *she*,' said the arrogant young man. 'Isn't *she*. That is what you say. In fact, it isn't appropriate to say that anyway.' With that comment, he rolled his eyes to the emerging stars. Maia watched Mahmoud's face, but even at this disdain for him, nothing flickered, and his grin remained fixed and frozen upon his face.

'I see, the Historian's new assistant,' said the effeminate man, and a short silence ensued. It was finally broken by the large woman. She looked as if she was the sort of person who could not bear to remain silent for long, and Maia was grateful for this.

'Have a little drink with us,' said the woman. 'It's so pleasant here. A little run down, but rather charming all the same.'

'If you insist.'

'I do insist! Lucy Bambage. Hello! So you are an artist? Have I seen your work?' She was a very jolly sort, and, assumed Maia, well intentioned, if slightly overbearing.

'I cannot tell you, Mrs. Bambage, perhaps you have.' Maia examined her more closely; she was a dough-faced woman, immediately

83

identifiable as one desperate for affection but determined to hide it. The heavy makeup made her pathetic even in the fading light. Maia was able to see the grease, sad and ridiculous on her face, the gaping crimson mouth, an open gash grinning madly, like the Joker on a pack of old and used cards.

'Well, where would it be shown then?'

'London. The odd gallery.'

'Stop it, Lucy. You'll scare the poor child,' said a large man coming from the bar who appraised her with goggling eyes. He possessed the manner of someone who was subjected to excessive nagging.

'Well, you are lucky enough to look like one!' she said, and grabbed Maia away from Mahmoud, who seemed happy enough to relinquish her. With an unfortunate lantern jaw and such a large body, Maia looked upon her with a mixture of trepidation and pity. Lucy seemed like a name fit only for a young girl, but this woman was in her sixth decade at least, and she had not aged well. She possessed that florid, floral look so beloved of middle-class English women who have spent too long under a foreign sun. Maia gathered that Martin Bambage was some sort of salesman who had made enough money to pass his time taking his portly wife on as many holidays as possible. The couple talked about themselves so much, or rather, Lucy Bambage talked for them, they had barely any time to listen to Maia.

The tanned man's face was symmetrically handsome, but his beauty was marred by a constant smirk of disgust, which made him irksome to his companions. Maia had entered in the midst of a conversation about food.

'My dislike of Moroccan food,' Lucy Bambage was saying, 'derives from two of my major food hates. There are not many foods that I dislike but two of them are deeply linked with the food of Morocco. Horror number one is the combination of fruit and meat. And the second is mint. Time for a gin and tonic,' Lucy Bambage barked promptly, to nobody in particular.

'You are quite simply unadventurous, Lucy,' said the young man, lying back languidly. 'Why not admit it?'

'That is how I feel about it, Rupert. I would never expect you, of all people, to agree with me. You only care about the waiters!'

'There is no need to be so very crude, my darling,' said the young man who Maia now knew as Rupert.

'Have you been to Tangier, Maia? How did you find it? We came from there . . . '

Maia recalled her own time in Tangier, a city where the heat seemed to have allowed

85

her to relinquish all responsibility. When she had looked around, it was full of awful little hills that channelled the energy of the town down to the waterfront where the developing world was still slavering to get out. Visiting the city was like being in a time warp, filled with scores of old cafés, relics from the days when Tangier had played a more significant international role. Tangier was still holding on to its former charms, reminding her of a beguiling, but ageing beauty who had now grown a little long in the tooth. She erased her memories and fought her way back to the present.

'We got so very lost in Tangier, didn't we, Martin?' she was saying. Her husband didn't reply; he was too busy snuffling over his food. Maia watched him; Martin Bambage and his wife resembled each other, a couple who over the years had grown to look the same. They had the same wide jaw, the flaccid face and sagging skin, the thick, glutinous lips. Rupert saw her watching Martin and he caught her eye. He evidently thought himself a superior being, and his dislike of the couple was obvious. Lucy Bambage was desperate to talk, so Maia enquired about their journey and health, but she soon discovered that questions asked innocently served only to encourage another unwelcome monologue.

Maia attempted to change the subject. 'How did you find the souk?'

'The place was revolting! So many awful, shuffling people, and then there were the children, always following, begging, so disgusting. We got ourselves lost and went into a shop and Martin, can you believe it, left me alone!'

She could believe very well. Martin looked up from his plate; he was a man with a face like an angry toad. His eyes protruded and a vast inane smile filled the entire lower half of his face. His arms were too long for his body, and looked strangely out of place. Lucy Bambage continued, breathlessly, keen to empty it all out onto somebody sufficiently unwitting to listen to her. Rupert rolled his eyes again. She wondered why Rupert stayed with these people if he disliked them.

'And then there was the smell. Putrid, just putrid. All the boys were shouting at me in French, but I could barely understand anything. The last time I studied French was at St Alban's secondary, and that was many years ago.'

'What exactly did the boys say to you, Mrs. Bambage?'

'Call me Lucy. They shouted something like *balene, balene*. They kept repeating it and running after me and they just would not leave me alone. It was awful. Do you speak French? If you have been granted a job here, I certainly hope so.'

Maia could only smile at her comment. She spoke in that proprietary manner that is so typical of tourists who come to feel that they own a slice of the places they are visiting. She made it sound as if Maia was a privileged impostor.

'I'm afraid that I can't actually tell you what the boys were saying to you. I seem to have forgotten that word.'

'Saying to me? They were calling me something? How can you forget a simple word like that? You said you spoke French!'

The two women stared at one another with a mutual suspicion that neither yet had the grounds to voice.

'Obviously I don't speak French quite as well as I thought I did.'

Rupert was smiling at her again, one that the redoubtable Lucy Bambage did not miss.

Maia stood up. 'I'm going to the bar. Let me buy you a drink. What would you like?'

'Well, my dear, I'll have a brandy.'

'*Quelle surprise*,' said Maia for absolutely no reason at all, and for the first time in the brief interchange, Lucy Bambage looked somewhat discomfited. As Maia walked to the bar, her voice did not recede, but remained excruciatingly loud. Maia decided that she needed a vodka.

'But you said she could speak French!' she was saying.

Maia allowed herself a small smile. From the bar she watched these people; their false influence, the accumulation of their manners, which were not so scrupulous as to appear innate. So quickly she had been drawn into their group, and then just as quickly she was cast out. Lucy Bambage was continuing her monologue.

'I didn't listen to them really. I was just trying to get Martin's attention. He can be so intolerably slow.' Maia looked back at the woman, whose jaw was wobbling emphatically. As she repeated her story, she relived the experience; the injustice that she perceived had been done to her. Maia was amused. The woman was a truly comical sight.

As Maia waited at the bar, someone tapped her arm, and she turned to find herself accosted by Rupert.

'Hello.'

'Rupert.'

'I know.'

'Where do you normally live, Maia, when you aren't working for shady historians?'

'Shady? Is he shady?'

'Well, the great Mihai Farcu does have his detractors. So where do you normally live?'

'Sometimes in Paris, sometimes in London.'

'And what brought you here? Wait — don't tell me, a lost lover, a broken heart,' and he began to snigger at his own witticisms.

'Don't be so ridiculous.'

'It isn't so ridiculous, Maia. Most of the people I meet here are running away from something. Are you?'

'You are a little inquisitive, aren't you?'

'I'm just curious.'

'In London I bumped into an old university Professor, who found out I was at a loose end. He mentioned the Historian, and, *voila*.'

Rupert nodded, apparently satisfied with her explanation. She had nothing else to tell him. She certainly was not going to go into details.

'And what will you be doing for Mihai Farcu?' asked Rupert.

'You seem so different to that couple. What exactly are you doing here with them?' said Maia, swiftly changing the subject.

'She is my mother,' said Rupert, and winked.

'I don't believe that for a second!' Then, discerning his true meaning, Maia could understand the strange enmity between Rupert and the husband. Martin Bambage was a cuckold, being routinely humiliated by his unattractive

90

wife. She did not trust Rupert; she had caught a facetious look in his eyes.

'They both have their little eccentricities,' he said.

'Lucy Bambage is in charge of both you and Martin.'

'As you say. She supports me, anyway. She has her needs.'

'Whatever do you mean?'

Rupert lowered his voice and whispered in her ear. 'Poor old Martin. He just can't keep the pace any more. Anyway, I've sent him straight home!' and he cackled wickedly, slipping away from her, taking Lucy Bambage's brandy with him. Maia stared at him in horror as he left.

Under Mahmoud's watchful eye Maia avoided Armand all night, but still she seemed to gravitate towards him. As she heard him speak, his words had all the urbane fluency of a highly educated man. Later in the evening she saw him sitting at the bar, flanked protectively by two dark women, both anxiously competing for his attention. As she passed, she looked at him puzzled, and as he smiled at her, she unsuccessfully tried to avert her eyes from his. Neither of them spoke, and Armand looked at her questioningly, raising a sardonic eyebrow.

Maia realised that she had drunk far too

much. Mahmoud had handed her so many differently coloured drinks prepared by Tariq, that she lost count.

Later that summer, she could recall only flashes of that first night at the Grand Tazi bar. She remembered Tariq's pitted face and the father and daughter at the bar, whose grieving faces were painful to look at. The father was sobbing and inebriated whilst the daughter remained pitiful and silent. It turned out that the commotion that Maia had encountered that afternoon as she had made her way to the bar was due to the death of a British woman named Pamela. The family had been living in the city for some time, and the father had decided to give his wife what he thought was the most romantic gift of all: an amorous camel. It seemed that incident in the streets with the camel had attracted more customers than was usual.

The lime-green light that spewed forth, casting a theatrical glare upon the bar, lent Mahmoud's listeners a ghoulish appearance as Mahmoud extolled on the excitement of the Friday afternoon camel market. The family had been perusing in their search for the perfect present. The camel market sounded very much to Maia like a weekly feast of drama and cruelty. Beaten into defecating ranks, the hobbled camels were overseen by traders who disregarded the emaciation of the animals; dead beat from their long, hard trek across the Sahara desert.

'The strength and the speed of a camel can be discerned by the legs, the chest, the eyes, the ears and the position of the hump.' He swayed slightly, with the effect of the drink heavy upon his frame. Mahmoud was enjoying himself. His head began to bob up and down, like a buoy at sea. His audience stamped its feet feverishly and gave shrill cries of delight. Mahmoud's thunderously low laughter revealed the enjoyment he got out of life. 'I, I too was once a camel trader myself. I know. I know!' He grabbed Maia's arm with excitement. 'If you ever decide to purchase a camel, I insist that you must take me with you.'

Maia smiled politely. She didn't know why Mahmoud imagined that she might ever purchase a camel, but she chose to humour him; his delight at being surrounded by the enthusiasm of an attentive crowd was evident. Maia had passed by the weekly camel market before, and was disgusted by the way in which goats and camels were exchanged while Moroccan merchants gossiped over their sweet mint tea, unperturbed by the throat slitting and the disembowelments beside them.

'You must look for the teeth. They reflect

age. You also have to look for signs of irritation, such as a conflated mouth sac, ferocious slobbering and gurgling.' He wouldn't be stopped, although Tariq made a half-hearted attempt to persuade him to come down.

'These signs are most evident during the mating season. Now! No wonder the camel was amorous!' He slapped the back of the man who was hunched over with grief for his wife. 'You should have come to me first. I would have advised you.' A preposterous image came to her of Mahmoud standing by a huge animal, its face snarling and lips bared back to reveal its hideous tombstone teeth.

Confidently, Mahmoud insisted that it was this lack of knowledge that had led to Pamela's unfortunate demise, the ignorant European's inability to discern the true temperament of a camel.

Maia was amazed at the onlookers as they gathered to listen to Mahmoud's lecture. Their curious contentment to stand around the bar and watch the father and daughter grieve. She winced at their cowardice. But neither did she speak.

Armed with her new knowledge about Rupert and Lucy Bambage's bond, Maia made her way towards the British group. The misery of the father and daughter had lent her a new surge of confidence, and Maia despised the

94

clientele's supercilious amusement. Fragments of their conversation drifted over to her:

'I hear the husband bought her an amorous camel.'

'An amorous camel, what is that?'

'But surely you must know. Don't pretend . . . '

'It is the season, they say.'

'They are staying at our riad.'

'I only know them by sight.'

'But why would anybody want one? Such ugly creatures.'

'Yes, they do get so over-excited.'

'It's a tragedy . . . '

She knew they prided themselves on not staying in another faceless hotel belonging to an international chain. Anonymous luxury was not what they were searching for. In finding the hotel alone, they believed that they had found the true meaning of adventure. Here they could step out of their usual surroundings, fraternise freely with these ephemeral travellers, people with whom they would never again meet. Instead, in the faded glory of the Grand Tazi they could wallow in the debauchery of the upstairs corridors, lie beneath the high ceilings amidst the fermented stink of Arabic coffee and stale food. They were looking for history, colour, spice and the space to breathe away from the competition in their lives at home. Everything that was so luxuriously provided for, they believed that they had obtained for themselves through their own efforts.

'Whale,' Maia told Lucy Bambage, 'I just remembered. *Balene* means whale in French. So sorry about that. Children can be so cruel.' With a detached distaste, Maia watched the muscles of Lucy Bambage's face spasm. 'I didn't want to hurt you,' Maia said lightly, and could only laugh as a look of such malevolence was thrown over her. As she walked away from the group, she heard them all talking in those ridiculous theatrical whispers, 'She's the type of person who will never be happy.'

Maia wondered if what they were saying was true. There *was* a void within her. Somewhere along the line she had made a wrong choice and every further turn had been a mistake. She had never stopped to wonder where she was. For a long time she had lived passively, and now at certain moments she was prone to remembering her past with regret. She relied on a certain brittleness to conceal her vulnerability.

She looked back to where Armand had been sitting with the two women, and seeing his seat was empty, found herself wishing that he had not left with them.

She went down into the deserted streets and returned to her room at the Historian's empty riad. As she opened the front door it struck her for the first time how far she was from home, and how completely alone. The street was silent and the closed houses formed an impenetrable façade.

5

In a tangled, clotted mass the people poured into the streets, while above them, a wailing was emitted so beseechingly from the mosque. Everywhere there were hands feeling, prodding, poking, and always the unrelenting, merciless stares. At first Maia tried to force her way through, but soon found it impossible and allowed herself to be carried through the streets. Body contact was frequent and unavoidable. Sunlight continually dripped onto her face, as she fumbled through noise.

At the entrance to the medina she broke from the heaving crowd and, having stopped in a moment of weakness, allowed herself to be picked up by an American who unwittingly saved her from a ferociously overexcited carpet salesman who had been choosing the right moment to pounce.

'Jacopo,' said the tall American, holding out his hand to her. Jacopo believed that he had chosen Maia, but really Maia had been following his filthy panama hat all the way through the crowd like a beacon. He was insistent on making conversation in that enthusiastic American way, and as they walked together through the chaos, shafts of light fell onto his face through the wooden slants separating one shop from another. In the direct sunlight, his complexion was pale and waxy.

Jacopo was unbearably inquisitive; he intimidated Maia with his eagerness. 'Where are you from? Why did you leave London? What are you doing here?'

Maia behaved as if she could not help but be constantly distracted by the people surrounding them. 'Thank you for showing me the way, Jacopo. But now I must go.'

'No! Now we have met, you must stay. Please stay with me!' Jacopo grabbed her arm and pulled her towards him. His gaze was intense and Maia saw the hurt in his glazed, bulging eyes. As he stepped closer towards her, Maia wrenched her arm from his grip, and began to hurry off. She saw that he wanted to call out to her, but she had not told him her name.

Maia walked at random, negotiating her way through the maze of narrow and twisting streets, the aroma of spices drifting from the stalls. She walked on, the city morphing into a dream, a circus, with wandering donkeys burdened down with packages and dark Berber women sitting cross-legged upon the ground, laying out their wares. Car horns blared and people shouted to one another.

The shops were selling handcrafted items, intricately styled bags, jewelled gowns and shoes, leather book covers and candles.

Through the cobbled, climbing alleyways, she walked in uninterrupted gloom amongst beggars who stretched out their hands to her. Maia felt that she was being followed. Only an occasional ruin allowed light and space and the odd glimpse of trees. She could not understand where she might be and several times she found herself exactly where she had begun.

A hand grabbed her arm, and Maia went to shrug it off. But as she turned, she saw that it was the man from the Grand Tazi with the photographic eyes.

'Have you been following me?'

'Yes, Maia. You seemed so lost. I couldn't let you go on like this.'

'How do you know my name?'

'How could I not? The Historian is an associate of mine. And this is a small city. Now let me take you out of here.'

'I can find my own way,' said Maia, but secretly she wanted his help. She didn't want to appear too eager as she felt the full force of his stern gaze.

'No, you cannot. You have been trying for too long. Come with me.'

Maia acquiesced, and he smiled down at

her as he took her arm.

'Where are you taking me?' She was discovering that she enjoyed the sensation of allowing him to take charge. 'Armand, tell me now, where are you taking me?'

'And how do you know my name?'

'Mahmoud told me.'

He reached down and lifted up her chin. 'So you admit you have some interest in me.' He took her hand and led her through the rutted alleyways and out into the waning sunlight. His grip was firm.

'Where are you taking me? Tell me now!'

'To a friend's café.'

She laughed. 'This sounds familiar. To my friend's shop, my uncle's café, a hotel, to find you a taxi. Do you want to try and sell me a carpet as well?'

'Don't be sarcastic, I want to help you. I cannot allow you to walk on through here alone. It is not safe. Besides, I am intrigued. Why exactly are you here?'

'So I intrigue you?'

'I am curious, I admit it. I want to know what you are doing here at Mihai Farcu's place.'

'I paint. He needed an assistant. I met an old university Professor who mentioned it to me. That is all.'

He didn't reply, but looked at her. 'So he

hasn't yet involved you in any of his real business?'

'What business is that?'

Again, he didn't reply.

Maia looked at him. His darkness, a long, straight nose; blue, narrowed, unreadable eyes. He spoke English with only the faintest intonation.

'I wouldn't have thought you would need company,' she said. 'I imagined you would have plenty of friends here.'

'Whatever made you think that?' He grimaced. 'I have no friends.'

She had revealed her own emptiness in the blink of an eye. He saw what she wanted and with surprise he realised that he was willing to give it to her, attracted by her helplessness in the face of the unknown. As they walked, she looked closely at the buildings and the people now entering and leaving them. They arrived at a café, The Parador, which was filled only with men and a dense fog of smoke. As they entered, the men stared at her with undisguised curiosity.

Through the smoke, Maia caught the pungent smell of strong coffee, and heard an Arabic tune playing on the radio; through the guitars and the beats of the tambourine a soulful female voice broke through.

Outside, the sun was setting and the sky

was turning red as the muezzin was sounding the call to prayer, but these men sat still. Maia thought of how everyone else was rushing around, but these men failed to move even for prayer. She envied them their contentment.

Armand attracted the attention of the waiter and he walked over to the bar. All eyes in the café were on her and she cringed beneath their gaze. As Armand returned, their eyes quickly swivelled away. He returned with a carefully carved cream box.

'What's in there?'

He opened it. 'You do play chess, don't you? You look the type.'

'To be honest with you, chess bores me.'

'It is a game of strategy. I don't know why, but I assumed you might be good at that.'

'I don't know why you would think that. My life is actually very disorganised.'

Maia helped him set up the wooden pieces, and Armand took the first move. He placed his pawn forward by two spaces. 'Did you know that the pawns symbolise little boys?'

Maia shrugged. 'Pawns grow up.'

'But they can never become King.'

'Why are you telling me this?'

'It is interesting, no? All the history, the psychology behind the game.'

'Perhaps. But so many cultures have their

own ideas. One might surmise anything. But did you know, Armand, that the Queen never became the most powerful figure on the chessboard, as she is seen today, until chess was introduced to the West? A direct reflection of our differing attitude towards women, do you think?'

He laughed. 'Evidently. But don't start that nonsense with me.'

'It is not nonsense.'

'I am intrigued. Why would you want to stay with the Historian? He is not . . . a friendly character.'

For a moment, Maia was speechless. The question was utterly unprovoked. 'I was not even thinking about him. I was wondering where to move my rook. But, since you ask, his research interests me.'

'I don't think that it does. I believe that you will come to despise him. But I also see that working for him, living with him affords you certain . . . opportunities. I know of his connections.'

'Of course, you might imagine that. My motives are not purely altruistic. But whose ever are? I came here for my painting, for the sunlight.' He smiled at her to continue. 'The light in London is terrible. The scenes too. The people boring. So ordered. So familiar.'

'Familiar?' he interrupted. 'So you came for

the exotic, the light. You want to paint decorative pictures of a foreign land.'

'I have never claimed to be original.' Maia wondered at the deep dissonance in his words; his sudden hostility.

'Well, you are French. What are you doing here?'

'I live here. Sometimes.' Armand waved his hand dismissively.

'Fine, you are here on holiday then. If that is all you want me to know.'

'It is all you need to know. Now, why do you like painting so much?'

'You actually do have extraordinarily long eyelashes, Armand.'

'I asked you a question.'

Maia recalled the same discussion she had with the Historian. Evidently he and Armand were of the same opinion.

'Perhaps you will find it difficult finding a woman who is willing to sit for you. You may have to go somewhere less than respectable.' He looked her over, and smiled slowly. 'But I am not sure you are too concerned about that. I know Mahmoud will be able to help you.'

'No!' Maia was sharp. The thought of being in any way further indebted to Mahmoud filled her with dread.

'You know, you are working for the

Historian here, but you can let off some steam now and again. I think you need to.'

'And why might you think that?'

'You are very uptight. Relax.'

'That is not true!'

Armand smiled, knowingly. But Maia knew he was right. The Historian left her without company, without real instructions. What did he expect her to do? Armand was taking her side, and she felt a rush of warmth towards him. He was interested in her.

Maia thought about the unpleasantness she sensed emanating from the Historian, and she wondered for how long she would be able to tolerate his hospitality. She found her initial excitement at the opportunity fading. But she needed the money. She thought about the woman she had met at the café. She wanted to stay and paint.

Suddenly Armand's features tightened, his heavy eyebrows drew together, and his previously calm face concentrated upon an unseen point.

'What's wrong?' Maia asked.

'I get a little down every so often,' said Armand. 'It is so difficult to escape, once you are involved.' Maia had no clue what he was talking about, but she nodded. 'We are all here hiding from one thing or another.' At that, Armand seemed to collect himself. 'It is nothing, just that sometimes I feel a little empty.'

He was looking at her, she imagined with hope. His strangeness was attractive, his present clouded by a distant past and unreadable emotions. She had found the distraction for which she had been searching.

Over Armand's head, Maia saw Rupert slouch into the café. Maia caught the look of utter delight that showed upon Rupert's sly face as he took in the sight of all the gathered men. He was in his element, and he was making his way straight over to them.

'Hello, Maia!' Rupert was effusive, but Maia was confounded by his friendliness, and she remained cold towards him.

'What are you doing here, Rupert?'

'I heard this was an interesting place to come, you never know who you might meet,' and he winked at them both.

Bemusement flickered across Armand's face.

Rupert peered down at them and leaned his body against their table. 'So tell me, my friends, how does this compare to the fabulous Grand Tazi?'

'Did we invite you to join us, Rupert?'

He placed his hand on her shoulder. 'Oh, Maia, Maia. Please don't blame me for the other night. It was nothing to do with me.'

'I pity you. That woman you are with is dreadful.'

Rupert squealed and jumped around. He leaned back down again towards them and whispered, 'I'm trying to get away from her. She just won't leave me alone.'

'I thought you had some sort of mutually profitable arrangement.'

Rupert pulled up a chair and Maia relented. He seemed genuinely despondent. 'I regret ever getting involved with them now. That woman is like a vampire! She wants me all the time. And the husband . . . I just can't stand him anymore, with his hangdog air and awful jibes.'

'So why are you here?' said Armand.

'To check out the talent, of course!'

Maia and Armand exchanged a silent and surreptitious look.

'You're drunk,' Maia said. 'You prefer men, don't you, Rupert?'

'Do you have a problem with that?'

'Of course I don't, Rupert. But it makes me wonder how you bear being a woman's manservant, especially one as unattractive as Lucy Bambage.'

'Don't call me that!'

'But my friend,' Armand said softly, 'that is exactly what you are.'

'I know,' wailed Rupert, and half the café's

clientele turned to look at him, 'it's so awful.'
Maia suspected that Rupert was finding
material luxury no substitute for thwarted
passions.

'How did you know where to find me?'
Maia asked.

'It wasn't really you I was looking for,' he
said, and winked. 'But I asked around.
Apparently the locals don't find it so difficult
to spot a Western woman trying to blend in.
What are you doing here?'

'The company is better. I found Armand in
the street. Or rather, he found me.'

'How coincidental,' said Rupert.

'Yes, I thought so too,' said Armand.

'Have you two met before?' asked Maia.

Armand looked down.

'But of course we have!' laughed Rupert.
'Armand is a regular at the Grand Tazi. He is
rather tight with Mahmoud and your Historian.'

'Really?' asked Maia, thinking about
Mahmoud's warning the other night.

'*J'adoute!*'

Armand and Maia both looked at Rupert.

'Armand, you just touched the knight!'

Armand looked at him blankly.

'I'm afraid I'm rather strict on the subject
of chess. I believe that if you touch a piece,
even inadvertently, you must move it. You
must say, '*J'adoute*'.'

'That is ridiculous, Rupert. I might as well start on you with a lecture about the phallic symbolism of chess pieces. Ignore him,' Maia said to Armand. 'This man is just a gigolo.'

Armand smiled at them both benignly. Rupert was looking around the bar, shifting in his chair as the look of desire flitted over his face. She wondered how he was able to tolerate the arrangement with the Bambages. Despite his slimness, there was a certain vulnerability about him. He had the face of one plunged into corruption.

A moment later, Rupert's attention was fixed once more on the chessboard.

'So, my friends, did you know that chess originated in India, probably around the sixth century? The sixty-four squares of eight by eight is the *mandala*, the symbolic representation of the Universe. It was a game of warfare and fate — '

'It still is,' said Armand.

Rupert trailed off as he realised that Armand was staring at him. Maia was astonished to see the self-important Rupert silenced with a mere look.

Armand stood up. 'I don't think we will continue with the game. Maia, it seems you have won.'

'Armand, don't be a bad loser.'

'Of course not, Maia! It looks as if you have

110

won. I can't hang around here all day dragging out the game.'

'But I will play with you instead!' said Rupert.

'I don't think so. I'm taking Maia down to the Grand Tazi. I have something to discuss with Mahmoud.'

'Then I shall accompany you!'

'Shall you?' Armand raised his eyebrow.

'I don't mind.' Maia was becoming fond of Rupert and his eccentric ways. She was pleased by his decision to align himself with her after Lucy Bambage's comments. She accepted Armand taking charge, and found that she enjoyed it.

6

When they reached the Grand Tazi the violet
sky was filled with shadows, and storks lined
the city walls. In the dark, smoky recesses
crudely carved into the stone behind the pool
sat several Russians and Arabs quietly convers-
ing, their heads bowed closely together. It was
becoming obvious to Maia that the Grand
Tazi was a popular venue for unsavoury exiles,
for expectations and transactions. Beneath the
darkening sky, Maia saw how Mahmoud's
shabby yard might come to appear almost
luxurious, despite the weeds twisting around
the fixed stone plinths, the cracked, peeling
walls, and the filthy, ragged curtains. Emerald
tiles lay broken beneath her feet, and Mahmoud had added several small lemon trees in
huge terracotta pots placed around the pool.
Light glowed gently from intricately worked
wrought-iron lamps of tinted glass, which hung
from the walls.

Maia's stomach dropped as she turned and
saw the Bambages. Watching them interact
with one another and their paid escort,
Rupert, who had returned straight to them
just as surely as a dog returns panting to its

master, Maia wondered how the purple-faced Martin Bambage found it possible to tolerate such an unbearable situation. All these people had something in common; they had nothing in mind but a taste of oblivion whilst remaining cocooned in their wealth. Fleeing expectations that they were either unwilling or unable to meet, they were sidesteppers of life, who were more than willing to leave everything behind and wait out their time beneath the North African sun.

Armand and Rupert disappeared off somewhere, and Maia hesitated to approach anybody. Mahmoud was nowhere to be seen, and no other familiar faces were visible. As she approached the pool, she noticed the Historian sitting on the edge, dangling his legs in the water, his trouser legs rolled up. His arched eyebrows and patrician face, his high cheekbones and straight mouth set in the stiff entirety of his face, she sensed a real dishonesty about the man. His trousers were dirty and splashed. The sight of the reserved and distinguished Historian sitting there was an amusingly strange sight. He looked to her like a small schoolboy playing truant.

Maia sat down beside him.

'And how is it going with you this afternoon?' said the Historian, as if she saw him every day.

Maia was learning to play the game. 'Very well. You do look a little overdressed for paddling.'

The Historian had brought a man with him back from the bar, who was standing just behind. 'Hello.' The man reached down to take Maia's hand. He had long, thin fingers and they were icy to the touch. An enormous gap between his two front teeth lent him an unassuming lisp.

The man's name was Konstantin and he had a bald, marble-looking head, upon which spectacles perched. Konstantin moved in an awkward way, his trunk seemed unstable, and as he spoke he swayed like a willow tree in the breeze. Amongst the hordes of vacationing foreigners, Maia had come to recognise the occasional individual who appeared a little more accustomed to their surroundings. The world of foreigners in Morocco existed separately whilst remaining at the same time part of the broader society. They had their own economy, myths and code of ethics. At first Maia thought they were, for the most part, the frauds, the freaks and the failures who could not make it at home, but by now she was prepared to admit that their stories were more varied and complex than their appearances would suggest and the Grand Tazi was the social hub for this transient tribe. Konstantin followed the Historian obediently around the bar. Every time the Historian moved, his bulbous eyes swivelled to follow him and they barely left him for a moment. He glared at Maia as the Historian talked, his animosity palpable.

'What is this statue?' asked Maia, and she pointed to a grotesque statue, which had been placed awkwardly on a raised plinth at the furthest corner of the pool. Carved in grey stone, it was a small, awkward creature with a hugely swollen, obscenely large member. It was grinning lewdly at her in the dusk. Maia wanted to tear her eyes away from the creature, but it stood directly facing the guests, commanding their attention.

'That is the Priapus. Mahmoud keeps it here to guard his garden,' said the Historian, managing to maintain a serious expression.

'Really?' said Maia, incredulously.

'Oh yes,' said the Historian, 'the Priapus was the ugly child of Aphrodite, cursed by Hera, who made him offensive in his ugliness.' Maia inspected the statue; he seemed to lend the hotel an even more hedonistic air.

'Priapus was born from Aphrodite's womb with a huge belly, feet and hands, nose and tongue, and this gigantic, continuously erect phallus. It seems that Aphrodite was so offended that she cast Priapus out and abandoned him.'

'How cruel,' was all that Maia felt able to say.

'Very cruel,' continued the Historian, 'but due to his voracious fertility, he is presumed to protect gardens.' Happily he quoted, ''O, wayfarer, thou shalt fear this god and hold thy hand high: this is worth thy while, for lo! There stands ready thy cross, the phallus.''

Maia looked on, sceptical. Everything that the Historian was; her suspicions of his dishonesty, his chequered past, his secrets, were inseparable from this hotel. The Grand Tazi kept drawing her in; she was intrigued by the oddness of it all. When Maia was around the Historian, she was starting to have the horrible suspicion that he was mocking her.

'Who said that?' asked Maia.

'Virgil. Be careful not to transgress.' And with that, the Historian sauntered off to speak to Mahmoud, and Maia was left alone with Konstantin.

'Mihai tells me that you are an artist,' he said, 'and that you are obsessed with painting the female form.'

Maia sighed. 'I have already explained this. You must admit that especially here, the social presence of women is very different to that of a man. To be born a woman is to be born into the keeping of men, into an allotted and confined space.'

'Have you finished?' Konstantin asked, in his bizarre lisp.

She continued, though slightly taken aback, 'Do you not understand that a woman must constantly watch herself? Here, I must always watch myself. It becomes a little tedious.'

Konstantin smiled. His accented English was stilted. 'I feel I must tell you not to worry. I prefer men.'

'I am sorry. Then I suppose that you have visited The Parador bar?' said Maia, recalling the café she had visited with Armand.

'Of course, but usually I come here. I have seen several of your new friends there, however.'

Maia was intrigued. 'Which friends?'

Konstantin only tapped the side of his nose with his long fingers. He leaned towards her. 'Don't trust him.'

'Trust who?'

'Anyone.'

'Not even you?' Maia tried to joke. She didn't like the turn the conversation was taking. 'Do you mean Armand?'

'I was not referring to him. But, him too. I am sorry for him.' He said this with a tone of superiority.

'Why is that?'

'He must run to the Historian's whims; he is desperate for success. He runs too much.

They do not like one another.'

'I know he has suffered,' said Maia.

'No, you do not know what you think you know. Armand makes many other people suffer too.'

'So he is damaged. That is not so unusual.'

'Be careful. Armand suffers no internal conflict. If the theory is correct that feeling is in the head, then ... the Historian is the worst. He likes to weave his webs.'

'Webs? What do you mean? I thought you and the Historian were close.'

Konstantin beamed proudly. 'We are. But that does not mean he is without fault.'

'What is it exactly you are trying to say?'

'The Historian likes to research people.'

'People?'

'Yes, he likes to test them.'

'Does he test you?' Maia was laughing now in an attempt to cover up her feelings of discomfort.

'In the past, he did. Now he has no need to test me further.'

Maia was forming her next question as Armand walked over to them, accompanied by Mahmoud and the Historian. Together they passed the rest of the night as other clientele wandered aimlessly around the bar. The Historian remained deep in conversation with Mahmoud, whilst Maia and Konstantin talked together quietly.

When he looked at her, his eyes were warm, and Maia sensed that Konstantin was able to get away with almost anything he wanted. Around them people exchanged their meaningless pleasantries. As Maia felt Armand's cold eyes penetrating her, almost immediately she contemplated surrender. She curled up on her chair.

'I'm feeling very sleepy,' she said quietly to Armand. With a subtle smile she offered herself to him, and a silent and surreptitious look passed between them. The Historian caught their glance, and smiled. They left Mahmoud with the Historian, and Armand walked her back to the riad.

In the room alone with him, it struck her how small and airless the space was. He placed his hand upon her thigh, and she looked away. She knew what was to come, and she didn't mind. She had resigned herself to its inevitability. The heat allowed her to relinquish all authority. He stood only a foot away from her, but she was unable to step towards him.

'I was watching you — '

'I know.'

'I want to talk to you properly,' said Maia.

'What is the point of that?' smiled Armand.

'I need a friend here.'

'We will not be friends,' Armand said, pulling her closer. Later, she realised that would have been the moment to stop.

'Why not?' asked Maia, closing her eyes.

'Because all of the interactions between a man and a woman are sexual.'

'I do not believe that.' She opened her eyes, pulling away from him. 'Why has the Historian never returned to Europe?'

'He has never wanted to. He likes it here.'

'Then why is he so bitter?'

'The Historian's former colleagues were ungrateful.'

'Do you know what happened?'

Armand shrugged. 'They did not get on. They were not cooperative. You should ask him.' He knew that she would not. The Historian was far too intimidating. 'But you don't want me to be your friend. You want me to conform to the needs of your unhappy life,' he said.

Maia didn't reply. What Armand didn't know was that behind Maia's passion, she believed that if she could be seen as the property of Armand, she could continue to visit the bar at the Grand Tazi, liberated from Mahmoud's advances.

He traced the lines of her face, her nose, the corners of her lips. He pulled her closer still, and there were his hands on her waist, the exploration of her breasts. She succumbed to him.

'I feel as if I've always lived in exile, never belonging.'

'You are very sentimental.'

'I can't help it. That's the way I am.'

Even to her own ears she sounded ridiculous. The truth was not so romantic; she always felt as if she were missing out, as if the party was somewhere else. Now she stood naked before him, and he came towards her.

'What do you want, Maia?'

'I want to lose myself.'

'I can give you that,' he said.

There was a darkness and an expectation, and an exciting vulnerability, and then it came hot and stagnant, eyes closed and bodies enlaced. With his thighs pressing down upon her she dissolved herself into a frenzied emptiness. She longed for annihilation, life without responsibility, and at some point she must have murmured this to him, for he raised his head to her and acknowledged it. He thrilled her, with his uncertain past and unreadable emotions, and bonded by sweat she abandoned herself to their nocturnal pleasure.

She knew she had demeaned herself. That he wanted to leave as quickly as possible. That she disgusted him. There was silence in the room and a growing aliveness outside.

She felt lightheaded, the events of the night before unfolding like a dream. She followed him down to the front door of the riad. Ina was standing in the corridor leading to the courtyard, looking at Maia as she passed her by.

'*Putain.*' For a moment Maia was uncertain if she had heard the whispered word, but when she turned round Ina was staring up at her maliciously.

Maia ignored her and returned back up the stairs to her room, where she lay discarded and silent upon the bed.

★　★　★

From their first night together, Armand knew that he had her hooked. The power he felt himself holding over her was delicious in its irresistibility; the memory of it made him wince with desire. But Armand was the type of man who thinks that he loves women. He loved their shape, their warmth and their scent. But he despised the way they made him feel, their pull on him and all their sordid manipulations. And even when they came to understand this, still they found him fascinating. He pitied them. For Armand, Maia was a woman to pursue, and nothing more.

If Maia had known Armand's thoughts,

they would have horrified her. But now as she looked herself over, she felt only repulsion for the person she had allowed herself to become. She washed her face and wiped the sleep from her eyes, watching the transformation take place as she made herself become all that she showed to the outside world, whilst inside she was still able to remain detached.

Nobody disturbed her as the day dragged on. In the afternoon the streets were empty, abandoned to indolence and heat. The sun climbed in the sky over the ochre-hued city and then began to fall. When she woke, covered in sweat, as the wailing muezzin called the faithful to prayer, it was to a silent house. The room was suffocating. She opened the door, padded out over the smooth stone slabs and called to Ina. There was no reply, only the sound of water tinkling in the courtyard. She went to dress. In the tiny bathroom there was only cold water but she cared little and stood under the cold trickle for a long time. She dressed in light jeans and a loose shirt and went onto the roof, to drink what was left of her bottled water and smoke the first cigarette of the day. Somewhere she had read that these flat roofs had once been the preserve of women, from where they could watch the life on the streets yet remain invisible. She surveyed the homing pigeons on the rooftops beside her and peered downwards into the endless, seething labyrinth of side streets. She sat there for hours, before a drumming sound awoke her from her daze, and she could see the men making their way towards prayer.

The view from the roof let Maia peer into the ordinary lives of women engaged in their daily chores. She began to photograph them, and then having gathered the shots she needed, she could paint them as she had wanted to from the start. She depicted the light at all times of the day, the varying shades, the sunset over the city, the women who are hidden behind its walls. She enjoyed the noise she could hear rising up from the streets, the occasional shrieking of children, the playing of a strange, dirge-like music, with wailing voices that stirred in her a vague, distant longing. It was a very different city from the one in which she had arrived. In those days she rarely wanted to go down into the crowded lanes, dreading the attention, the suffocating heat and the stench of the bodies in the crowds. But now, curiosity took her in its firm grip and she went down into the pink city streets.

For a time she believed she was content. She worked hard; and when she saw the Historian he sighed, 'Well, I suppose you'll

124

get it all done eventually. Good work with the library.'

Armand appeared with three drinks and placed them on a round table, which he pulled up to the pool. The evening was still early, when the sun had just gone down and the courtyard lamps were being lit. The fig trees were stretching up to the darkening sky; their fruit, soft and bruised, lay discarded around the tree trunks. He smiled at her, and Maia wondered what the Historian knew about him.

Maia resolved not to give the Historian any further information; he could think what he liked of her. She told them that she had been exploring in the streets when Armand had found her, but the Historian seemed disinterested and he got up and went into the hotel. Maia was curious to know what Armand's business was in Morocco. She reasoned that what he did was really no concern of hers. Instead they discussed the Historian, and his eccentric behaviour.

'He is so secretive. I have no idea where he goes or what he does. We haven't even had a decent conversation, apart from the time when he showed me briefly around his riad. And I do admire his work. That's also why I'm here.'

'Really? It has nothing to do with living

rent-free in the centre of the medina?'

'I do all the work he asks me to do.'

Armand leaned towards her. 'Don't concern yourself with his business, Maia.'

She ought to have been irritated by his patronising tone, but somehow she didn't mind at all. She was unreasonably delighted to hear her name on the tip of his tongue.

'I see.' Maia stared at his lips. She looked at him, recalling her past innocence, and the strong belief she had held that love was for once only. She had never before been open to other possibilities of pleasure.

'How is your painting going?'

'Slow. I've been painting city scenes, that sort of thing.'

'No women then?' He was laughing at her.

'Not yet.' She was lying to him and continued talking to cover up her unease.

'There is a painting I saw a copy of in a book. I thought of you. It's a close-up of the genitals and abdomen of a naked woman, lying on a bed and spreading her legs.'

She laughed. 'That is a little obscene. I'm not sure why you thought of me. But I do know the one you mean. It is *L'origine du Monde*. Courbet, oil-on-canvas. I think it is beautiful.'

'It is quite obscene. So tell me, do you believe that the world originates from women?'

'In a way the world does originate from women. I don't know why so many religions worship a male god. Who knows what changed. But I can tell you that during the nineteenth century, art changed the way the nude body was displayed, and Courbet was one of those painters. He rejected academic painting and its smooth, idealised nudes. I like that.'

'Why do you admire his work so much?'

'He was a realist. He pushed the limits of what was considered presentable. And he didn't depict the woman's face; he had a certain admiration for women.'

'So you believe that women are the origin of the world?' said the Historian, who had returned from the bar and, stood hovering over them with a drink and a smile playing upon his lips. Armand nudged the Historian and to Maia's surprise the Historian did not seem hostile to his overt friendliness. In fact he seemed almost pleased.

'So, you do indeed believe that women are the origin of the world?' said the Historian. 'Was it the chicken, or the egg?'

He laughed slyly at what he imagined was his own witticism and Maia wondered which question she was supposed to answer first.

'What is your style of painting?' asked Armand.

'I'm not quite sure. I haven't tried to define it. Perhaps it is most similar to Fauvism.'

'Surely that is an excuse for laziness,' said the Historian.

'You are entitled to your opinions,' she said.

'I'd like to see your paintings,' said Armand.

'I haven't shown them to anybody since I've been here.'

'Then perhaps you will show them to me.'

Her whole body screamed against this. At that moment, there in the bar she experienced a terrible dislocation; an insight into the relationship between them. An awareness that despite his hold over her, not only were they wholly incompatible, but neither did she trust him.

The bar was beginning to get busier now, and brass lanterns were lit around the edge of the pool. The Historian reappeared by the table; he was swaying slightly. Maia was surprised; originally he had seemed so controlled.

'Stop bothering with the past, Maia. It won't do you any good. It hasn't to me,' he said.

Maia was surprised, judging by the world in which he now consumed himself. 'But you are the Historian!'

The Historian eyed Maia, and finally he said coldly, 'I really don't think you know what sacrifice is.' He turned his back on her, and Maia went cold. The snub was obvious; his true feelings towards her were becoming impossible to ignore.

Every so often the Historian stretched his long neck back and laughed at something. Konstantin was nodding his small head approvingly as the Historian was exclaiming, 'There are so many lives to be lived, if only one doesn't care about the opinion of mankind, money and material success.' He turned challengingly to Maia and his eyes were sharp. 'Don't you agree?'

'I don't know,' said Maia. 'Doesn't the opinion of others matter at all? It keeps many of us on the right path.'

The Historian glared at her. 'What is the right path? Please, tell me. For I think I may have diverged from it long ago.' He held up his glass, and Konstantin smiled in adulation.

The way that Konstantin looked at the Historian, Maia could not help but assume that he was the Historian's very own acolyte.

'Don't we have something to discuss?' Konstantin said to the Historian.

But the Historian brushed him off with annoyance, and he left with Armand to find Mahmoud.

Konstantin smiled. 'Excuse me,' he said quietly. Slowly he moved off in the direction of a group of leather-jacketed Arabs.

Since spending the night with Armand, Maia had not showed her face at the Grand Tazi. She had preferred to stay away for a while, concentrating on the use of perspective in her art and doing the work that had been set for her by the Historian. She was not particularly keen to see Armand, despite not hearing from him. She felt that during their last night together she had suffered an embarrassing loss of control. She was suffering from that most dreadful of afflictions: hope. Hope that he might begin to feel something for her too.

Eventually she found that she could not keep away from the Grand Tazi, and she was pleased that for a while, at least, she didn't see Armand. Instead, she passed her evenings with Konstantin.

On one of these evenings, Konstantin made a comment about the Historian in French — too fast, its meaning obscured. He said something about suicide, and she tried hard not to think about it. They came to know one another well, and Maia felt protected in the face of Mahmoud's disturbing enthusiasm.

Mahmoud had a fondness for both Moroccan and European pastries. He kept them stocked behind the bar, and he licked his fingers incessantly. 'Try these! They're called *rghaif.*' He pushed a dozen, smeared with honey and jam, towards Maia and Konstantin, who looked at the plate with disgust.

'Try one!' urged Mahmoud. Maia tried one, and she retched at the taste of the sweaty, uncooked dough.

'You shall have to get used to them here!' boomed Mahmoud, and he went over to the next table to amuse some Czech tourists with his false bonhomie. Mahmoud's sycophancy disgusted her. He laughed immoderately at everyone and everything. She suspected that the warm façade concealed a definitive nihilism.

That evening, on her way to the Grand Tazi Maia stopped at the Place of the Dead. By day, the square was an ordinary, large and quiet place, but as evening fell it teemed with shifting crowds of onlookers. It was enchanted. There were snakes, lizards and other wild creatures of the desert. A group of blind beggars were singing for their suppers in rows of ten at a time. Kerosene and spices hung in the air and blended unpleasantly with the dust and exhaust of the battered cars.

Just as she was leaving the square she passed a tiny stall where a herbalist sat on the ground. Odd-looking potions in unlabelled jars were set out before him. In the backdrop, the Koutoubia Minaret glowed and she watched the shifting circle of onlookers and fruit sellers shouting their wares. Apes were being led on chains, and there were musicians and a troupe of young dancing boys. She was cut off from her past life; all this had now become her world. Her life was contained within these streets; her painting, the guests at the bar. No news from outside could permeate. She passed the days in an indolent state.

On that particular evening, Maia was unsurprised to find Konstantin lolling at the bar by the pool, wholly immersed in the possibility of his next drink. It was a little early, even for Konstantin.

'Another whisky, Tariq,' he slurred in the vague direction of the barman. 'Where have you been today?' lisped Konstantin. His breath was heavy and stale in her face.

'Painting. It is very interesting what you can see from the rooftops.'

'Pigeons? They make pastries out of those pigeons. A flaky cinnamon sprinkled pie stuffed with pigeon livers and eggs.' Gleefully he rubbed his hands together. 'Delicious, makes for a lovely meal.'

'Konstantin, you would be surprised.'

His loss of interest was visible. Five small whisky glasses were lined up before him on the bar. Konstantin was a fastidious man, and

Maia had become used to the long pauses before he spoke.

'I have trouble,' he pronounced slowly.

'That's nothing new, Konstantin.' Everyone she had met in this twilight quarter were evaders of one sort or another, ill-fated sidesteppers of life, drawn to the life where very little can go a long way. He was evidently drunk and for a moment Maia was of a mind to warn him that he must watch his wallet. But Konstantin must be used to their ways by now. He was a peculiar mix of cynicism and naiveté. As she grew to know Konstantin, Maia became fond of him.

Konstantin slumped down on his stool, pushing back the wire-rimmed spectacles that were always on the verge of falling from his head. He possessed a certain innocence, which endeared him to those who knew him.

Outside the hotel, Maia heard as if muffled in the distance the call to prayer. She watched the twitching of Konstantin's small features and the round head perched atop the unusually tall neck. He spoke again, more slowly than ever: 'No, it is not new.' He showed Maia a letter, which he snatched back immediately. 'I can't show you. But it is very bad. I shall probably have to stay here a while longer.'

Maia asked Konstantin nothing. This was

the unspoken rule at the Grand Tazi. One did not ask questions, and accepted the half-truths and fabrications of the regulars as if they were the most delightful revelations one could ever hope to hear.

'I wait,' he said. 'I wait and I wait, for a final answer from Athens.' Rather sorrowfully, he banged his whisky glass down on the bar. A fat tear rolled down his perfect moon face, as cold and as white as marble. His hair was almost all gone and his clothes parodied the long black gowns of a priest's tunic.

Poor man, thought Maia. The cloister was all that Konstantin had ever known, and now he was stuck here, with the rest of them. So he could only wait, spend his time drinking, and perhaps maybe find more of the same trouble which had sent him scuttling here in the first place. When Maia thought of this, she was unable to muster any sympathy for him. He clasped and unclasped his fingers, gnawing at his bloodless lips. Beyond them, the city was nonchalant, unaware and unconcerned by the offences of its foreign inhabitants. Konstantin was holding his head in his hands and whining, 'Oh, Jesus, everybody is against me, I had the urges, you see.' He was sobbing violently, his face white and puffy. 'I am so ashamed. It is so brutal. Brutal. Wrong.'

'Yet still you do it.'

Even in his size he exhibited a lanky innocence. He was after all, Maia told herself, merely a victim of his own desires.

Konstantin looked at her stupidly, as if he might have expected some other reaction, some indulgence from her. 'I can't stop myself.'

'You do not want to stop yourself. You believe you can get away with it. Did you imagine that you might find refuge here, Konstantin? You thought he would protect you, didn't you?'

For a moment Konstantin looked at her appraisingly, with an unusual coolness. 'I thought he cared for me. But you should not trust him. No-one should trust him.'

'I haven't seen the Historian for a while,' she said.

'I wouldn't expect to. The Historian suits himself. He comes and goes.'

'I don't know why he stays here,' she continued thoughtfully. 'He could teach and write anywhere.'

'Not now, he would have to do some work.' He looked at her face, and seemed to catch himself. 'I mean . . . listen.'

Maia made no reply, thinking of the crumpled-up papers that filled the drawers of his study.

'I wish someone would tell me what was going on here,' said Maia.

Konstantin gave a short laugh, tinged palpably with bitterness. 'Oh yes, Maia, so do I.'

She sighed, and went to leave.

'Wait.' Konstantin had his bony hand on her arm. 'The Historian is not all bad. He was experimenting . . . research.'

'Historical experiments? What sort are those?'

'He studies everything. Not only history. Behavioural. He needed funds. His department was unhelpful. He had to get it from somewhere. He owed everybody.'

'Fraud?' said Maia. 'That's almost too banal for him.'

'That is the truth.'

'Why tell me this? You seem to hate him.'

'I do not hate him, I love him!' His mouth gaped; he looked aghast, and he dissolved again into tears. The lines of his face took on the significance of his suffering, of the deepest dejection. The Historian did not love him; he rejected him and Konstantin was humiliated.

'He doesn't want people to know his situation. But he is in trouble now. That is his problem.'

'Maybe you care for him more than he cares for you, Konstantin.'

'You are right. He should be nothing to me. But he is everything,' he said with a melodramatic flourish.

His endless self-pity was beginning to bore Maia and she looked around for a distraction. She imagined the parties once held here, which had filtered through from the hall into the dried-up old courtyard where the fountain had tinkled alongside the voices of ladies, where now lay two men, smoking away the days.

The bar was starting to fill now, although Maia doubted that the clientele were all of the kind that Mahmoud was so desperately hoping to attract. Amongst the foreigners living out their sterile expatriate lives, there were a few Berber-looking men in cheap leather jackets, men with sufficient means and attractive business interest to mix with the bar's clientele, swarthy men with jaded imaginations and evil intentions. There was corruption here, and it was palpable.

Maia attempted to change the subject, now that she saw that Konstantin was completely unwilling to discuss her own interests. He was utterly self-obsessed, yet in so many ways he was charming. 'I can't stand those two apes down at the entrance. They are always staring at me. I hate having to pass them. They are intimidating.'

Konstantin looked at her and laughed, as if humouring some petulant child. 'You know why they are here.' He tried to sound soothing, but failed.

'Yes. Security, apparently. Well, Mahmoud needs to do something about them. I really cannot stand them.'

Maia did not feel that she was a woman to be intimidated by men, especially here, where she suffered the constant calls in the street. Even in the haven of the Grand Tazi she felt their greedy eyes looking her over.

An Arab man, who Maia had noticed watching her lasciviously at the door earlier, came over to them and gripped Konstantin's slender arm. The man's eyes were blank. He ignored Maia and she found that Konstantin had suddenly turned his back on her. Maia had seen several men like that all over the city; they were evidently a sign of punishment. Being outwardly gay looked like trouble amidst the shifting sands of Moroccan sexuality, a very delicate balance. With public space universally gender segregated, the city was a place of seductive contradictions. All Konstantin's attention was now focused solely on the man, and Maia watched the pair's interactions.

Eventually, Konstantin left to complete his exchange, and Maia was alone at the bar. The Grand Tazi was about the only place she felt she could sit unaccompanied and have a drink. She never stopped being captivated by a city where so much of the population secreted the overpowering scent of being on the make.

Tariq the barman was suddenly in front of Maia, gazing at her intensely with his peculiar stare.

'What will you be doing now you have been left all alone? I suppose you might want to paint me?'

Maia went to leave.

'Wait, you pay.'

'No, Tariq. For free. Always for free. Mahmoud promised.'

She went and watched the other guests from the foyer at the foot of the stairs, which went spiralling up into the enclaves of the old hotel, where Mahmoud kept his rooms free for other transients, and who knew what else. It was whispered that every night drug fiends stretched out upon the ragged rugs in the upstairs halls and undemanding women looked for effortless work in the long passageways.

For a long time she sat alone looking at the chattering crowd through a dim haze of boredom, as people came towards her and sat down and went away again, filtering out as the sun came up. There were days when Maia did not even trouble herself to return to the Historian's riad. At the Grand Tazi there was always a party. She wanted to lose herself in the sun and fleeting moments of pleasure she thought she could glean. One afternoon she had not meant to fall asleep in the sun, she awoke to the sharp sounds of jabbering; Maia's head hurt terribly as waves of nausea came upon her. A sense of utter shame, of near nakedness before the hotel guests as their eyes rested upon her. She managed to gather up her clothes, heading blindly into the hotel and up the staircase to the room Mahmoud allowed her to use before anybody might notice. She went to shower, then came back into the room and pulled down the shutters.

Several hours later she woke, refreshed, and studied herself in the bathroom mirror, before heading down to reception.

The two men at the door only allowed people in on the advice of Mahmoud, but now it appeared that they were letting in their local friends. Maia knew that Mahmoud was attempting to cater for a more cultured clientele, but from the people here it seemed that this policy was failing. Maia was sitting quietly, smoking and listening to the lone guitarist playing, when there was shouting and a commotion.

'*Salloum allaykoum,*' a young man was shouting as he charged bullishly towards the pool area.

Now Mahmoud appeared, his face red and bulging. He was hurling abuse at the two men who were supposed to be guarding the entrance. 'How did this cretin get in here? Get him out!'

The young man dived straight into the empty pool, and came up spluttering a few moments later. The two guards grabbed the intruder by each arm, lifting him out of the water he squealed in pain as his arms were stretched. As they kicked him, so viciously that each rib made a grotesque cracking sound, he curled himself smaller and smaller into a ball until he lay huddled upon the ground whimpering to himself.

'You will leave now,' Mahmoud told him.

But the man still had spirit, even as Mahmoud's bulk shadowed over him. 'I am from this place too. I have right to be here. I can enter.'

'Huh. *Wa qul bravo.*' Mahmoud changed to English, so that he could properly display his linguistic skills before his guests. 'This is my hotel. I say who enter. You want to mix with foreigners? Now I tell you not try to come in here. Go away now. You make big, big fool of yourself.'

'No,' came a small voice.

'Do not argue with me,' Mahmoud said, and he kicked the man in the stomach. 'You are in real *harira* this time, little man. I know your type.'

A tussle ensued, ending with Mahmoud sitting proudly astride the man as his men held down the man's flailing arms.

'*Je suis moi le patron*,' bellowed Mahmoud, elbowing his way through the gathered crowd. 'Now, is all above board, above board,' he repeated loudly; it was evidently a phrase he had once learned well.

Security took the man, who by now was completely wilted, his fight having deserted him, and dragged him outside.

To her revulsion, Mahmoud came towards her and stroked her hair. 'You be safe now here. Do not worry. Never worry.'

7

On the afternoon that Konstantin decided to
introduce Maia to his rather intimidating
female friend, the sweltering air stifled Maia,
pulling tightly around her neck like a
steaming vice. As Konstantin took her arm
and led her across the room, she was finding
it difficult to breathe. At first, Maia saw only
a slim back wrapped in a navy dress, and
dark, bare feet. The woman threw back her
head and laughed.

'Konstantin,' gasped Maia in surprise, 'she
looks like a cat.' The woman was sleek and
angular. She was just on holiday, he insisted,
an extended break. The two had known one
another for years.

'I think you get on very, very well,' said
Konstantin.

'How did you meet?'

'In Roma. I met him through work.'
The tall Roman woman took Maia's hand
with a light, practiced touch. Her name was
Cassandra Magliozzi, and she was the former
fashion editor of a well-known Italian gossip
magazine. Maia was surprised when she
revealed how she had met Konstantin.

143

'I had no idea that Konstantin modelled.'

'He doesn't generally. I was directing a fashion shoot set in a Catholic Church. Some of the girls were wearing cassocks and sitting with the priests. It was a little naughty.' Cassandra gave a sharp laugh.

'But I thought he was Greek Orthodox.' Maia was somewhat affronted, and Konstantin looked embarrassed.

'Oh, never mind about that. It is the concept that is important.'

Her voice erupted in short, staccato bursts. Delicate attention had been paid to the moulding of Cassandra; she was dark and slim, with hair that caught the sun as she moved.

Cassandra attached herself to Maia all afternoon. She felt flattered by Cassandra's attention, but when she confessed to Cassandra her recent liaison with Armand, the Italian was unsympathetic. As soon as she opened her mouth, she knew that her revelations were a mistake, but after the long days alone she was lured by the prospect of feminine companionship. Maia's obsession with this man was obvious to Cassandra, who promptly decided that she would like to see him for herself. Cassandra knew without seeing Armand that he was not the irresistible prize Maia spoke of; he was just a man, like any other.

'This uncertainty, my dear, it is the vital

element of all seduction.'

Maia's face fell, but Cassandra commented disparagingly, 'This attachment you talk of, it is false. You know nothing yet. Why do you come here?'

Maia shrugged. Already she regretted confiding in this woman. The truth was Mahmoud's bar offered company, and an opportunity to be taken outside herself, into the intrigues of his guests. But she would never reveal this to Cassandra, and as she wiped the sweat from her brow, she noticed that Cassandra's own brow was cool.

She did not know where Armand was, and she was not sure she cared. Abroad, away from her life in London, nothing much seemed to matter anymore. Maia was now able to admit to herself that she simply wanted to feel nothing at all. The prospect of becoming a recluse was becoming more appealing the more time she spent abroad. Anxiety was caused by other people, and she did not want to form attachments; she wanted to have nothing to do with them.

Sitting under the ragged curtain that Mahmoud had hung so unevenly over the bar, Maia watched Cassandra emerge from the pool, glistening and sleek. She wore her face with a nonchalance that belied the exquisite attention she paid to it. The Grand Tazi was a haunt for those who could afford its secrecy, giving the opportunity for men who practiced their businesses under the façade of respectability and those who did not, come together without fear of retribution from the authorities. Some tourists seemed to imagine that this dilapidated version of chic was the latest place to be, as Mahmoud reaped the benefits from them. Maia returned to the poolside, but beside Cassandra with her enviable body, she felt mediocre. The woman was a marvel of beauty, an advertisement for conspicuous consumption and leisure. Armand entered and he saw Maia, but immediately turned to talk to someone. While she watched Armand, he knew all the while that she was looking at him. Beside her she heard Cassandra continuing her languid monologue, her soul given to a shallow cause. Maia fixed a smile on her face; the perpetual, unchanging smile of the doll-like woman. She went over to the pool, and sank under the water where she felt a transformation take place. Above the surface, dark figures were moving about, but they were figures from another world.

But she could not stay submerged beneath the surface, and when she came up for air, she saw Armand standing nearby. He did not approach or acknowledge her, and so Maia lounged beside Cassandra in a secluded alcove, which was set back from the pool. She watched with interest as all afternoon his eyes sought out those of Cassandra.

Maia noticed Cassandra watching her rather strangely and she realised that she must have been laughing to herself.

'You know, Maia, you do look quite ugly when you laugh like that.'

'I can't help it, I have a highly developed sense of the ridiculous.'

Cassandra possessed the sort of personality that might be classified as borderline. When they first encountered one another, Maia was immediately impressed by Cassandra's charm and warmth. Only after they had spent more time together, when Cassandra simply refused to go away, did it dawn on Maia that Cassandra had a unique talent for sensing the vulnerabilities in every person that she met. She quickly became aware of how Maia might be flattered, and how easily she could be hurt. An extraordinarily skilled manipulator, she managed to do this with both force and subtlety. Whilst Cassandra was skilled at emitting a golden, seductive glow, she liked to drop little barbs into the conversation, intensely personal ones, which she made just to remind Maia about her weaknesses.

Luxuriously, Cassandra stretched on the sun lounger beside Maia and the oil on her body glinted in the bright sunlight. She was studying an old French magazine, her legs the colour of dark mahogany, and the ease of her life reflected in the softness of her flesh. 'We are the real seducers, Maia. Not the men. We are superior. Don't allow them to usurp you. Men should worship us. They must prostrate themselves before us.'

Looking at her, Maia imagined that men prostrated themselves before Cassandra rather too easily.

Maia lay back, exhausted. In the orange trees above her the birds sang to each other, and the light made circles before her eyes. The perfumes of the oils mixed with the blue of the tiles in the pool made waves inside her head, and in the advancing heat she dozed.

When Maia awoke, she was unbearably hot. She looked to her left: Cassandra had left and was now on the far side of the room with Rupert and the Bambages. Maia turned and smiled at Armand, who was talking animatedly to Rupert, but he didn't notice her. Cassandra was standing in the centre of the group, with all eyes on her. These were the people who weeks earlier had unanimously rejected Maia. Seeing her new acquaintance accepted with such ease, she suffered a sharp thrill of envy that struck her like a blow to the chest.

Cassandra crossed the room, back to where Maia was standing. 'We are going for dinner tonight. You can come too.' A casual invite, somewhat instructed upon Maia.

The entire evening might have turned out quite differently had they all not agreed to accompany Rupert to meet a man he had met that same evening. Konstantin said he was busy; he didn't reveal his reasons.

'Armand knows his way around,' he said, smiling at Maia ingenuously. Lucy Bambage was openly resentful, but they appeared to have negotiated a new deal, and a key element of that deal appeared to be Rupert's temporary freedom. Martin was the provider of the finances, and Maia was coming along for the ride. The day was ending; it was an unusually dull, overcast evening as Maia watched the others in their disparate group moving slowly along the streets.

'I found a fabulous place this afternoon, but it will only be opening now,' said Cassandra. Maia looked around at all her associates. Armand looked impenetrable, and the rest were quiet, as if already they had run out of conversation for the evening.

'So, Cassandra, why don't you show us this place?' Maia said, in a vain attempt to be civil.

'This place you're taking us, Cassandra,'

Rupert interrupted. 'I can't stay for too long. I'm busy later.'

'Well you can go on later then. But you'll see that for now, this place is perfect.' Already she was assuming an unearned authority.

They arrived outside the city walls, on a wide road that was teeming with people and taxis. Maia was feeling out of her depth; these people would abandon her without a second thought. She planned to spend some time alone, to explore the city and regain her independence, the independence she had so enjoyed before she had come to rely on Armand and his support.

Maia feigned interest whenever Martin opened his mouth, but still she suffered a longing to disparage him. The man invited it, but from pity she remained quiet. They were surrounded by cafés into which streamed hordes of young men. Maia could not help glancing at Rupert, who appeared to be in his element. Maia had to admit that she found the place exciting, promising herself to come back again.

'This is the place. It's secret,' said Cassandra, with her curving, sly smile.

'Cassandra, if it is so secret, how do you know about it?' asked Rupert.

'I — '

'I know!' said Rupert. 'You read it in some magazine.'

Maia laughed quietly, but Cassandra seemed smug. All of the signs of complacency were apparent in her features.

An old sign read 'The Continental Palace', and on the steps of the building sat a very large woman guarding her oversize luggage. They were standing beside an iron staircase leading underground. A squat, bulky doorman was standing outside beneath a hanging lantern. He squared up to them in an attempt to appear threatening.

'Very exclusive,' Rupert muttered under his breath.

'Appearances can be deceiving,' retorted Cassandra.

They were one of the few customers in the dimly lit restaurant. Several miserable couples were dining at tables spread far away from one another, as a miniature casino at its far end was blinking incessantly. Tucked away in the corner was a stage where an elderly, sad-looking Elvis was working his way through a decrepit version of 'Roll out the Barrel'. The room was decorated in dark maroon velvet, which Maia found fondly reminiscent of a Parisian brothel she had once visited, purely out of curiosity. Then, she had found the place amusing. Now, she was furious.

'What is this dreadful place you've brought us to?' Maia asked. 'It's empty. This is so exclusive, there is no-one here!'

'Don't you think it's atmospheric?'

'Oh, you mean it's supposed to be ironic!'

'Ironic?' Cassandra repeated stupidly. She was not stupid, but it suited her for the others to think so. 'Anyway, I am so hungry.'

Maia was appalled to hear the murmurs of agreement, and they all sat down and buried their heads in the red leather-bound menus.

'I really don't understand this at all,' Maia proclaimed.

'But you speak French?' asked Cassandra.

'I do — but this is a mess. The language is totally confused and the food is in no particular order. It's also overpriced.'

'That's no problem for us,' said Martin proudly, and Maia glared at him. Martin was not malicious, merely oblivious.

The place was squalid and dull. The uniformed waiters brought a series of starters and placed them on the table, managing to glance at Cassandra's chest as they did so.

'Don't they all have remarkably large teeth?' Cassandra remarked while the men were within listening range. Maia flung what she hoped he might perceive as a conciliatory gaze.

The meal began with lamb tagine and Maia watched in horror as Martin launched himself upon it. He tediously explained how the dish was cooked carefully in Moroccan earthenware, laughing in inappropriate places. This insufferable laughter punctuated every other word so that she was barely able to catch the gist of what he was saying.

'The process keeps the meat unusually moist and tender,' he said. Vacantly, Lucy Bambage placed something in her vast mouth and gobbled.

'So Martin, does the cooking of the tagine take quite as long as your explanation of it?' asked Rupert, and as Maia watched Martin's flabby face fall she immediately felt dreadful. Now that she was eating the tagine, she felt quite nauseous, and then noticed that Martin had chosen an entirely different dish.

The roasted peas with cumin reminded Maia of English skin under the sun. With uncontrollable pleasure, she recalled Armand's olive skin, the grooves around his mouth, and the dark stubble he scraped across her neck. She looked at Armand but he did not return her glance. He was only too aware of how fatally Maia was compelled by him. Cassandra was of a different calibre. To add to her discomfort, Maia was forced to watch Cassandra and Armand sitting opposite, whispering to one another as they shared a rich stew. Maia sat stony-faced, steadily downing one drink after another.

'Watch her go at it!' bellowed Lucy Bambage, drawing the group's attention to Maia's drinking, but Maia barely registered her; she was too far gone to be ashamed. A delicious blur ensued. She was discovering how she might lose herself, a habit she had never before explored. Every so often, Cassandra threw her a conceited glance. Rupert, who had long finished his food, was sat there chain smoking, surveying the room disdainfully. Martin was gobbling down something meaty, his breath heaving noisily as the fork dived in and out of the mess he had created upon his plate. So eager was he to force the next mouthful down that he didn't bother to chew, but stuck out his tongue and plunged the next morsel down as the sauces splattered across his shirt.

'Just melts into the mouth,' he gurgled.

Rupert looked at him. 'Delightful. An authentic feast. But then you think all food is delicious.'

The others laughed at him. Martin lacked the wit to respond. He was tolerated for the luxuries he offered and was so grateful for their company that he never noticed he was being taken advantage of.

In her drunkenness, Maia lost control, lunging at Cassandra, who was sitting there passively across the table. The other men were too transfixed to attempt to stop her.

Tears glinted in Cassandra's eyes and with a sinking heart Maia realised that she had played straight into her hands. With this sudden revelation, she fell back into the chair.

'That's enough!' Armand sat back, and put his arm around Cassandra. He was silent, alternately gazing at Maia, and examining his fingernails. It infuriated Maia that she couldn't elicit more of a response from him. He was utterly immovable. Not for the first time, she wondered if Armand was totally devoid of the ability to feel emotion. He was cold, ruthless and uncaring. At the moment, however, he was infatuated with Cassandra. Finally, he spoke, 'You're being hysterical.'

Lucy Bambage sat with her arms around Cassandra, who was now sobbing into her shoulder. Maia looked on with a detached disgust, as she sobered up. Armand stood.

'Where are you going?'

'For some space.' He grabbed Cassandra, who obediently followed him out.

'I think I'll go with them,' said Martin, and he began to cough uncontrollably.

Rupert laughed. 'Has all this excitement been too much for you, Martin? Have some water.'

Martin was struggling to get up, and by the time he did, Cassandra and Armand had left without him.

'I'm meeting a man soon.' Rupert smiled, chuckling to himself as Maia realised he was drunk. Lucy Bambage looked deflated.

'In the medina, I suppose?'

'Yes. Quick, cheap and easy to meet. Lovely. Just lovely.'

'What exactly do you know about him?' said Maia.

Rupert took a drag on his cigarette, and blew a large lungful of foul-smelling smoke directly into her face.

She tried not to reveal her amusement. 'Don't be rude, Rupert.'

'He's an architect called Yasser. I've seen his photo. He's gorgeous.'

'His real photo?'

'We'll see,' winked Rupert. 'Aren't you going with your boyfriend? Or are you just going to leave him to Cassandra's clutches?'

'I just don't have the energy,' said Maia, slumping on the table.

'Of course you do. Don't be pathetic. Run along.'

They settled the bill and caught up with Armand and Cassandra who were strolling along with the glutinous Martin, who followed like their lumbering manservant.

Cassandra threw them a spiteful glance as Armand gave Maia a rueful grin, hoping to recapture her affection. Maia felt that she couldn't harden herself towards him.

Maia found herself walking next to Martin. She tried to be kind. 'What are you thinking about?'

'My wife . . . '

'I know. I'm sorry.'

They walked on in silence. She wanted to be away from him, from all of them. Maia felt a tap on her shoulder, and she turned around to see a young man clinging on to Rupert's arm. Or perhaps it was the other way round. They were so tightly entwined it was difficult to tell. He pushed the boy forward. Yasser was tall and slim, and by the looks of it, had only just passed puberty.

'This is Yasser,' beamed Rupert. Then he noticed the gloomy look upon Maia's face. Over her shoulder, he could see Armand and Cassandra wrap themselves around one another. 'Oh darling, whatever did you expect?'

Maia took Yasser's hand. 'Hello.'

Martin stood watching with a strange grin pressed firmly upon his face. Armand and Cassandra suddenly pushed themselves forward, eager to meet the new arrival.

'Yasser is studying to be an architect,' Rupert said as he took the young man's hand. Maia was sceptical.

'And where did you meet this charming

157

young man?' asked Martin, with all the sleaze he could muster.

'An architect?' said Cassandra. 'What do you design?'

'Buildings.' As contempt flittered across Yasser's face, Maia was pleased to see that he had taken an instant dislike to Cassandra. 'My family adore English people. Why not come to us for a drink and something to eat?'

His English was surprisingly fluent. But Rupert looked dejected. 'I thought you might show me some good places to go?' It was uncomfortable viewing, but Yasser was determined.

'Of course, we would love to meet your family.' Armand was strangely polite.

Cassandra was excited and she began to squeal. 'Just think of all the wonderful photographs I can take.'

Yasser looked at her with thoughtful disapproval, his head cocked to one side. His home was in the suburbs, south of the city. In the taxi there, Maia sat beside Rupert.

'What do you think of him?'

'Polite. Interesting.'

Armand caught her eye. She looked at him, wondering what he was thinking about her, but he was unreadable.

They left the taxi, deep in the slums. Rupert looked about him with undisguised disgust. 'I am afraid, Yasser, that this is not quite the atmosphere I was led to expect.' He had gone very cold, and his frostiness was tangible. He made a move to get back into the taxi before it drove off. For the first time since they had met that evening, Yasser rushed towards Rupert and squeezed his hand.

'Please come. My family are expecting you. They love to meet foreigners.'

Despite Maia's doubts, she followed the others deeper into the slum, where rivers of dirt flowed between lazy mountains of old rubbish and rotten vegetables.

Lucy Bambage was muttering pitifully to herself. 'Help me, Martin.'

To Maia's delight, Martin was leaving her to struggle as her ludicrously sandaled feet sank deeper into the dirt.

Yasser's home was at the centre of this desolate, rusting suburb, in a block four floors high. A group of boys were kicking around a tired-looking football and they stared at the tourists with unfazed curiosity as Yasser led them through the maze of grey tenement blocks and up the crumbling stairs to his flat.

An unsmiling woman opened the door and eyed the group. Yasser spoke to her in Arabic. He smiled broadly at the group. 'My sister.'

Maia watched Rupert to see his reaction. He seemed a little taken aback, if not wholly unsurprised. But the others were undaunted. Maia stood on the doorstep. She was unwilling to take part yet something made her stay. It was the interplay between these characters that made them all so intriguing.

The woman escorted the guests into the main room, as Lucy Bambage came stumbling up the rear, exhausted from the steps.

'This is our living room,' Yasser told them proudly. Filled with low tables and violet floor cushions, the room was decidedly Eastern, if the quality of the furnishings was far from luxurious. For one moment Maia was thrilled in having managed to see the other Morocco, the one unseen by hordes of tourists.

Yasser uncorked a bottle of red wine. He was evidently not religious. Maia sensed a strange atmosphere; something was amiss. She stood up. 'Yasser, may I help your wife in the kitchen?'

'His sister,' corrected Martin.

'Of course, my mistake.' They were all smirking and she felt ever more uncomfortable. She disappeared into the kitchen, where the woman glowered at her and refused her offer of assistance. Back in the living room, she found that the party was getting underway. Another bottle of wine had been opened.

'I thought Muslims didn't drink, but Moroccan wine is really quite excellent,' Martin slurred.

'But this is a free society,' said Yasser excitedly. Rupert slipped his arm around the young man and a beautiful young woman appeared. She was around fifteen years old, with long black hair and a sullen expression. Maia was amused to notice Armand staring at the girl with lust in his eyes and Cassandra watching her carefully.

'Meet Mariam. She lives close by. She is an expert in giving tattoos. Henna and normal, if you are no coward! Very special.'

Maia smiled at the girl. 'No, thank you so much.' The idea was ludicrous. Who knew exactly what was in that dye, and she was certainly not going to allow a teenager in a desolate suburb to experiment upon her. The situation seemed to become more surreal by the minute.

'You are all my brothers and sisters now!' said Yasser. He grabbed Cassandra's hand and gazed intently into her eyes. 'Henna?' he shouted into her face. Cassandra's eyes widened. 'You want henna. Is beautiful!'

Without Cassandra saying anything, Mariam grabbed her hand and began to draw in dark ink. It didn't look beautiful at all; it was repulsive. Cassandra's face was pure terror as she squealed at Mariam's strong grip. Maia noted Cassandra's puerile vanity, but then realised that Mariam was using a needle. Maia thought for a moment to intervene; but then she sat back. Cassandra had caused her enough trouble. The tattoo would look faded and dull in the morning, like smeared mascara at the end of a party.

Mariam began binding both of Cassandra's hands, swathing them in filthy bandages. Everybody else was too drunk to protest or even to notice. Armand was now sitting on a cushion and ignoring Cassandra, staring straight at Mariam. Cassandra was evidently miserable, now also completely drunk and hunched over with a pain she could not hide. For a brief moment, Maia felt sorry for her. Maia was pleased to see the exquisite Cassandra looking vulnerable, yet at the same time she despised herself for the pleasure she took.

The guests sipped more wine as a circus began to materialise. Strong, broad, dark men began wandering in and out of the small flat as Maia began to feel even more uneasy. Even the rest of the group: the besotted Rupert, the bulbous Martin, the unusually subdued Lucy, Armand and Cassandra, all began to look uncomfortable, as the hostility brewing in the room begin to rise.

'I don't think we should be here. I don't

feel comfortable with all these people.'

Armand shrugged Maia off, irritated by her presence. He was beginning to despise this woman so willing to be at his side. Maia sensed his irritation, and it chilled her. She had caught a wisp of the personality he hid deep down.

'Always a nasty little wasp in my ear, aren't you,' he sneered, his fine features twisting horribly. 'But now I can sting you!' He was laughing almost hysterically.

'I'd never have imagined you to be such a sloppy drunk, Armand.' He was acting out of character. He was usually so controlled, and she began to wonder if the wine had been drugged. She realised that Yasser had not taken so much as a sip, and she had only drunk a little herself.

Yasser opened another bottle. He threw caution aside and began to drink from the bottle, abandoning any concerns for the appearance of civility before his guests. He even forgot that he had introduced the fat woman as his sister and began to pat her on the bottom as she emerged from the kitchen.

'Yes, I did wonder why he was kissing her on the lips,' Martin smirked.

Rupert looked dejected. Mariam was going round the room, holding out her hands for money. Maia saw that Mariam's own hands were free of tattoos. At first, Maia took out a few coins from her wallet, which Mariam seized without thanks. It seemed reasonable to her to pay a small amount. They had drunk Yasser's wine, they had been offered food and experienced the local hospitality, although she had not enjoyed one moment of it. But as the group gave more money, the mood of the room shifted further as more men began to appear.

Mariam noticed the change, and she took the opportunity to take her leave. She stopped in front of Maia, spitting out the only two English words she seemed to know. 'More money.' Now Maia shook her head. She was damned if she was going to donate any more of her money.

Yasser came to life and shouted, 'Sixty dollars!' He slithered towards Maia, and his manner changed. 'Henna is not free.'

Armand surprised her by placing his hand reluctantly in his pocket and shoving the notes into Mariam's palm.

'What did you just pay her?' demanded Rupert.

'About sixty dollars.'

'But that's more than a month's wages here,' said Martin.

'Who cares? Let's just get out of here!' said Rupert.

'You brought us here!' screamed Cassandra, now in obvious pain.

At that moment, the fat wife brought in a huge pile of couscous. Yasser was growing more drunk, and shoving Rupert aside, he placed himself on the cushion next to Maia. For such a wiry man, he was surprisingly strong. He presented her with a crude leather necklace, which he attempted to tie around her neck, stroking the soft nape. 'This will protect her against evil,' he slurred.

'The only thing she needs protecting from is you,' said Rupert, who was evidently affronted that his potential lover had turned out to be blatantly heterosexual.

'Don't be jealous. Just look what a lovely young girl she is. Nice skin, she has such lovely pale skin.' Yasser slumped clumsily forward in a vain attempt to pat Rupert's knee. But he suddenly fell forward as Rupert moved away and they all laughed as Yasser clutched at thin air. Even as he was falling, Maia found Yasser's hands fingering the front of her shirt. She glanced up and saw Cassandra watching her, a strange smile upon her face. Maia's pity evaporated.

There now seemed to have been an unspoken, unanimous decision to eat their food as fast as they were able, to avoid further offending Yasser and his friends, and his wife or sister, whichever one she might be.

Cassandra plucked a few vegetables from the platter. Yasser noticed, and beamed over her monstrously. 'You don't like? But you are so beautiful; you must not worry about your weight.' He turned to Armand. 'And they are both yours? Such beautiful girls. Congratulations.'

Despite their desperate situation, Armand sat on the cushion looking indescribably smug.

Yasser grabbed Maia around the waist and this time she violently threw him off. Her impulsive reaction and the total passivity of the others left the prospect of finishing their food, in ruins. Maia was enraged. Martin was staring vacantly at the plate, her selfish lover was engrossed in Mariam's chest, and Cassandra was sitting on the floor looking bedraggled, and significantly less sophisticated. Maia stood up, scrambling to put on her shoes when the entire household exploded into panic.

There was a struggle, but between whom exactly, Maia was unable to see. Her view was blocked by two large men who had come rushing through from the kitchen.

Yasser was shouting, 'How can you go from here? I am too drunk to drive. And the buses have all stopped now. No more, no more. You must all stay the night here.' Mariam and the fat wife both stood at the door to the kitchen, watching the scenario unfold with unabashed delight.

Maia ran for the door and opened it, as each member of the group filtered out.

Now Yasser was pleading with them. 'Please, my friends, do not leave.'

Stumbling down the collapsing staircase they found themselves staring at one another in the empty street. For a moment they waited, but by some miracle, they were not being chased. Maia spoke first. She was furious and could not contain her anger a moment longer. 'So Rupert, do you think he is interested in you?'

'Shut up, you bitch,' he said, and began to giggle. The street was empty, but like an apparition, a taxi appeared and they managed to persuade the driver to take them back to the medina.

As the taxi began to move, they were all quiet. Looking back, Maia could see two men standing in the road, watching them go.

8

It was a clear morning when Maia awoke to find the Historian still gone. She steadily rose from the bed, wrapping a shawl about her shoulders. She passed Ina in the hallway. 'Has the Historian telephoned to let us know when he may be returning?'

Ina merely grunted at her and turned away.

'As helpful as always, Ina,' said Maia.

Ina turned and stared, her eyes flashing, but she remained silent.

Maia executed the Historian's tasks, and spent more and more of her free time painting, convinced that the images she was portraying were bland, with none of the vivacity that she had originally sought. She worried that the mediocre paintings she produced were replicating her state of mind. Maia was convinced that the images that she so studiously portrayed of the city and its inhabitants were featureless, useless and interchangeable works which would never be appreciated. She found corners in which she was able to sit for hours and observe the people who passed by, sketching the expressions upon the faces of young children, of merchants, and of the slippery entrails of slaughtered animals which lay sprawled across the ground, but still she felt that she lacked a true insight into the lives of the people around her. She became convinced that life here was too impenetrable for an outsider to portray it as it genuinely was. She spent whole nights painting, attempting to catch the vibrancy of colours and atmosphere.

In this way, her obsession with portraying the lives and position of women in the city grew, and she began to take photographs from a distance, but she was never able to get close enough to see their faces. The Historian had been right. These women were devoted to the creation of spectacles, and she was finding it impossible to penetrate their façades. They were hard, and when she looked at them, their bodies refused to offer themselves up for speculation. When she spoke to them, she found they kept their softer selves hidden.

Frustrated by her attempts to reach these women, Maia concentrated her efforts on the study of the inhabitants' backgrounds. The glowing bright and earthy tones, the quartz-pink and vivid red pigments of natural earth, all the varying colours of the iron and wood stirred her. Against the mud-coloured buildings, she used varying hues; the way the sun danced upon people and buildings seemed to turn them blue and flashes of cobalt lit up the sky.

The sunlight was so strong that it cast dark shadows, but she did not want to use black. Black was too harsh; instead she found that indigo could make the scene take on a sinister effect. Sometimes the effect was to make her subjects look as if they were hovering in the sunlight. In her art Maia sought to capture all the tension and ambiguity that she saw everywhere in the streets, in the fraught relations between men and women. She painted absorbedly, trying to depict shapes and colours from varying viewpoints, with different degrees of clarity.

Starved of company, Maia found that the heat began to carve away all the self-consciousness that she had carried with her from London. She drifted from day to day, no longer striving to improve nor monitoring her progress, losing herself in paint and sleep. In the evenings she returned to the bar at the Grand Tazi, but she did not wish to see those people again. She wanted to force all thoughts of Armand from her mind, and after a while she believed that they had all left. She drank at the bar whilst Tariq prepared her more concoctions, and she wondered what Mahmoud desired from her company, until one evening he told her.

'Will you paint for me? I hear you're very good.'

Mahmoud was a jovial man, laughing immoderately at everyone and everything around him. It was impossible not to warm to him, and she enjoyed his presence.

'What would you like me to paint for you, Mahmoud?'

'I want paintings of all this!' He exulted in his empire; the hotel was his pride and joy.

'Of the hotel, you mean?'

'You are my guest; you would be doing a great favour for me. With your help, Maia, the hotel will be everywhere! It will feature in all the guidebooks. Tourists will flock here!'

'Like sheep?' Maia was unable to resist a slight laugh at his expense; his plans were so unrealistic. She knew that foreigners would never throng the long and dark, dusty corridors of the Grand Tazi.

'No, no, not like sheep! Why do you say like sheep? My clients are not sheep!'

Maia was amused at Mahmoud's use of English; he often spoke as if he were repeating some loved phrases he remembered from an old English textbook.

'What do you want me to paint?'

'I tell you what I like,' he said, leaning forward. 'I like you to paint my clientele. Especially the women. Pretty, pretty women

171

for the walls of the bar.'

'I don't think that is going to lure in the foreigners you are hoping for, Mahmoud.'

Mahmoud slapped his thigh and laughed heartily. 'Ah, you think they see too much female flesh at home, do you? Well, they haven't seen our women, have they? You watch, they will love it!' He lowered his voice and leaned even closer towards her, so that his lips were almost brushing her cheek. 'I think you are too negative, Maia. I think you will not give things a chance. You will not let things happen naturally. And this is the ethos of my hotel. To let things happen naturally!' he said, and sat back in triumph. 'It is very popular now, this country, no?'

'Very popular, Mahmoud. But perhaps the tourists will be expecting a different experience from the one they will find here.'

'What do you mean? This is very good experience.'

'I don't know, Mahmoud.'

Suddenly he became very serious. 'Your job is to paint, my job is to please my guests.' She saw then that Mahmoud did indeed care about his guests, for his hotel, for its very reputation as the focal point for a certain sector of the city's nightlife. Quietly he masked his true character. He was a sly man hiding behind a jovial façade. But he did care. Not for money, but something else.

'Please, Maia. Everything is starting to fade away. There is competition now. Things are not the same. I need to keep them coming back. Will you help me?'

'Of course, Mahmoud. I will paint you something,' she relented under the pressure.

'I pay you!' he said. 'I can give you only a little, but still I pay you. I am very honest.' Mahmoud stretched out his arms, to show her the extent of his sincerity.

Maia laughed at him.

'Do you not trust me?'

'I don't trust anyone.'

'Oh, you are too harsh to your old friend!' said Mahmoud.

'We are not old friends.'

'But I am old!' shouted Mahmoud, and heartily he slapped her thigh.

Maia sighed, and smiled at him, but as he revealed to her the extent of his financial difficulties and the huge debts that he owed, as he complained to her about the extortionate cost of the renovations and she observed his laziness in the sun, she became aware that his ambitions for the Grand Tazi would never come to fruition. But still, in the empty afternoons and evenings, the atmosphere, the drinks, the people of the Grand Tazi drew her in.

Now when Maia visited, she often went directly upstairs to sit in the rooftop terrace café, where she had first come to meet the Historian. Up here, she relished her afternoons. She was able to observe the Moroccan people rather than the familiar expatriates and tourists she met by the bar at the pool.

'My artist in residence!' Mahmoud would shout. When he came to watch her work, he stood behind her, clasping her shoulder, and his huge presence loomed and made her nervous. Maia watched out for the crying woman who had smashed the glass on her first meeting with the Historian, but she never saw her again. Deprived of women to paint outside the hotel, Maia went back again and again to the Grand Tazi.

'You know I want portraits! Real portraits,' Mahmoud boomed at her. 'Who are you painting now? Paint her! No, paint her! You are too cut off, Maia. Your imagination is indeed very vivid, but I want you to understand that you must paint my customers as they are.'

'You do not understand, Mahmoud. I am painting them exactly as they are. I can only paint them as I see them. Do you see the tired eyes, the pain, the laughter lines, the age spots? I cannot paint people perfectly.'

He looked at her thoughtfully. 'You are too

honest, I think! People do not want to see those things.' But for once, he gave in. 'Well I suppose that we must see something different in them.'

Mahmoud wanted Maia to paint everyone as beautiful, the surroundings as glamorous. But Maia saw the dirt, the cracks in the walls, the mismatching colours and the character in the faces. And still she found the women she painted in the café too open, too provocative. They were too self-aware. Instead she wanted to attempt to reach below the veneer of Marrakech and reveal the skin of the women who lived underneath it.

She was becoming desperate to paint not just women but also the naked form of women. A woman's body was constantly changing, dependent on the unremitting rhythms of nature. So she began to paint herself, using the cracked mirror in the bathroom. At first she was nervous and tentative, but then as she felt her curves she relaxed. She mixed the colours of flesh tone for her skin; she factored in the shades where the rays of sunlight fell in through the shuttered windows against the afternoon heat and made her skin translucent. Faithfully she illustrated the shadows, the curve of her stomach and the shape of her thighs.

Only one particular painting that took her

weeks to complete managed to please her. She left the face blank because she felt that the faceless woman gazed back at her, turning her back on the male viewer. She thought that by not painting her features, she might be able to escape the eyes of men.

As the Historian stayed away from the house, the apprehension she felt at his presence dissolved. But her comfort did not last long. By now, painting had totally consumed her. She became used to living alone, attempting to develop her own understanding of life, and resenting any intrusions upon her solitude. She was unable to sleep at night, suffering flashes of nocturnal brilliance that lasted for hours. When she tried to sleep she suffered a now-familiar, terrible groaning before dawn. When she would reawaken in the afternoons she was unable to see what had so inspired her in the night. Maia considered when she looked at her nude self in the mirror that perhaps by depicting her naked body, she was only further imprisoning herself. Surely viewers of this painting would be viewing her only through the lascivious eyes of men?

Maia did not want to reveal the facial features of the painted woman; it was a feeling she could not articulate but she wanted to leave the faces of all her women blank. A man would always project his own fantasies onto the feminine, regardless of the woman's identity. She had the idea that this technique would be somehow less voyeuristic. However, when she painted Mahmoud's customers, she did not shy from the faithful representation of their faces.

In the late afternoons, when a cool breeze was beginning to take the edge off the heat, Maia wandered the streets. One evening, at the end of an alley on the edge of the medina, she stepped into a jewellery shop. It was a dark place selling religious artefacts, and it was swathed from floor to ceiling in cedar and thuya wood, cartouches and symbols smothering the walls. It was a cavernous bazaar, filled with antiques of obvious falsity, with battered copper pots and sabres encrusted with semi-precious stones hanging along the back wall. The old man at the counter watched her, sitting silently upon his stool. He was a tall, thin man with a short beard and a mournful face, dressed in a sharply cut suit of olive tweed which had become somewhat shabby with age; the elbows were patched up but his shirt beneath was starched and white. The entire outfit lent him the reassuring air of a European intellectual. His only flaw was his cracked, beige teeth. He had evidently profited from the fascination foreigners had with the town. She looked around, admiring the beauty of the craftwork. He followed her around the shop.

'They are all antiques, my dear.'

'I doubt it,' Maia smiled drily. She looked around the shop. A necklace caught her attention. The silver chain led down to a carved eye.

Immediately the owner appeared at her side. 'The Hand of Fatima,' he whispered, fastening it around her neck. 'I am happy you didn't choose gold.'

'Why, what does it matter?'

'Because we Berbers believe gold to be the source of all evil.'

'I am not a Berber.' Maia laughed as she handed him the money for the necklace.

'Why are you laughing, girl?'

'Because you say that you don't like gold, and yet you are happy to take mine.'

The old man looked her straight in the eye. 'I believe, daughter, that you already have al'ayn upon you.'

'I don't know about that,' said Maia.

Here, people seemed to be convinced in the power of the evil eye. At the entrance to houses Maia spotted the hand of Fatima; that very day she had seen a doorknocker sculpted in the shape of the hand. In this way, the home was presumed to be protected from evil.

'You know the story of Fatima?'

'No.'

He stopped her from taking her purchase. 'You can't buy it without knowing the story.'

She decided to humour him, and remained silent.

'Then I will tell you. The *khamsa* is the five-fingered hand that in Arabic we can use to arrest the evil eye. Fatima was the compassionate daughter of the Prophet Mohammed and several miracles are attributed to her. When she prayed in the desert, it began to rain. Watch out for jealousy.'

It seemed absurdly superstitious. But she agreed with him anyway. 'There are plenty of those people around,' said Maia, thinking of the jealousy that Cassandra provoked in her, and the feelings she suffered over Armand.

When she left the shop, the streets were emptying as the call to prayer was sounding. As she reached the Grand Tazi, Maia was surprised to find the Historian.

He greeted her abruptly. 'How has my work been going?'

'I have finished it.'

'I know you have finished it.' He smiled. 'Did you imagine that I wouldn't check up on you?'

179

'I am sure you will find it is all in order.' She thought about the crumpled letters and criticisms, and wondered for how long he intended to maintain the charade.

'I have no idea. I'm leaving again tomorrow for Europe. I don't know how long I will be gone for, but I trust you will carry these out,' he said, handing her another list of tasks.

'Of course.' When Maia was around him, she felt that her very presence was an irritant, and she wondered why he wanted her there, in his home. Even as she tried to stop it, her hostility and resentment towards him grew.

As she left, Mahmoud and the Historian were murmuring together at the doorway and then together they looked at her.

She continued her visits, but a lull had settled over the Grand Tazi. She laid her head on the cool surface of the table. Maia had felt her energy levels dropping, and she became incredibly morose.

'What are you thinking about?' asked Mahmoud.

She lifted her head up off the table. 'About Paris, about my last experience of it.'

'Ah ha.'

She smiled. Something about Mahmoud made her desperate to impress him.

'Mihai told me that he forgot to say he will not be back in Marrakech for a long time.'

'What is a long time?'

Mahmoud shrugged. 'Whatever Mihai deems it to be.' He beamed at her with delight.

The days passed while Maia painted, interspersed with her nightly visits to the Grand Tazi. One evening, on her way to the bar, she took a different route, and made her way to the Bab Agnou gate.

'Enter with blessing, serene people', announced the gate that for centuries welcomed the black people who arrived in the city from beyond the Sahara, whilst the fair-skinned aristocrats had their own gate to pass through. Maia wandered the streets before she decided to return to the Historian's empty riad. She resolved to eventually return to the Grand Tazi, for in the next few hours before delirium and inebriation took over, she would at least not be alone. Maia found that all the afternoons she passed were stifled and depressed. A life alone in a massive mausoleum would lead anyone desperate for a drink.

9

For days, Maia felt defeated at her lack of direction and purpose. Now she began to miss the rain and the abundant greenery of England, the oak forests that travelled for miles and its comforting redbrick buildings. She forgot about the coldness of the land, of the people, of having felt that it was simply just another place to which she would never belong. She continued with the tasks the Historian had set her, and sitting on the roof, she painted and smoked incessantly, distractedly lighting another cigarette before she had even finished the last, as she watched the dust swirl up the street.

The city seemed to be closing in upon her. She lay in her room, drowsy in the shadows, listening to the faint voices outside. Some days she felt so listless, she could hardly get out of bed. One morning, when Maia was emerging from a vague and elusive dream, a rapping was being played upon the door to her room. Walking wearily over to the door, she opened it to find an unusually dishevelled Armand.

'Why are you here?'

'I was in the house already,' he said.

'And how did you get in?'

He held a key up to her face. 'I keep one for myself. The Historian trusts me to take care of some business for him.'

'I see,' said Maia, hesitating. 'I never knew you had it.'

'Why would you?' he said, and Maia wanted to ask him if he had been in the house without her knowing.

Armand came towards her. 'I know what you are wondering, and the answer is yes.' He brushed past her into the flat.

It seemed to Maia that he had not washed for several days. He was carrying a small, leather brown bag and as he kissed her, his breath smelled of alcohol, stale cigarettes and other women.

Half reluctantly Maia returned his kiss and as she did his stubble brushed harshly upon her chin. It took only a moment for her to forget her resentment towards him and Cassandra. When he pushed her down onto her unmade bed she was too overwhelmed to stop him. She wanted to forget all her boredom and failure, and from the window outside she watched the sky darkening.

Several hours later she awoke to the clattering from her tiny kitchen. In an alcove with two hobs, the Historian had left her with a few necessary kitchen utensils, pans, knives. In the kitchen she found Armand, barefoot and dressed only in his jeans. Maia resented that in such a short time, he had succeeded in making her the victim of an insatiable lust.

Maia tried hard not to be disappointed. She often had the distinct feeling that the only person that Armand desired was himself. As she looked at him, she was pathetically grateful for the small attentions he paid her. She placed her hand upon his arm, as if searching for some reassurance that he really was still there.

'I want to escape, Armand.'

'Have you ever tried *majoun*, Maia?' He was searching her cupboards, opening and slamming the doors until he found whatever it was he had been searching for. Suddenly he grabbed her by the waist and kissed her, she was delighted, but just as quickly he backed away and began muttering to himself. Blending nuts and oil in the frying pan, he poured in all the spices he had found with an entire jar of her honey. Taking a plastic bag from the back pocket of his jeans, he added murky-looking herbs to the mixture, blending and churning until it was a huge brown mess. As he added butter, Maia hoped he would not force her to eat this mixture. It revolted her.

He directed her to the roof where he rolled a cigarette with the mixture he had cooked, and sat there smoking rings into the city. Despite it being close to midnight, the air was dry and hot. Maia watched him smoke with an adoration, close to hatred. She wanted to ask him why he was here with her, why he sought her company but then rejected it, why he paid her so much attention if he didn't want her. At the same time, she felt an irrational appreciation for any glimpse of affection from him. When he did deign to look at her, he gave a frisson of delight, which in all the years they had been together, George had never succeeded in eliciting from her.

'Is this where you view your women to paint them?'

'Sometimes.'

'Are they ever naked?'

'No!'

Armand saw her watching him and handed her the roll-up. She took it from him and breathed in deeply, before retching. The sweetness of it sickened her. Armand laughed, taking her hand. 'The Historian holds a certain fascination for you, doesn't he?'

A silence stretched out between them.

'He is plausible in his explanations,' said Maia eventually.

'He is very clever.'

'You don't need to tell me that.'

'I've had enough of this city. How would you like to get out for a while?'

Maia did not hesitate. 'Didn't you hear what I told you before?'

Armand didn't bother replying. He had already assumed she would follow him. For a moment she thought about leaving her paintings and the responsibility she had with the Historian. The *majoun* had made her feel remarkably free and lightheaded.

She was decided. 'Of course I do. Do you really want me to come?'

'I wouldn't have asked you, if I didn't mean it,' replied Armand, looking bored.

'I always wanted to escape somewhere.'

'And have you got what you came for?'

His eyes met hers, and she knew in that moment that she was a mere amusement for him. Despite all this, Maia was unable to walk away from him.

Armand stayed on the roof and smoked while Maia collected her things together. He appeared at the bedroom door, his leather bag in his hand. He was impatient. 'Let's go.' He grabbed her arm. 'The car is parked near the square . . . ' He held up her face and gripped her chin. 'You need a change of scenery. I've been looking at your paintings. They're . . . *merde*.'

Maia was crestfallen. She was hurt by his abrupt condemnation of her work.

He went to stand beside her. 'These women are very ugly.'

'I did not paint to please you. I see character in their faces.'

'Where did you see them?'

'In the souk.'

'You paint like a child.'

The blues and yellows merged on the canvas, so that just in looking at them she relived the excitement and urgency she had experienced when she had painted it. She looked at the shadows in contrast to the pure sunlight and wondered at how rapidly she had managed to improve her technical ability. Radiating energy and light danced across the canvas, but when she stood back from the canvas, she wondered if he was right.

'You need to retouch this area,' Armand told her, and he touched a corner of the painting with the tip of his finger, seeing how it pained her. At first, her growing attentions had flattered him. Her passivity had excited him. But as he looked at her, he saw that the more he demeaned her, the more eager she was to please him.

'I don't feel that it is necessary to retouch.'

'Feel, feel — you always concentrate on how you are feeling! You take yourself far too seriously. It is not the most attractive state, you know, for a woman.'

'I know someone,' she said, giving a laugh she did not feel, 'who takes himself far too seriously.'

'Do not laugh at me, Maia,' he said, coldly.

Maia stared back at him. 'I have nothing to hide.'

'All you women have something to hide.'

They stood there for a moment, looking at the painting. The female collective fascinated Maia; all the love and the subjugation, the mistreatment, exploitation and neglect, but Armand's face was twisted in disgust. She waited uneasy, suspended. The only reaction that she had elicited from him was disgust, and Maia realised this was another man who wanted women to wear masks. But still she accompanied him; and on the staircase they passed Ina, who barely acknowledged them. Maia left the Historian a note on the kitchen table and she went out with Armand into the empty street. As they drove together, the city fading behind them, Maia glanced at his shadowed profile. She knew she was mad to leave with Armand, but she was past caring. It was inexplicable, but something was propelling her forward.

She must have slept for most of the drive, and when she awoke, the sun was just rising.

Here, the roads were treacherous and they stretched out before her under a clear sky. On one side, a jagged mountain rose up, whilst on the other, a huge ravine fell down steeply.

Armand's window was open and a cigarette was dangling from between his lips. He looked at her, as though for the first time, but said nothing.

The road was slow going, eternally twisting. A roof of soft sky stretched out endlessly. Between rock and sky, the air was held motionless and below them there was only the rough, bare ground and the starkness of the ravines, and then, far below them, the odd tree clinging precariously to the mountain-side. As Maia stared down into the valleys, she saw the neglect of this part of the country. The view of the dirty scrub road soon became monotonous, and the parched landscape was cool and eerily quiet as the sun went down. She must have fallen asleep again because next time she awoke they were at a police road block. Maia was horrified to see that the driver's door was open, and Armand was no longer there.

Ahead of her, she saw him talking with an official. As Maia stepped out of the car she watched the two men shake hands. Armand marched back to where she was standing confused, one hand placed on the burning roof. A swarm of people came out of nowhere and they began to surround the car, pestering her, asking if they wanted hashish. Armand took out a pistol and two shots blasted sharply into the air. The noise resounded around the valley and the crowd dispersed.

'Get in,' he snapped, and ushered her back into the car.

Moments later, Maia couldn't hold her tongue any longer. 'Do you want to tell me what all that was about?'

'Not at all,' Armand replied.

She looked at him and another intense rush of desire claimed her as she settled back down into her seat. The balance of power between them was all wrong, and again she felt a fool. It occurred to her that she may have simply exchanged one master for another. He made her so passive, to the extent that she felt far removed from whatever it was that he might be dragging her down into.

She opened the window and felt the cool, clear air. They were high up into the mountains, and as Maia looked down, she saw the red tiled roofs of tall, bright blue buildings, all converging upon a square. The car was descending steeply through the rust-coloured hills, and Maia's sense of unease was blurring into excitement.

Armand booked them into a small hotel, called 'Pension Etoile', where the windows were high up in the mud brick walls, guarded by old cedar screens.

At the desk sat a bored, haggard old woman who spoke to Armand, before leading them upstairs. She was taken aback to find that Armand had arranged for two separate rooms. Too surprised to respond, she stood looking at him.

'I'll see you downstairs in two hours,' he said, and promptly closed the door on her.

Alone in her single room, Maia used the tiny bathroom to wash before lying down on the narrow bed. She could hear Armand on the phone in the next room, talking abruptly in French. His voice rose and fell, alternately angry and threateningly calm; she fell, undisturbed, into a deep sleep. She dreamt she was back in London, amongst the tall grey buildings and the scurrying people underground when she awoke with a jolt, filled with a vague longing.

Later, while preparing to meet Armand downstairs, he burst through the door. 'Ready? We're going.'

'I haven't even unpacked.' She thought they would be away for a few days at least.

'We're only here for the day. I want to show you the area.' Armand pushed her out of the door. The shove he gave her was light but insistent.

Back in the car, Maia looked down as they drove above the desolate valley. These villages were timeless, with mud brick houses, which clung to the mountainside, and ribbons of smoke rising from their chimneys. The road twisted until Maia caught sight of a desert *ksaar*, which rose up against a higher rocky cliff. Armand stopped the car suddenly and took her hand. The desert sky was an intense, clear blue and a man with buck teeth opened the gate of the *ksaar* for them.

Inside, there were narrow whitewashed buildings with high shutters and staunch, iron grilled windows. The man led them through a shady cobbled square, to a house with a huge brass door. From the outside, there was nothing to be seen, but as they walked through a long corridor Maia realised the building's vastness.

They were permitted to sit in a peaceful garden area, with a citrus tree in the centre. A lean-faced young woman came from within the house and poured mint tea into small glasses. Armand ignored them both, and looked towards the entrance into the house.

10

Two men holding rifles against their chests came in and stood by the door. They stared at Maia, and gradually it dawned on her that Armand was not objecting to their leering.

'What is going on, Armand?'

He ignored her, and leaned back in his chair. Something was wrong. It dawned on her that she knew nothing of Armand's business. She wanted to be angry with him for bringing her here, but then he was opening up a whole new world, and part of her felt strangely privileged. Two older men then came into the garden. The first was dark and rotund, and the second was pale and angular. Standing before her was the Historian and Mahmoud. As Maia's heart began to race, she tried to calm herself; after all, these men were familiar. The Historian stood with his hands clasped in front of him, and Mahmoud beamed at them.

'Welcome to my house,' he said cheerfully.

'Yes,' said the Historian. 'We often come to the Atlas to escape the summer heat.'

Maia had no chance to speak, for Armand said abruptly, 'Who are those idiots you employ? I had some moron try to stop me on the road. If you want to do business with me Mahmoud, those are not the sort of people I will deal with.'

So that, thought Maia, was what had happened with the road block and the policemen. What a shame she had been asleep and missed such excitement.

'They tried to force me off the road.'

Mahmoud was strangely apologetic, obsequious even. Maia was embarrassed to see him that way. She saw him only as an authority, always in charge as the host of the Grand Tazi, the owner of all that he surveyed.

Armand was outraged. Maia wished that he would not be so angry with the men; she was just now beginning to be comfortable with the Historian, although there was always the intangible awkwardness, a stiffness that remained. She sensed a power struggle, and Mahmoud was at the bottom of the league.

The men continued to converse, only now in Arabic. Servants came out to set the food on the table: fresh goat's cheese, which they ate with flat bread, oranges, apricots, cactus fruit and olives.

Sweet black coffee was served, and Maia was beginning to enjoy herself when she noticed the conversation switch to English.

194

'The girl must leave. We have some important matters to discuss,' said Mahmoud.

'You can take a wander through the town, Maia. Someone will find you. It is very small here.' The Historian was quiet and courteous.

'I read your guidebook. You never mention the Grand Tazi, why is this?'

'It was not yet open at the time.'

'But it was!' erupted Mahmoud.

'My mistake. But please, we have something to discuss, before I drive back to the city. I will see you soon.' He impatiently tapped his long fingers on the wooden table, but his voice was perfectly controlled; still and calm.

Maia was aware she was being pushed out. It was not the business of women, perhaps. Mahmoud and the Historian surprised her with their demeanour. The possibility that they were all involved together intrigued her.

Maia walked slowly through the town, although it seemed more of a stronghold. She wondered who was in charge here. Surely it could not be the Historian. He was a foreigner, but he had lived here long enough. It couldn't be Mahmoud.

Maia was certain that she knew why they were here. This was *kif* country, and high in the mountains they would be safe from the scrutinising eye of the authorities. She didn't care about the illegality; wondering at the ingenuity of the criminal mind. As she walked through the streets, she saw that the inhabitants of the town appeared to be Berbers rather than Arabs.

The small town was cooking under the sun, and Maia worked up the courage to enter a café. The place was filthy, the rot of idleness having sunk into the cracks long ago. She was the only woman in the place, and the men looked up at her with evident interest. While seated at a round table, she found herself surrounded, and decided to buy them all mint tea.

Her benevolence endeared her to them, and they resumed their normal conversation: discussing their dislike for the foreign tour groups who had begun to enter in the areas this deep into the mountains. They took offence to their unreachable wealth, the men who wandered around in their shorts, and their uncovered, untouchable women with their patronising behaviour, taking photographs without permission with their expensive electrical equipment.

Their broken English became a rabble of disagreement.

'These motherfuckers!' shouted one man. 'We can't even speak to them, offer anything.'

Maia was amused. They were disgruntled at not having the opportunity to rip them off.

The tourists had plenty of money to spare. For a man here it might mean a week of food for his family. She slipped away, leaving the men squabbling amongst themselves.

At a dead end, Armand appeared before her.

'I've been wondering where you might pop up,' she said.

Maia was delighted to see him. Her jaded nerves craved the excitement he gave, and the fear he instilled in her. She wanted to tell him about the men she had met in the café.

Armand placed his finger over her lips. 'Not just now. Come here.' He enveloped her in a kiss.

'Are we going to eat dessert?' she asked.

'Not yet.'

The day had grown dark, and leaden clouds were settling low over the mountains. Armand took her back to the house. For a moment he left and she heard him talking about her as she stood at the door. From the little she was able to gather, the very man who had attempted to stop them on the road was to help organise the smuggling for a kamikaze run to Spain, so close that a speedboat could make the shore in fifteen minutes.

Armand went out past her and then back in again, carrying something. Mahmoud was sitting at the table in the courtyard. The two men with rifles were leaning lazily against the gate. Inside she heard voices, the conversation continued.

'Don't worry; she'll go along with it.'

When she entered, she noticed one person missing. 'Where has the Historian got to?'

'He has already left, my dear. He sends his regards,' said Mahmoud.

Maia felt a niggling doubt creep in. 'What's going on?'

'We are not eating,' said Mahmoud. Maia was sure a smile was playing upon his lips. There was a shift in the atmosphere. Maia was stricken, and she reached over to Armand, but he pulled away from her.

He was now bending down over her, and she felt his lips brush her ear. 'I find this is the best way to end every meal. We just need your help with something very important.' He took her arm and began rolling up the sleeve.

'What the hell are you doing, Armand?' She tried to snatch back her arm, but he was too strong. She saw his face was grim, and she felt ashamed as he uncovered her before these men. She could barely believe it. She had never been tempted to touch the stuff and she had promised herself that she never would. Now she found herself being injected with it.

Armand opened the intricately carved box

before them. Maia tried to lean forward to look inside it. Armand was furious.

'Get back!' he shouted. Grabbing her arm, he began to whisper nonsense in her ear. He stroked her hair, gently pushing back her head, and kissed her neck. 'I'm going to give you something now. You'll be doing us a favour.'

Armand was gripping her arm tightly and Mahmoud was sat staring. The ritual that Armand was performing intensified Maia's sense of anticipation. He took a spoon from the table where the fruit still lay, mosquitoes beginning to hum around in the evening air. He took a silver lighter from his shirt pocket and cooked the brown drug over the lighter. The viscous liquid dripped onto the table, and he took out a syringe. Maia flinched, but Armand kept his grip. She wondered if she really understood his intentions, here in this remote mountain village; a forcible experience from a man she barely knew. The acknowledgment of her own stupidity came crashing down upon her and as she looked at Armand's face, for the first time she did not admire the ruthlessness in his smile.

He pulled the belt tightly, drew the mixture up into the needle, and plunged it into a vein that throbbed in her arm. There was a painful shock before bliss took over. She turned over her hands and saw the blue veins pulsating wildly. Paralysed with terror, she put her hands before her eyes but they fluttered like butterflies. The sensation was like a feather-filled pillow pleasantly smothering her. 'What a beautiful nightmare this is,' she murmured.

Armand said nothing. He was taking delicious pleasure in her trembling fear, thrilled with his power to dispense both life, and, if he willed it, death to whom he chose.

She was aware of the men watching her, aware of the emotions that must be flitting across her face. She heard their voices in the background, but she no longer cared. A chasm had opened up and sucked her in; inside it was pleasurable and warm.

Looking at her peaceful face, Armand suffered no remorse.

'Look at her, she's oblivious now,' said a voice that Maia did not recognise.

Time slowed down, warmth spread through her body, she was cocooned in an inner temple of delights that left her breathless with pleasure, her mouth was incredibly dry and her limbs became heavy. She awoke, and saw that she was lying on a low bed in the centre of a white room, with a thin blanket placed over her. The room was bare, and cockroaches scurried across the floor. She felt drowsy and wakeful, warm and content. Here, as at the

Historian's house, there were carpets and hanging silks. She spent those days in a drug-induced haze as the curtains grazed her ankles in the breeze coming off the mountains. Sunlight streamed dustily through the ragged curtains. Maia fell in and out of sleep, and when she awoke she found that Armand was watching her.

Then he was in her, but now she saw that something about her disgusted him. She tried to stop him. 'You hypocrite!' she tried to shout, but no words came. His hatred and fury were bursting out towards her. Why had it taken her until this point to understand the extent of Armand's cruelty? Maia watched his detached expression as he pushed himself into her. He gazed off into the distance above her head; the same blank gaze of the dog copulating in the souk until all control shuddered away from him and the expression slid from his face.

★　★　★

They stayed at the *ksaar* for several more days. She barely saw Armand at all, and he came only to give her what she now so desperately required. In the narrow bed she stirred, moaning fretfully. Later on, all that she could recall of that time were the voices and splinters of light that emerged through the high grilled windows at certain times of the day.

When Armand came to fetch her, she could hardly look at him. She slept as he drove back to the city and it was already dark when they entered the walls, driving slowly through the shifting crowd of onlookers. Out of the window, Maia watched a young man whose tooth was being pulled out. She was horrified. He was sitting nervously on a stool waiting. The tooth puller was standing down looking at him, grinning sadistically. Maia heard the scream pierce the air and she shuddered and turned away.

Armand watched her. 'It may seem crude to you Maia, but it is all most people can afford.'

'Why did you give me that stuff and not take any yourself?'

'Why, didn't you like it?'

Only to herself would she admit that she did. 'You forced me. And I don't need to depend on it.'

He turned and stroked her face. 'But you are so unhappy, Maia, you already do.'

'No!'

'You have no choice.' His voice was harsh. 'You need it now. We made you need it.'

So many times he had heard this

conversation. The formula was always the same. This reaction he elicited in women had begun to be unutterably boring. He wanted to laugh at Maia, but her innocence chilled him. She clung to him, and it made him more determined to hurt her. There are women who one has an irresistible desire to worship, and others who demand to be abused. At one time, he had been an empathetic being, but now he was a man who preyed on others.

In Maia's head she was busy creating all sorts of stories and myths to justify his actions. He too had been a victim. This, she knew, was how the world worked. She could not believe in mere sadism, it was too far-fetched. She still wanted to release him from his compulsion — as yet she gave no thought to her own. He had suffered; he was suffering still.

They stopped at a café and he offered her a hot, spicy drink.

'Why did you use me? What do you want from me?' she asked him.

He watched how she projected all of her own desires onto him. The idealised view Maia had created of him increased his enjoyment in destroying it.

'Maia,' he said evasively, 'each man kills the thing he loves.'

She looked at him, unfeeling and hard, and

with horror she understood there was a deep ugliness within him, an ugliness that she had never known before in anyone.

'But Armand, we barely know one another. You do not love me.'

He smiled at her kindly, and stroked her arm. 'All the more reason for it then.'

Maia sat back, shocked at how horribly she had misjudged him, how a mere dalliance had nearly destroyed her. In the square the *Gnaoa* musicians danced; they sat in silence watching them and smoking. Later on the only people still remaining in the square were a few lute players, the dealers and the gigolos, old rolling Europeans whom she recognised from her nights at the Grand Tazi.

'I need to know why you did that to me.'

'You really do take this all too seriously. Did you not come here to escape?'

'Not like that. I wanted to be free, to express myself.'

'Well, we all want that. You want to go to the Grand Tazi? Your friend might be there.'

'What you did to me is a crime.'

'All of it?'

'I trusted you.'

He smiled his canine grin, and placed his hand over hers. 'I don't share your opinion.'

'And you think I am happy now? Are you happy, Armand?'

'Happiness is something which does not interest me.'

The man sitting before her cared nothing for the misery he had brought to others. Never before had Maia met somebody who was so self-possessed and so utterly devoid of a conscience.

'You don't get past me,' he said. 'You wanted excitement, wanted to do things that you could never get away with back home.'

'I don't know what you mean.'

'You wanted to lose yourself. And now you will. I'll take you back.'

'I don't want you to. I don't want you near me.'

'Oh, but you do,' he said, and despising herself, she let him take her hand. Maia was wondering how she would face the Historian now. How much did he know?

When she returned, Ina was waiting in silence. She handed her a small envelope, and turned away. When Maia reached her room, she found hundreds of crisp notes inside. Everything fell into place. She had been the pawn in a game. But what use was she to them? Her senses were too dulled to be angry, although she knew that was how she ought to feel. Here was the suggestion that she could be bought, and she resolved to return the cash to the Historian the moment they met again. But for now, she could only stand beside her bed, holding the envelope, drained of all energy. She could not shake the sense that she deserved it, through her naivety, her hope, her fascination. She had allowed herself to be drawn in, through her desire to be accepted.

In the weeks that followed Maia frequented a café known as 'The Chaumiere', but the atmosphere was never the same. There was no sense of frivolity, no figures of dubious influence, no musicians or people with interesting stories to tell. There were no other foreigners with whom she could talk, and rather than being able to sketch and observe the clientele, Maia found instead that it was always her who was being observed. Maybe she had experienced the oblivion she had so longed for.

Weeks later, she ran into Rupert in the street. He was unshaven and behaving evasively. He would not meet her eyes and told her he was leaving; when she invited him to join her for a tea he was apologetic, but he had no time to spare.

'One last tea, Rupert.'

'Fine. One last tea.'

In the café, she could barely get him to speak.

'Why are you leaving, Rupert?'

'I might as well ask you why you are staying. You seem so . . . diminished.'

'I don't know what you mean,' said Maia.

'I think you know exactly what I mean. I really do like you, but I don't think that we are cut from the same cloth.'

'Don't use clichés with me, Rupert,' said Maia, sharply.

'I must leave,' he said, sighing dramatically. Then, with a sharp laugh he raised his drink to his mouth, made a vague gesture, and promptly disappeared from her life.

11

As the weeks passed Maia found her cravings impossible to ignore. She had become completely engrossed with her painting again, and only ventured outside for her daily trip up and down the main rue. In the evenings Maia looked at the lights in the small windows carved into the walls as she walked down the street.

She eventually found herself tracing a familiar route. The way to the bar was etched indelibly in her mind.

At first, Maia had been reluctant to see Mahmoud. She was too consumed with the influence of the drug to be angry with him, too weak to feel outraged. In the event, Maia need not have worried. When she did find the courage to return to the Grand Tazi, Mahmoud was as welcoming as always.

As she entered, Maia passed by several intricately handmade lamps in stained glass, the light shining through different shades of red. Mahmoud startled her, grabbing her arm. 'You like?'

'Very nice, Mahmoud.'

He grinned. 'I knew you would come back.'

'This was no choice, and you know it.'

'Of course my dear, whatever you say.'

'This deceiving, Mahmoud. It can't go on. It should never have happened.'

'Whyever not?' he asked, and turned on her a wide and disarming smile, before bumbling off to lure some more tourists into spending money at the bar.

With the passing of innumerable nights and easily forgettable personalities which faded immediately from her memory, Maia's longing for pleasure and relief took place so quickly that she never had an opportunity to recognise it. Armand always delivered exactly what she needed in the required amounts, and he never tried to force himself on her again. He had no need to. When she lay awake in bed, showered in the cold trickle of water, or watched from the roof the black-clad figures of women moving slowly around under the scathing sun, she wondered about the motives of the men and the strange web of their relations. Her suspicions grew; unformulated thoughts arose in her mind, hazy in the heat.

Although she could hardly begin to deny the pleasure into which they had introduced her, she did feel betrayed. They all knew she would never have willingly ingested the drug; that once it caught her in its warm, black void, it would never willingly relinquish its hold. They had wanted her to trial it for them. Yet they could easily have chosen someone else, another who was already inducted. They had targeted her because all three of them had taken a perverse delight in getting her hooked. She was lethargic; it was only the constant desire for release that kept her awake in the stultifying heat. Even in the shade, exhaustion took over.

When Armand was late, and her supplies were dwindling, she became anxious. And when he did not come at all, she suffered. He gave her weeks of uncertainty.

Looking in the mirror she was sure she could see lines on her forehead and around her eyes, which had not been there before. Her face was thinner, her cheekbones were more defined than ever, but now her ribcage was visible. She believed that all the excesses of her life were gradually becoming displayed on her face. It was horrible; the dread and anxiety suffocated her. Each day, as she got out of bed, she pulled the bandages back over her arm. Every day was the same.

At the Grand Tazi, Mahmoud was greeting his guests enthusiastically, and advancing beween the tables, behind a pleasant, welcoming mask. Maia found Konstantin in his usual spot by the bar. Mahmoud came over to join them. He looked her over. 'You do look a little gaunt.'

'I've been so busy painting.'

'Well, don't become a recluse,' said Mahmoud, and then he laughed energetically for no reason at all.

It was nearly a fortnight after she had returned from the Atlas before she saw the Historian again. As she sat with Konstantin, the agreeable sense of lightness slipped away from her. Then his voice was in her ears and she turned to find his face bending down over her.

'Excuse me,' the Historian said, 'I must introduce you to somebody important.'

'I have been waiting to speak to you. You thought you could buy me. I want to speak to you alone.'

He bent down towards her. 'Not now, Maia, I beg you. You will embarrass yourself. Don't you think you have done quite enough to damage your reputation?' He smiled and stood up; placing his hand on her hair, he ruffled it. 'This girl is like my daughter now!' he announced to no-one in particular. His grip on her scalp was firm.

He pulled her up onto her feet and began to fuss over her, calling to Tariq for drinks and asking her about her paintings. Maia had been prepared to speak to him with as much coldness as she could muster, but now she was trapped, confused by his sudden interest.

The Historian sat down, bringing with him a man she had never seen before. She wanted to ask him so many questions, but she knew that this was not the time.

The Historian's friend was carrying an aloof air for one who was so short of stature. His hair was curly and black, and the informal way in which he wore his luxurious fabrics with a crimson silk scarf bestowed a charming appearance of eccentricity. Maia had become suspicious of the Historian's friends. She thought the man had the air of a faded screen star, who had once been handsome and still hoped to be found so. He extended his hand to her. 'Dr Mathias de Farcas.'

Maia knew who he was. 'A medical doctor?'

'No!' said Mathias de Farcas defensively, confirming her doubts. 'I am actually a Professor of Islamic art.'

She felt that he looked upon her as a bird of prey looks upon its next victim.

'Can I get you a little drink?' asked the Professor.

'I am feeling a little sleepy,' said Maia. 'It must be the sun.'

'I insist. Mihai tells me you have been a

great help to him, and that you are an artist?'

'I love the light here. There's beauty in the mosaics, the sculptures, all the jewellery.'

'Maia is here to do some work for me first and foremost. But she is interested in painting. Painting women in particular.' The hint of contempt in his low voice was unmistakable.

'Aren't we all,' laughed the Professor, signalling to Tariq for more drinks. 'And what is your style? What materials do you use? Where has your work been shown?'

Maia saw the type of man he was. He wanted her to justify her every move, to render herself acceptable in his eyes. The truth was that she didn't have her own style. She was still only developing it.

'I paint in symbols,' said Maia, although this was a lie.

'Ah ha, a surrealist is what you are. You are very cryptic. Never fear, my dear, I shall find you out sooner rather than later,' said de Farcas, a sly smile playing upon his lips.

His threat disturbed her. She felt his eyes exploring the contours of her neck and shoulders, lazily roaming down the rest of her body.

Looking away, Maia noticed Cassandra enter the room. She hadn't seen her since that disastrous dinner at Yasser's. Both she and the Bambages seemed to have faded into the ether. She was unrecognisable from the woman she had watched crouching on the floor in pain. She had drawn on her mask; gold and black makeup smeared heavily across her eyes, lending her the appearance of an Egyptian queen. Several men came over to the bar to talk to her, but she looked at them with disdain and turned them away. Cassandra was pure glamour; she was both hard and available at the same time, inciting her male onlookers and provoking the female ones to compare. Maia could only stare and wonder how she had achieved that self-possession.

For the first time that evening, Maia saw Armand. She watched as he went over to speak to Cassandra. She knew she could do nothing about it.

Konstantin noticed the look on Maia's face. 'I beg you, pay no attention to him. I've seen him at it with so many women over the years.'

'Thank you, Konstantin. That makes me feel so very special.'

'I'm afraid that is the truth.' He peered down at her through his spectacles and cocked his tiny bald head.

Before the first word was uttered, the agenda was already decided. Cassandra and Armand looked at one another. Cassandra pushed back her hair, did something with her lips, and fluttered her eyes at him. Armand smiled debonairly. Maia already knew how this game would end. Armand was certain that he could not be resisted, and it could not be more obvious that Cassandra was willing to surrender to him.

'I prefer to paint the female in all situations,' Maia said to the Professor. 'Fully clothed, surrounded by realism, so that the reaction of the intruding male is not necessarily erotic but merely mundane.'

'I see. You wish your paintings to be mundane?'

'My women . . . '

'Listen to her! My women!' said the Professor.

Ignoring the interruption, Maia continued. 'I wouldn't exactly label my paintings mundane, just because they are not pornographic.'

'What do you think of the *niqab?* The veil that some of the women wear.'

'It is not often their choice, and it must be unbearably hot. Men want to cover them up, but then they get upset when they cannot see a woman's face. I find that mindset interesting. The women can see but they cannot be seen. It encourages a completely irrational notion of exotic sensuality and mystery. A woman ought to have the right to cover her face.'

'You do take yourself very seriously, my dear,' smiled the Professor, 'but you do go on and on about the female body. In the West, do you not think that society is so rigidly sexualised? Men don't stare at you in the street, but they stare at other women in magazines and newspapers instead. You have exposed, naked women everywhere. I bet you find it strange that the men there bother only with unattainable women.'

'At least the men there never bother me.'

'But you must admit that the relationship between the man and the woman has lost all of its playfulness, all of the energy of seduction? It simply does not exist for you anymore. I would be willing to wager that sometimes you wish it would.'

Maia thought about this. She saw the men here as inadequate, loitering indolently in the cafés and on the street corners, unable to control their urges. But perhaps he was right; in her own country, almost everything had become sexualised. Men did not stare at her in the streets, but on the television, and in the clubs and the bars, in all the confined spaces the heavy charge of sexual expression was unavoidable. Romance had been replaced by freedom of expression, and Maia wondered if her way was any better.

Eventually the Historian spoke, and when

he did, Maia noticed a smile playing around the edge of his lips. 'But the Mona Lisa looks out at us, with that knowing smile upon her face.' He taunted her, leering. 'I bet you too wish that you were viewed so sexually. This perverse desire of yours . . . this perverse desire of all women.'

Maia shrugged. 'Perhaps you are right. There is no freedom from the eyes of men or women. But it is the asymmetrical gaze I am talking about, the exhibition of a totally unequal power relationship. Then, it is only women who fit the ideal of feminine beauty who enjoy this gaze. I think that men are upset about the veil because a woman can look at you, but you cannot see her.'

'Upset me? How does it upset me?'

'The man is superior in society. He does not like to be watched.'

'I do!' said Konstantin, in an attempt to lighten the conversation.

Maia laughed, and patted his arm. 'I know you do.'

The Historian was smoking a long, thin cigarette as he watched their exchange. 'But still it persists, this notion that the male looking at a painting is the intruder. Ridiculous. Women look too, do they not?'

'They do, but I don't feel it's in the same predatory way.'

'Are all the women in your paintings beautiful?' asked the Professor.

'Certainly not. Sometimes unattractive women have the greatest character. They have had to learn to be interesting, to earn the right merely to be noticed.'

The Professor laughed. 'All cats are black in the dark, I suppose.'

They ordered dinner, and as they ate, the Historian and the Professor became particularly vocal on the role of women in art.

'I prefer the buxom woman,' de Farcas said, staring obviously at Maia's chest.

With a certain yearning, the Historian sighed, 'Michelangelo's David is incomparable.' And Maia was beginning to see where his preferences lay.

De Farcas leered at a passing waiter, and asked him for more wine.

'*De suite, monsieur*,' said the waiter, bowing obsequiously.

'There is something, Maia, that you ought to know about men here,' said the Professor. 'They never mix love and sex. You may find that the two are mutually exclusive. And sex, you see, may be performed with anything from a goat to a dead salmon!' He laughed heartily and felt for Maia's thigh underneath the table. She pulled away sharply, and looked at the Historian to see if he knew what was happening, but he gave no hint.

'You will betray those ideals of yours. It is inevitable.' The Historian spoke as if he was tasting, savouring the words as he spoke them.

As she sat there, watching the men contemplate her in their varying ways, Maia toyed with the possibility of contacting the Professor who had sent her here. In her head, she composed several letters, which she already knew that she would never send. In any case, what could she say? That he had misled her; that the Historian was not the man he had known, that he had forced her into an arrangement? Could she accuse him of enslavement, or even corruption? There was nothing to say; there was no proof of intent or even of involvement, direct or otherwise. It was all of her own accord, it was all suspicion, and she had allowed herself to be lured in.

An announcement was made. Mahmoud was in his element. 'Make way for my dancing girls,' he shouted, 'make way!' The belly dancers passed by their table, shaking their hips to the beat of the drums, strings of coins hanging loosely around their waists. Maia had anticipated youth and beauty, but instead she marvelled at the expansive girth of the women who passed by their table, bearing plates upon their heads as a trick for the tourists. When they brushed past Maia, she smelt not perfume, but decay.

Now they lay back on the velvet couches, drinking sweet mint tea and cocktails. Here, just outside the medina, alcohol was easily available, intoxication almost immediate. Cigarette smoke hung in the air, as dense as fog, as thick as her thoughts. Yet despite their age, the belly dancers pulsated with sensuality.

'This pandering to the male fantasy of the Eastern woman is absolutely pathetic,' Maia said, derisively. Immediately, the men were on their guard.

'Do be more specific, if you don't mind,' said the Professor.

'It seems to me that men want to control the female body. For you lot, a woman is either hypersexual or completely asexual. In your minds you have this strange contradiction between the sexual belly dancer and the constrained, covered woman. She is demure in public, but a slut in the bedroom — all forms of disguise for the object of the male fantasy. Just look at these women. Their only reason for existence is to cater to your whims!' Her tirade had exhausted her, and she sat back in her chair.

The Professor sniggered. 'And what do you think is wrong with that? Perhaps they enjoy it.'

'Nothing, I suppose.' Maia decided to exude

graciousness. But she despised the male fantasy of the Eastern woman. She saw that it was slavery that he desired, slavery without any responsibility. 'If you see how shallow it is.'

'Depth! Ha! Depth has never been my concern,' said the Professor, and he sneered at her.

Tariq was lighting the lanterns, and flickering on the tables they illuminated the guests with the ghastly glow of green. The men questioned Maia on her opinions on the role of women in art, but she feared that the alcohol had made her less articulate, and that they were mocking her. Maia could not help but despise the men she met here. Deprived of opportunities for employment, men young and old crammed themselves into crowded cafés that were off limits to their wives, mothers and sisters. Here they sat on the terraces watching people go by as if the city was their own theatre, downing syrupy mint tea by the gallon and sucking incessantly upon cigarettes. They had nothing to do but argue and engage in their own favourite parlour game: politics. A game in which they would forever be utterly ineffectual. Maia felt that when she walked in the city streets, these men made her want to erode her own beauty, to become a gargoyle, if only to spite them. Maia looked at the men sitting before her.

I am simply an image for them to look at. Yet I breathe, I rot, I emanate stench just like you, Maia thought. They only wished to perpetuate the image they had formed of her. They looked at her to assess her quality. Maia attempted to describe this to the Historian and de Farcas, but they both laughed at her.

'You should be flattered,' de Farcas admonished her. He genuinely believed that she should be grateful for their harassment of her.

Konstantin joined them and Maia sensed he was feeling particularly promiscuous. He was drunk and recalled in vivid detail the indulgences of a time when he lived in Cairo.

De Farcas leant over to whisper to Maia, 'You know he prefers boys. Platonic, of course,' he said, and giggled horribly. It was a stage whisper, and Maia was embarrassed. She raised her eyebrow. He made the gesture, just below the table, to indicate their height. At that moment she glanced at Konstantin, and somehow he knew that he was the subject of their conversation. He lowered his head, but just before he did so, he caught the brief flicker of dislike flash across her face.

Maia was filled with dread, and an even newer horror about the workings of the city. She wondered who these people were, who walked in the dark, who longed to purge themselves of the former lives that cling, and what it was about this place that afforded them such refuge.

'Excuse me,' said Maia, hoping that they did not catch the look of disgust on her face. She walked inside the twisting bowels of the hotel and found an empty room in which she could prepare her ritual in peace. She always carried the usual paraphernalia with her: the belt, cotton wool and the stained silver spoon. The craving had by now come to dominate her life, but still she never failed to find the act itself shocking. She pumped her arm in frustration and the syringe broke her creamy skin. She watched the vein fill with her red, sticky blood, breathing a sigh as relief took hold of her.

Afterwards she stood a while in the foyer hoping Armand would pass through, but he was nowhere to be seen so she went up the staircase, and lost herself in the hallways, roaming along through the foul-smelling passages, passing the tiny, recessed rooms. In these grim corridors, there lingered a palpable odour of dried sweat, and she heard low voices coming from one of the rooms. Pushing open the heavy wooden door, the walls were covered with an artistic series of black and white photographs depicting various areas of Rome. Even from a distance she was able to see the photographer's yellowing card; 'Blake Cram, Roma, 1976,' read the inscription proudly.

On the faded, psychedelic carpet, with its brown and yellow swirls, Cassandra's shoes were placed neatly against the wall, and for a moment Maia stood perfectly still in the rancid, airless corridor. On all sides, the plaster walls rose above her, in an apparently ceilingless gloom. Then there came Armand's voice. Opposite the door was an old mirror, through which there ran a large crack. Flames shot up through her as she saw herself reflected: an open-mouthed, ivory-skinned woman, the lips a little too thin, black wide eyes placed far apart, more the face of an unadorned Venetian carnival mask than that of a human. Unable to help herself, Maia slowly turned round and saw them struggling with one another. As she stood there breathless, frozen and appalled, she felt her ribs contracting with misery and a hot sick feeling rising in her chest.

She walked over to the gilt-edged mirror, a tribute to Mahmoud's taste, and as she heard them move, her blood pounded deafeningly in her ears. She looked at her face: a soulless, grotesque mask, ash-white, with the consistency of moulded clay. She took a crimson lipstick from her bag, which she ran thoroughly over her trembling lips. Wondering how she appeared to others, she compared herself with Cassandra again, the exquisite, mysterious Cassandra who now lay sprawled beneath Armand on the bed, giving little gasping sighs. Maia looked at Cassandra quite differently, now that she had viewed her in these soiled surroundings, her glamour somewhat tarnished.

Walking purposefully, Maia went back outside and descended into the courtyard to join the Historian, the Professor and Konstantin. When she returned to the table, her face remained like a mask.

She sat detached and still in her chair, aware of their eyes resting upon her.

'You have become very quiet, Maia,' said the Historian. 'Have you nothing more to add?'

Still she found that she couldn't speak, and suspected that they were fully aware of her humiliation. She felt the shame was discernible through her clothes.

Strangely, the Historian appeared sympathetic. 'He is a useless man,' he said. 'Armand has his weaknesses. He likes to imagine that he is tortured, but never has a young man been so lucky, or had so many opportunities offered up to him. He is cold-blooded, an egotist,' he went on, not fully realising the irony of his statement. 'He sees himself as a wanderer. But at the same time he is anxious.'

'How?' asked Maia, intrigued by the Historian's analysis of her lover's psyche.

'You speak of him so disparagingly.'

'He is worried about the fate of his masculine freedom in a world full of feminine distraction, tossed around upon a sea of lustful breasts.' And at this vivid image conjured up by his master, Konstantin laughed politely. Unlike his master, however, Konstantin did not despise women. Rather, he envied their feminine allure. It was the incense of women, their gentleness and softness that he sought to emulate.

'You are sad, my dear,' said the Historian gently. 'Besides, all life is ephemeral. Armand, for instance, is himself a very transient character. He was just another young Arab man in Marseilles. I met him many years ago, and I helped to educate him. He reinvented himself. And then he saw what we have here. That is what you imagine you love, Maia — a mere creation.'

'But we are all creations of our circumstances,' said the Professor, who was in turn ignored by the Historian. These were callous men, and with a lurching passion she resented them and hated herself. They had opened a cesspool for her and then welcomed her in. Out here in Morocco, nobody could reach her. She had allowed herself to become stranded. She had welcomed it.

'Very well, then. I think we might have exhausted this subject already.'

Maia could not answer. She was sweating and shaking. Soon afterwards, Armand and Cassandra joined the table, and Maia watched the Historian as he arranged his mouth in a careful smile. The air was thick with tension. Her companions wanted to see her reaction, to have the evening's entertainment, but she would not show fear or distress before them. With her sweaty arms sticking to the chair, their eyes clung to her, her neck, her calves, her ankles, searching her for any small morsels of emotion, dissecting her for any betrayal, any muscle reflex in her face or her body which would reveal her unhappiness. They were all of them inescapable.

An image of being with Armand flashed up in her mind, and the taste of acid flowed up bitterly into her mouth. Maia hated him, but hated the fact that someone else could have him, even more.

Konstantin prodded her. 'Are you alright, Maia?'

She forced out her words through a tight throat. 'I'm fine. I think I am going to get another drink.'

Beside Armand and Cassandra, she felt small, inadequate. She was no competition. When she looked at him, Maia was stricken. Until this point she had not realised the full extent of his indifference to her. She tried to smile at them gently, with all the benevolence that she was able to summon. 'Where have you two been?'

She was accusing him now, and Armand ignored her and joined in the conversation, while Cassandra left their company. She resented Armand for this ability to change her opinion of him from moment to moment.

Irrevocably now, Maia was a participant in her own destruction. Armand did not want her, but still she wanted him. Any slight kindness that he showed her, she took as a sign that his feelings might be changing. But Cassandra was invincible. The most attractive woman that Maia had ever met, Cassandra was able to slink in and out of clandestine involvements and freely participate in them without ever being spoiled by them.

Cassandra surveyed Maia, but Maia met her straight in the eye. She was quite aware of her own magnetism; it was her lack of power that troubled her.

As the conversation developed, Maia stared about her abstractedly; at the curving bar and the guests milling around it, each struggling for the limelight amongst the pitiless clamour. She felt thousands of miles away from London, from the clean lines and the neat rows, Sunday afternoons, rain and freshness, familiarity. Then there were her neatly folded clothes and the jackets packed away at the back of her wardrobe in her flat, now rented out to a stranger who would be cooking in her kitchen, sleeping in her bed. She thought of the huge art galleries where she often spent hours alone considering the different types of brushstrokes made by other artists. She had left it all behind, but she still had not found what she was searching for.

These men were overly concerned with her view of the city, and they all wanted to give her their own interpretation of it. They competed viciously with one another. The Historian wanted her to see it as a city of ancient battlegrounds, of tribes, of historic references, a place between East and West where the desert caravans came to rest. Konstantin needed her to view the city as an expatriate refuge, as if here she too could join him in hiding something. Armand, she could barely understand. He reminded her of the Tuareg warriors who emerge out of the desert draped in white with only their kohl-rimmed eyes left uncovered. His suit was his armour, yet he too was another European who came here to take advantage of what the city could offer him. Armand was simply conducting himself with his customary arrogance.

Maia was suddenly tired of them all, and wished now to meet more Moroccan women, coy and aloof, not these men who were only interested in foisting their own opinions on her. These men wanted to break her down, and diminish her. They were, all of them, caught fast in the Historian's net, and all three of his disciples were irrevocably tangled.

She decided to try loneliness over subservience. The longer she spent here, the less anything surprised her.

'There are so many gay men here,' Maia said. 'Yet the men harass women terribly. Perhaps if relations between the sexes were a little more liberal . . . '

The Historian laughed bitterly. This was a legendary gay destination in a place were homosexuality was illegal.

Maia scrutinised the Historian carefully. At first he seemed so sensitive, discerning. Now his change was like that of a chameleon that hides, shudders and crawls from the light. This evening, the Historian was unusually talkative. When Maia complained about the incessant, unwanted attention she received from the men in the street, she was told to be grateful. She had never imagined he might be so garrulous. As she watched him, she imagined that she was watching a strange transformation, that of a spider emerging from its chrysalis. A sudden irritation at his quick change of character pricked at her.

Maia went outside into the street, and bumped straight into Cassandra again, who was just leaving. 'He went to look for you. I have an early flight tomorrow. Well, goodbye. It has been fun, hasn't it?' Cassandra smiled, with a slight wave of her hand, where Maia noticed the faint, jagged trace of a tattoo.

'So much fun,' agreed Maia, almost snarling at her, but she managed to restrain herself and the taxi took Cassandra away.

Maia went back inside and there was Armand still at the table. The light appeared to fall only upon her companions, giving her the sensation of being pushed out further and alone. The beautiful cut of their clothes hid all of their ugliness and the honest human traits, which would have made them up into real people. She longed for their masks to at last slip.

Occasionally Armand's eyes caught hers across the room. He wanted to check that she was watching him. And as she looked at him, the strength of her venom, her hatred and her desperation grew. Yet still she continued to smile, a smile that started to resemble more of a grimace.

Later, Maia was sitting alone at the bar when there was a terrible crash. She turned in the direction of the sound and she saw that the grotesque, leering Priapus, the chief piece of Mahmoud's garden furniture, had fallen into the pool, along with de Farcas, who rose to the surface, spluttering. He had been sitting on it just a few moments earlier, and she covered her hand with her mouth to hide her laughter.

'Isn't that rather dangerous? Have you ever fallen in here?' de Farcas was shouting frantically at Mahmoud. The entire bar was amused, and de Farcas looked furious.

Mahmoud was nonplussed. He held out his hand to help de Farcas to his feet as he climbed out of the pool.

'Oh they are falling in all the time,' he said, and began on one of his incessant courses of laughter.

That night when she returned to the house, she painted the belly dancers as she recalled them before she forgot their fluidity. She painted them in swirls of white and bright energetic colours, and their unlimited movement and flexibility reverberated across the canvas. For a few hours, as she stood alone and stared at the coloured surface she was creating, she revelled in the broad canvas that stared back at her, the twisted tubes beside it, the fresh paint squeezed and smeared along the hands of her brushes and the turpentine stench filling the room. She thought that she might once again learn the meaning of joy.

12

Maia woke early one morning to a dull ache that had plagued her for days. The fan whirred soullessly, and out of the corner of her eye she glimpsed a small cockroach scurrying along the cracks of the skirting board. She caught sight of her face in the mirror directly opposite her. Her eyes beneath the dark, almost purple grey lids, swollen from sleep, stared back at her.

Her sleep was fitful and erratic and her painting had reached another low point. Nothing came out as she intended. She painted with agitation. Every day, her incompetence screamed at her. She worked herself into a trance, crying and swearing as she staggered in front of each canvas.

As the dust of the changing season came swirling up the streets, Maia seemed to have lost her ability to see in colour. The light eluded her, and the paintings were finished in shades of grey, in tones of sepia and muddy browns, like an old photograph that for many years has been hidden away in a drawer. Maia had sought light and the bright sun for her art, but the Historian had brought only

darkness. The Historian's austerity, his absolute control, drained her of all vibrancy and
hope. Full only of apprehension for her future,
she breathed the stifled air of oppression. In
her imagination, she approached the canvas
aggressively and flung down the paint, using
jagged brushed strokes of violent crimson to
depict the sky. She dreamt in colour, in purples,
violets and crimsons, painted in thick, broad
streaks, which enveloped the viewer, but the
work she produced depicted only stagnant
dim shadows moving lethargically across the
canvas. She had arrived in a city full of mental
vigour, only to be confronted by a growing
sleeplessness. When she remembered her experiences, they made her recoil in disgust. Her
life had become so thoroughly dependent upon
the conscious whims of others, the imposing
presence elicited by the people who now surrounded her. She saw her future as bleak.

For several days Armand had neglected to
visit and she was becoming frantic with the
need that had taken over. She began to
wander the streets alone after dark, meeting
visitors both fluid and mysterious, slipping
through the opening and closing of the city
gates. She knew that in one way or another,
Armand would begin to expect payment. She
wondered if Mahmoud could help her, but
even her addled mind could remember his

involvement in the Atlas.

By wandering the streets alone, Maia was able to see sights that she would otherwise not have seen. Sights that fascinated and appalled her, reminding her of the otherness in this society, in which she had no place.

She came upon a small, quiet square, where a few men were gathered around a wizened-looking young man, long-haired and filthy, sitting upon a rug. Despite the thick layers of dirt that encased the young man's body and the dark, matted hair that hung around his face, his beauty was marred only by the slightly simian quality of his face.

Having edged through the crowd, Maia was now close enough to see that the marks he wore upon his arms revealed him to be a member of the fellowship to which she too belonged.

He conveyed an exuberant charisma that enraptured the crowd, who were listening intently as he began his story. His long pink tongue darted lizard-like across each side of his mouth as he spoke in English. Maia nudged a small, insipid-looking woman who was standing by her.

'What is his name?'

'Larbi. Women are not supposed to listen to the stories he tells.'

'But you do?'

The woman said nothing but inclined her head towards Larbi. Men leaned their rusting bicycles against the walls to stop and listen. One man whispered something unintelligible to her in Arabic and made a gesture with his hand, as if to send her away.

Larbi was flinging his arms around, making strange patterns in the night air. His English was surprisingly good, and Maia wondered if he had lived a very different life before the one that stood before her.

'This is the story of the girl who married a snake.' The crowd seemed to shudder in horror and Maia realised that she had arrived just in time.

The storyteller's voice grew alternately low and sad, then rising, his eyes narrowing and widening.

'Once there was a woman who married a rich merchant and lived on the very edge of the desert. He had two beautiful young children, a boy and a girl, but the man had lost his wife when she was a young woman. She died of a snake bite. But even in death she was a threat to his new wife, who hated the children. In turn, the children detested the stepmother, for she was a cruel and evil woman. She punished them and sought useless tasks for them to do. She beat them and scalded their tiny hands. In what little free time they had, the children would run freely in the land close to the house. But the boy was very stupid, whilst the girl was extraordinarily clever, and the stepmother saw this, which made her detest the girl even more.

'One afternoon, the children went for a walk, but became lost. For hours they walked around, unable to find their way. Several times they found themselves back in the desert, and try as they might, they couldn't find their way home.

'A huge, strange creature appeared before them, grimacing. I cannot go into too much detail for you all, for it is shocking, but let it suffice to say that the creature's skin was raw, as if it had shed its previous skin, its hair was sparse and it seemed as if all the brutality of the world was etched upon its face. They saw that the creature was a woman, and she took out from behind her back the huge net which she used for catching butterflies. The beautiful butterflies fluttered away from her, hiding from her net, but she used many tricks to recapture them. Forsaken in the shifting sands, which barred their way, hidden within the deep density of the palm trees, their stepmother had succeeded in finding them and she brought them back to the house where she committed horrendous cruelties towards the children which I am unable to relate.

'The children had long suspected that their stepmother was an ogress, and now she revealed herself to them. The father was often away a great deal, and the ogress was an expert in the art of witchcraft, so that he believed his wife was beautiful, kind, and loving to his children.'

Something about the man compelled Maia to stay and listen, pressed among the crowd in the saffron glow of the fading light.

'The father was away so often that the cruelty of the stepmother was never exposed, and indeed he was so enchanted by her, that had he learnt about her cruelty he never would have believed it. The ogress had all sorts of unnatural relations with animals, and one evening she found herself to be pregnant, and not by her usual partner, but by a serpent.'

A muted sound of collective horror flickered through the audience, and Maia saw them shift forward to listen even more intently.

'Soon afterwards, the father died on his travels, captured by thieves and left for dead in the desert. The children mourned for him, but they wept too for fear of the future that awaited them. With their last hope gone, the children, now slightly older, succeeded in escaping. They built a shelter so deep inside the oasis that the ogress was unable to find them. They spent evenings huddled together listening to her tread the paths nearby their shelter, calling out their names with a kindness that they had not known since their mother had been alive.

'One evening, as the sun set, the girl decided to leave the hut and her sleeping brother to see what had happened to the ogress, as they had not heard her shouting for quite some time. The girl knew that at this hour the ogress was often asleep, from the late afternoons until the sky was black and the stars could be glimpsed, in preparation for all her nightly exertions. The girl walked up the pathway to the house of sandstone where she had once known such cruelty, and now it was even more dilapidated than in the days when her father had been alive. Insects of all kinds scurried in and out of the windows. The shutters were broken and hanging loose, and the girl was able to see inside as she crept up to the window.'

Larbi stopped abruptly. He got up and began to walk off, but the men shouted at him. 'What happens? How can you leave us like this?'

The storyteller shrugged and continued

walking, but a stocky member of the audience grabbed him and forced him back. He smiled and sat down. It was all part of his act.

'Then, instead of finding the ogress fast asleep as she had expected, the girl found the ogress lying in terror upon the trodden floor, trying to scream. She was muttering incessantly for help, but the girl looked on with contempt for the stepmother she had learnt to despise.

'Yet the ogress was not giving birth. Not, at least, from between her thighs. A few moments later, she was forced to stop her screaming. Something grotesque was wriggling its way out of her gaping mouth, as the ogress and the girl's eyes met in a shared moment of horror.

'All of a sudden, the snake made its entrance into the world, slithering out of the mouth of the ogress. It bit its own mother, and as she died, the ogress rocked with all the agonies of poison and the girl simply watched the woman, transfixed. She had no time to run away, the snake was already fully grown and it turned its head to speak to her. It slithered over and was soon breathing at her neck and coiling itself around her. It tried to hiss at her seductively, and there was nothing the girl could do to fight back as it took her on the very floor where her stepmother had died and now lay motionless, the fluid of afterbirth pouring from her lifeless mouth.'

The crowd was transfixed.

'When the brother came to look for the girl at the house, he marched into his former home and found the girl and the snake together.'

Larbi stood up and shouted, 'Yet wait! There is no happy ending!' His eyes were magnetic and he smiled apologetically. 'If anybody would like to make a small donation for my upkeep, it would be gratefully appreciated . . . ' He pulled a small clay bowl from beneath his cloak and went around, offering it to the crowd. During this momentary pause, a snake trader brought his snakes into the centre of the crowd. The onlookers recoiled from them in delight and horror as the snakes horribly flickered their tongues through their stitched mouths. At the side of the square some other snake charmers toyed with defanged black cobras, whilst robed Berber men and a few women chewed upon fried locusts.

On the side of the street an old man was playing the lute, high sweet notes rose into the air and floated above her head and the cobra rose out of its circle, its scaly loops undulating and its reptile body upright, its small reptile head keeping in perfect time to the music as it bobbed its head about, its eyes moving almost lasciviously.

Maia saw Larbi sit down and someone brought him over some mint tea as several richer members of the crowd evidently took the opportunity to purchase some snakes. After a while Larbi returned to take his place once more, counting the coins in his bowl. Seemingly pleased with the result, he intoned a blessing in Arabic, and started the story again. His voice began to rise, then whisper, and his eyes grew large and wide.

'The snake kept the girl captive and the boy was forced to stay at the house. The snake presided over the household and soon began to speak against the girl whom he had forced to become his wife. He was forging a bond with the girl's brother, whispering seductively evil thoughts every day that the boy was finding hard to resist. The main desire in life for this creature was corruption. It resolved to protect the boy from what it had come to consider its wife's malevolence, for it was aware of how vehemently the girl still despised it. By this time, the girl was no longer beautiful, the hardships and trials of her dreadful life having worn her down. When her brother looked at her, he sometimes felt a rush of sympathy, but the opportunity they might have had to make their escape was long past, and he was now starting to enjoy the company of the snake.

'One evening the malicious snake and his brother-in-law hatched a vicious plan. As the girl was reluctantly preparing an elaborate evening meal, the snake slithered up behind her affectionately, and viciously bit her on her neck. Just as her stepmother had died, the girl began to writhe in agony, the poison coursing through her veins. The snake and the boy left together, leaving the girl alone in the house to die. But the snake had bitten her only lightly, and she survived.

'The brother did not mourn his sister. He felt that she had been lost to him many years earlier, when she had allowed herself to become the property of the snake. So the boy, now a handsome young man, together with the snake, went off together into the night, the snake as dedicated to destruction as it had been when it first came into the world, and the boy now addicted and utterly corrupted by the snake.'

Maia felt the entire crowd shiver, and then it erupted into applause as the ragged storyteller shuffled through the people. Larbi held his clay bowl stretched out for any extra coins. Maia dropped some in his bowl and fell away.

She wondered why it was the girl who had

to suffer, what had then happened to the girl, and why her punishment for existence had been a dreadful death. Abandoned because she had become old and ugly, childless, alone amongst the sand dunes, her virginity lost, considered worthless and now isolated, what would become of her?

Maia turned back towards the crowd in the hope of finding Larbi, but he and the snake sellers had already left the square. Maia stood still, jostled by the people walking past, but she could not feel them. She was thinking about the girl and her fate, and she felt that she too had been seduced into taking the plunge into a pool of terrible emptiness.

13

Larbi's story haunted Maia's nights. Her mind was becoming as cloudy as the dust that would swirl in from the desert. The inhabitants of Marrakech seemed to be even more restless than normal. Tension rose until it exploded, like a crescendo of wrong notes. Anxiety pursued with an intensity that shrouded the air, and grey clouds lurked over the mountains.

Maia now hadn't seen the Historian for weeks. In the afternoons, she painted and slept, and when Armand was in the mood, he visited her and they passed the time by making love. Yet there was now no pretence of any tenderness between them. Armand did not fail to supply her with her needs, despite her increasing narcotic appetite. But with desperation she paced her empty room, accepting the scant affection he bestowed on her.

In the evenings Maia found herself unable to stay away from the bar at the Grand Tazi. She drank the mint tea that Mahmoud offered her with enthusiasm, and every night Tariq delighted in creating new concoctions.

Her favourite was cold mint tea with vodka. Even Mahmoud commented on her intake.

'Are you not taking a little too much, Maia?'

'Why do you care?'

He laughed heartily.

'Because I still need you to paint! And it is not too good for you.'

'Why do you care about what I drink? You introduced me to something far worse.'

'I do not know what you mean, dear! You are imagining things. It is not the same!' He ambled off to charm some more guests.

But Mahmoud had begun to notice that the colours and shapes of Maia's paintings were as murky as her mind. 'Well, has the spider emerged from his lair?'

'Spider?'

'Mihai. Your Historian. You must know that you are his collateral, little fly, his collateral! My hands are tied, little fly.'

'Little fly? Why do you keep calling me that?'

'We are all caught in his web. Sticky, sticky!'

'I could leave.'

Suddenly he was serious. 'We both know that you will not do that.'

'And what makes you think that?'

'He won't let you go, you know too much about him now.'

'Not at all, Mahmoud. I don't know what you mean. The problem is that I don't know anything. I never see him.'

'That is no problem,' he said, and suddenly he looked extraordinarily depressed. 'I am being squeezed.'

'By who?'

'Who do you suppose? By your employer.'

'Not the Historian? I thought you were friends.'

'Who else? He takes so much from me,' and he looked down at the ground.

Against all her instincts, Maia was sympathetic towards Mahmoud. She was too weak to fight against any of them now, and she didn't care enough to bother.

'How can I have any sympathy for you, Mahmoud? After what you did to me.'

'It was not my choice,' he said despairingly. 'We were acting for the Historian. He made us.'

'Armand too?'

Mahmoud made a clicking sound with his tongue. 'That man acts on his own. And the Historian is not my friend. Nor yours.'

Across the bar Maia caught sight of Armand; she lowered her face for fear that he might see her. The bar swirled and warped with bubbling voices, the spiralling exhalations and the loosening of inhibitions.

Mahmound relaxed into the seat beside her and placed his hand upon her knee. Maia wished that he would leave her alone. He tapped a stubby finger on the table top to an unheard rhythm.

She left him in a mood of frustration, unable to elicit any sense from him. At the bar the guests dropped out and were succeeded by other people. Maia returned to the riad.

★   ★   ★

Maia painted women in natural poses, capturing them in moments of action, walking sedately in the serpentine streets. Now the wind was blowing, she found that her view from the rooftops was becoming useless, the women always fully garbed, dark, barely visible figures. They were depicted as only insignificant black dots on her canvas, for that was how they seemed to her, small and inconsequential.

As she slipped further into dependence and craving, a voice within her still reprimanded her for her days of indolence and futility, and she knew that the longer she stayed in this expatriate refuge, the further she would become corrupted.

Maia's fear was that she too would become

like the Historian, like Armand, nihilistic pleasure seekers on the periphery of a world which they would never be able to enter, and exiled from the one they had rejected. She knew that she had never found the bright light and inspiration she had been hoping for. Nothing good had come out of this escapade; no decent work, no friendships. The chance to paint nude women still eluded her. So she decided to enter the private world of women, and then she could draw the images and transfer them to the canvas.

Armand did not visit her for days and Maia wondered if she ought to go in search of a new supplier. But her craving was not yet so strong, and so she now worked up the courage to visit the *hamam* alone.

On entering, she undressed. She saw the other naked women wandering around without shame, bodies moving forwards through the steam. Maia looked at the women and imagined how she would portray their secret world.

It was a social ritual. This was where the male fantasy of the East came alive. Women of all shapes and sizes walked around unabashed, gossiping and laughing with one another.

A woman came to exfoliate her and began with some abrasive cleaning, before she was doused with a bucket of cold water. But as

Maia lay on her front and the woman continued to clean her, she was only able to think about the life of this woman. The attendant was silent, simply going about her job with methodical, mechanical actions. Maia sensed a misery about this woman, and felt guilty. This was supposed to be the ultimate Moroccan experience, but instead Maia could only think about how it must be to spend one's time scraping the backs of more privileged women. The steam was dense as she entered the next room, and she went to sit on one of the tiled benches. A woman came to sit next to her, smiling at Maia.

'I am Safira.' Her hair was as short as that of a boy and her eyes were huge and dark, her breasts feminine and full. Maia could think only of how she would paint those eyes.

Over time, Maia told her about the Historian, about her art, and about the Grand Tazi and Mahmoud, but she did not tell her about Armand. For the first time in months, Maia felt the joy and closeness of communicating with another woman.

Maia began to frequent the *hamam* daily, avoiding the Grand Tazi. The two women would pass their evenings together, wandering about the streets. She took Safira back to the Historian's house, and they passed Ina on the stairs. Again, Maia felt her penetrating gaze, but still she said nothing.

Maia had never kissed a woman before, but on the rooftop she felt a sharp, sweet taste and their new adoration for one another unfolded. A few weeks went by and Maia realised that the Historian was still away, and in that time she was yet to visit the Grand Tazi. With Safira's presence, Maia found her art was improving, the colours becoming clearer and brighter. She even began to be less dependent on her supplies.

Maia painted Safira in countless poses. In her paintings and studies, as in reality, the charismatic presence of her model was inescapable. She felt that the best depiction of Safira was in the nude. She lounged in a blue armchair, facing toward the viewer but at an angle, both hands held nonchalantly resting behind her head.

Maia's paintings were not decorative or superficial, as Armand and the Historian had suggested, but her characters advanced purposefully through the shades of red, carrying a fierce erotic charge. The broad, choppy strokes suggested an extreme disturbance; the stories suggested weakness, an enforced surrender. Looking at it she saw that each painting was a confrontation. There was something coarse and primitive in them.

Safira looked up at her from beneath

lowered lids as Maia told Safira about her broken past. 'We do not keep all our old sentiments. The mind is cultivated enough already. You must learn to let go.'

'People are always telling me that. But I don't know how.'

Maia believed that finally she had found a friend, an ally who supported her, not competed with her. They shared everything: Maia's bed, Maia's body, Maia's ritual. They shared more than Maia could ever have imagined.

As they lay together on the bed, Maia told Safira about the story told by Larbi. 'I didn't like this one. It was unfair.'

'I think I may have heard that storyteller. He tells a good story. You weren't really expecting a happy ending, were you? I've heard that tale so many times before.' Maia saw that her eyes puckered up on one side with contempt; for a moment she was unattractive.

'Indulge me,' Maia said. 'I am interested in your opinion. I thought it was unfair to the girl. She was condemned to a lonely life outside the boundaries of society. Silenced in the oasis of the unconscious.'

Safira let out a slightly embarrassed laugh. 'You are just as poetic as they told me. But that snake was just another representation of the male organ, the all-powerful male devil. Don't be fooled!'

Maia sat back and looked at the woman before her. Safira had no sympathy for the girl in the story. The girl is a victim; she sacrifices herself for her brother. She is captured and dominated, she has no independence, and when she is worthless she is cast out and abandoned.

Maia tried to explain this train of thought to Safira. 'Do you not think that the story perhaps shows how there is no place in the symbolic order for a used woman? And that when she is ruined she too becomes the stuff of men's nightmares?'

'Do not analyse so much, Maia. You have far too much time to think.'

'But it is true! Look, they have no time for female sexuality! If they want to talk about it, it is in these huge metaphors!'

'Please, leave it, Maia. It really is true what they said about you.'

'Who?'

Safira tapped the side of her nose. 'Just people we both know. No more questions!'

Despite the seed of niggling doubt, Maia stayed with her. For the first time since she had arrived, Maia believed that she might be be coming free and indifferent to shame and the rigid boundaries. She touched Safira's golden skin, that offered itself to Maia's gaze, flaunting, hands clasped behind her head in a smiling gesture of natural superiority.

'Show me which position you wish me to take,' said Safira, with the strong tilt of her chin, her eyes seeking out Maia's approval.

Maia's eyes drank in the elongated proportions of Safira's body. In painting her, Maia felt that she was painting herself. 'My mirror image,' she murmured softly.

Safira enthralled her; when they were together the sky became a darker, more vivid blue. It was Safira's sense of abandonment that she envied. But still a hollow laugh came out from inside her, she did not know where, and there was a deep, abiding coldness tight in her stomach.

★   ★   ★

Maia still saw Armand. Her cravings for him and the drug had not yet diminished.

Maia liked these daytime assignments, the lethargic afternoons and the comfort of the bed.

'I know Safira. I know all about you both,' Armand said to her.

'How?'

'I have known Safira for many years. Did you imagine that I didn't know?' He gripped her arm, so hard she knew there would be bruises later.

He tried to press more of the drug on her, more than she felt herself able to resist.

'You can no longer continue like this. You owe me.'

'I owe you nothing, Armand. You introduced me to this.'

Still they slept together, but now she sensed in him not only frustration, but also boredom.

And so the days passed in this mechanical way, with Maia growing used to the ways in which she used her body. She told Safira about the man who had caused her such discomfort, to gauge her reaction. To her great dismay, Safira seemed genuinely oblivious. She knew that Safira had met Armand. Why is Safira lying to me? she thought. But she said nothing. The seed of doubt, growing stronger.

'This could be another journey for you,' whispered Safira, snorting the odourless white powder from Maia's stomach. Safira had obtained this new pure batch from some unknown source she would not reveal.

'I don't need Armand anymore. We have your source now. Armand is not reliable.'

Safira sat back, and stroked Maia's thigh. 'But he could be. Take me to him.'

They went together to the Grand Tazi. But it was different somehow. She realised that no music was playing; there was just a handful of guests, seated around the pool. Such a drastic change from the lively, welcoming place that Maia had first walked into, only three months before. Mahmoud seemed dejected. 'The season is now over.'

Armand cared nothing for her, but Maia suspected a sense of neglect under his arrogant façade. He wanted to be worshipped. His ego would not allow him to be usurped, and particularly not by a woman.

His efforts turned to Safira as they entered the room. Armand's flirtatious manner and Safira's peculiarly coquettish attitude, a side of which she had not seen before, were a sickening sight. Maia realised she was unsurprised by this, nor was she hurt. She was simply surprised at herself, now she had become used to the deceit of this place and its inhabitants. How had she not thought of this sooner?

At the Historian's riad, Safira came towards the bed. She entered through the gap in the curtains, and the tangibility of the situation now frightened Maia.

Armand closed the door and went across to Maia. 'Is this what you want?' he asked, as if giving her a choice.

And before she could answer, there came a rhythmic moving. She could hear Armand's rasping breath, as she watched his silhouette in the candlelight. Her hips twisted in an imitation of desire. A woman's voice was whispering eagerly and limbs were wrapping themselves around her; a man's voice was commanding her. The smell lingered in her room, she sat numb, feeling helpless, just as Mahmoud had said, a fly in their ointment, a fly sticking and caught.

The two girls twined and entwined, spread on the bed like lizards skewered by the man's desire. Their pleasure unfurled as Maia felt Safira's tongue in her mouth. A sweet pleasure enveloped them, until the man stepped out. From that moment Maia felt his presence as unwelcome as Safira's. She lay there in the darkness, at the foot of the bed, feeling empty.

'You had better put your face in cold water.' Safira laughed — a deep, cynical sound.

Maia looked around her, dazed. A sense of shame and utter disgust flooded through her entire body.

She stood trembling after they left, shocked at how they had been able to abandon all inhibitions. The early pink sunlight was drenching the walls and she shuddered. Squeezing herself into the smallest corner of the room, she drew her knees to her chest.

She had been cleansed by the fresh start

she had attempted to make with the *hamam* and Safira, but in the aftermath, she felt tarnished. She wondered at how Armand might ever be satisfied. His lust too was insatiable. She didn't know if it was the effect of the drugs, or the chains of depravity from which she was still unable to break free. How were they able to? These people were without conscience. They had no time for remorse, or guilt, and she envied them wholeheartedly.

She stayed within the apartment for days, twisting behind her makeshift curtains. She never saw Safira again. For her, the episode had been a brief experience to satisfy her own curiosity. Safira infuriated Maia; her sly, knowing smile, her contempt, her strange satisfaction and ability to leave Maia behind.

She broke down, succumbing to her silent howls. Safira mocked her, the paintings mocked her. In trepidation she covered her canvases, fearful to see what horrors she had produced, terrified to see the person she had become.

The indolent evenings were a void, a time where nothing was ever remembered, and as they stretched ahead of her, she laid down her tools once more, and succumbed to oblivion.

14

When Maia sat on the roof she found it was becoming less scorching and unbearable, the luminous colours were fading. As darkness finally began to fall, curiosity took her in its firm grip and she went down into the city streets.

Maia went deep into the putrid souk, where the tiny food stalls sold proudly and metal workshops stretched back into dark recesses. Monkeys on chains gibbered triumphantly, and she passed a stall where old men sat stuffing mattresses. The multiple hands of Fatima were being sold everywhere. She remembered purchasing these, and, in a vain attempt to protect herself, placed them on her walls. To protect her from what, at the time she didn't know. Now she knew who, rather than what it was that she had so feared. Her fears had become manifested in people, in Armand, the Historian, Mahmoud, and in her insatiable cravings.

Although she had been seeking solitude, she knew that the Grand Tazi had again been filling up with tourists who came for a brief respite before the winter in their own countries. A wonderful relief from the long days of loneliness. As she prepared herself, she looked forward to the new characters that she might meet. She never blamed Mahmoud and the Historian. Maia had come to understand that betrayal was Armand's nature.

Mahmoud and Tariq greeted her as an old friend, which greatly amused her. She was trying to learn to take life as lightly as they did. Maia surprised herself with her resilience. She now yearned for the company of these desperate lowlifes as they so gladly presented themselves as the evening's entertainment. Maia relished the distractions they offered.

That evening, as Maia observed the clientele, Mahmoud was beaming at her, and waving some sort of stew under her nose.

'No, thank you,' she replied flatly.

'We shall have to fatten you up!'

'No, thank you, Mahmoud. I am not too hungry.'

'You know, Maia, it is not pleasant to reject a gift here?' smiled Mahmoud, his mouth parting in a wide and unpleasant slit. 'We really shall have to fatten you up, increase that small appetite you have. Eat my food!' Mahmoud shouted, rather more genially. He stood over her, the expansive, welcoming villain of his own show.

She smiled dutifully. 'I am afraid my stomach is very weak. Have you seen the Historian?'

'No, I am afraid he is still on business, my dear. I think you are missing our friend. That spider! He is all day long weaving his webs.' He shook his head, as if to kindly admonish the Historian. 'Are you lonely? We can always fix that!'

'Not really. I was just wondering. I have plenty to be getting on with,' she explained, but Mahmoud's attention was elsewhere.

He was watching Konstantin with a benign smile. Konstantin was sitting across the courtyard, flirting with a new group of men. With affection, Maia watched his awkward movements. He was standing, discomfited in the centre of a crowd of predatory men. Konstantin possessed a certain innocence, a naivety perhaps, which she always found endearing. He was unpleasantly drunk, slurring his words together and muttering unintelligibly. Maia noticed that red thread veins had begun to litter Konstantin's perfectly marble-white complexion, in the mere course of a summer.

'A man's capacity for delusion is unlimited,' Mahmoud whispered. As they watched, a much younger Arab massaged Konstantin's shoulder rather obviously. 'Konstantin is making many mistakes here. You see the young men he is

261

talking to? They do not like men. Not really. They want his money, perhaps a European visa. He falls in love again and again, but not one of these men will ever leave their families for another man. You ask me. I know.'

Konstantin saw her looking and waved for her to come over. He kissed her three times on each cheek.

'You looked busy, so I didn't head straight over.'

'I am never too busy for you! Meet Paola.'

The woman was sitting at his table, downing one vodka after the other, surrounded by people at the table, loudly cheering her on. She held out her hand to Maia. 'Paulo Straneo.'

The woman was more than overweight, with short, pudgy limbs and beady black eyes, which constantly darted around the room. Her face was squashed up like a toad, and her hair was black and frizzy, with dreadful breath as she leaned towards Maia.

'*Straneo*. That means 'strange' in Italian?'

'How perceptive of you,' said a sarcastic voice. A few feet away, Armand was fingering his wine glass. Another man was standing next to him, a man with a sneer upon his face.

'This is Florian,' said Konstantin. 'He is German!'

'No, no.' Florian was evidently affronted. 'I am Dutch!'

'Just look at all those girls.' Paola leaned towards Maia in what she obviously believed might be a shared intimacy, as she gestured to a group of women by the pool. Maia recoiled at the woman's dreadfully foul-smelling breath. 'Fallen women.'

'Fallen from where, exactly?'

'They're not to be trusted, you know. They're all prostitutes.'

'And how did you come to that conclusion?'

'Just look at them.'

'Look at yourself,' Maia said with contempt. She tried to walk away, but Konstantin gently held her arm. Maia knew she had made an enemy but she was past caring. She found Paola revolting. But she also pitied her.

The place was more quiet than usual, and as Maia wondered vaguely if this was just the last flux before desertion, Konstantin placed his hand clumsily upon Florian's shoulder. He was wearing a velvet jacket, which in this weather was still too warm. Maia thought he looked utterly ridiculous.

'Florian is having a party soon, aren't you?' said Konstantin. 'It is at his house. In the Palmeraie.'

Maia knew that the Palmeraie was the supposedly smarter quarter of Marrakech. She had only visited the area once, but had found that she had a distinct preference for the high walls of the medina, with their blank façades and hidden secrets to the modern mansions of the Palmeraie set in open gardens and wide set drives.

'Florian is holding this party in honour of an American photographer, Blake Cram.'

This grabbed Maia's attention. 'How interesting. I'm an artist.'

'Oh really? What do you paint?' said Florian.

'Women. How men look at us, and watch us. I like the way they are in daily life. I am interested in humanising them.'

'You like women?'

'I find their demeanour, and their bodies, deserve to be immortalised.'

'I tell you! You try to portray that old Madonna-Whore complex.' He was suddenly very excited. His cheeks were flushed, and when she looked more closely, Maia thought they looked a little too flushed.

'Well you must have been unlucky. You can come to my party. We will let her, won't we, Konstantin? She sounds interesting.'

'Yes, she is one of us,' said Konstantin.

Maia's opinion of Konstantin was waning. With his calculated smile he possessed that incredible ability of being all things to all people.

'I want to die violently instead of simply fading out,' said Florian dramatically. 'We've just been here, dissipating all summer.'

Maia could only wonder how she hadn't noticed him before. 'So only people you consider interesting will be your guests?'

'Oh no, my dear. Rich people too. Especially very rich men! I'm hosting the exhibition of this artist's latest work. You must come.' Florian's smile was fixed rigidly on his face, which was twitching frenetically. As if nobody was paying him sufficient attention, he suddenly threw out his arms. 'You must all come!'

Paola was staring at him with a disapproving look. 'I don't think your party is exclusive anymore, Florian.'

Florian's face fell. 'I just wanted to spread my love.'

'Look at him! He's so fabulous.' Konstantin was grinning ferociously.

'You will never understand me, Paola,' said Florian, tossing his thick hair. Then he beamed. 'Merely a trifle,' he muttered randomly, as if responding to some remark that no-one else had heard.

15

The next morning, Maia found the Historian sitting peacefully in the courtyard, thoughtfully sipping his mint tea and reading the review of his main rival's latest work in a New York paper. Maia could tell he was in a ferocious mood.

But Maia was becoming desperate. 'I need help,' she said and went over to sit beside him. The Historian shifted his newspaper away from her, and Maia's hard façade began to disintegrate. 'Please help me,' she repeated, tears forming at the corners of her eyes.

The Historian stared at her with disgust. 'Stop it,' he said, irritatably.

'How can I stop? I want to. I want to so much. But you know I can't.'

'You can,' said the Historian.

'Did you know? Please tell me; just tell me if you were in on this. I can't take these lies. Do you know what they did to me in the Atlas? What Armand and Mahmoud did? They say it is your fault. It was your house. But you weren't there! You didn't stop them! And now I'm stuck here. I need it; I can't just leave. And I never see you. You are never here.

Help me escape this!' She grabbed at his hands, and now she was sobbing violently as she caught her breath between bouts of tears.

'Did you not like what they gave you?' the Historian said coolly, like a scientist measuring the success of an experiment.

Through her tears, she looked up at him. 'Yes, at first. Of course I liked it. But now I hate it. Look at me!' she shouted, and it was true; violet shadows encircled her sunken eyes, and the blue of her veins was growing more prominent.

He drew away in disgust. 'You have merely let yourself go.'

'I will come off it. But I need more now.'

'You will always need more. That is not a reason for me to help you. You can begin now.'

'No! I can't start here. Not near him.'

The Historian sighed, as if he was relenting to a young child's demands for ice cream. He had made this girl pathetic, and it had been so easy. Now she was begging at his feet, stripped of all her independence. It was so disappointing.

'I will help you today,' he told her. 'But after this, no more. I will not help you again,' and he turned away.

Maia was torn between taking what he was offering, and confronting him. But she needed to know.

'So you know all about it?'

'No,' he said quietly. 'Why?'

His reticence provoked her. 'I will make it known,' she shouted at him. 'I will tell everyone. I will ruin you!'

The Historian gave a ghastly, mirthless laugh. 'And who will believe you against me?' Gently, he touched her arm. 'I will speak to Mahmoud and Armand. I don't know how they have been behaving while I have been away.'

Maia was confused. She wanted to believe him.

'Maia,' he said benevolently, 'I let you stay here, don't I? Even when I am so disappointed with you. I am your protector. Why don't you go for a rest, and I will see you tonight at Florian's exhibition.' He didn't even bother to look up from his newspaper, and now ashamed, she rose from the table.

Later that night, Maia dressed in flat sandals with a plain black dress, which fell below the knees, and silver necklaces and bracelets bought in the souk. Her shoulders were covered with a silver scarf. The taxi went slowly through the isolated Palmeraie, where the palms were dry and the roads dusty. The area was isolated, and along the ochre rubble she saw chameleons clinging. As she gradually approached the house, she saw white

268

fairy lights decorating a gigantic villa, already exuding the sounds of a party in full flow.

Maia got out of the taxi, and walked up the stone path to Florian's riad. She entered into the brilliant white light of the huge hall, and despite the engraved invitation in her hand, lingered at the door.

A wide flight of marble stairs was placed in the centre of the hall, and as Maia looked up, she saw Florian was descending, jerking sharply to the music of the tango, and clutching a tiny white cat in his arms. When he reached the bottom of the steps he did not greet Maia, indeed she thought that he may not even have seen her. Guests were draped not so seductively on cushion divans placed against the tiled walls, and handsome young men were proudly walking around, displaying themselves. A very fat Frenchman who smelt strongly of whisky came and stood next to her picking up one of the sweets, which lay upon a pile of sweet sugar pastries. Maia moved away before the man had a chance to talk to her.

Maia was the first person to greet Paola as she entered the hall. 'Is the Historian here?'

'I have no idea. I saw him this morning and he said he might see me here. Listen, Paola, I think we might have set off on the wrong foot. I don't really like the way women are treated here, and I think as another woman you might have been more sympathetic to that.'

'But you let yourself be treated like that.' Paola smirked.

'Whatever do you mean?'

'Don't pretend, Maia. I know all about you and Armand. Everybody here knows about it, and what he's like.'

'That is none of your business, Paola.'

But a condescending smile was already forming on Paola's lips. 'He started with me, you know. Although all that was quite a few years ago.'

'Oh.'

'Is that all you have to say?'

'What do you expect me to say? Things here don't really come as so much of a shock to me anymore.'

'How very jaded you are. Why are you still here, anyway?'

'I don't have much to go back to at the moment. The Historian gave me a job and somewhere to live, and my painting hasn't gone too badly.' She didn't know why she was bothering to explain herself to this woman.

Florian's gathering had been presented to her as exclusive. But as Maia looked around, she saw the usual gathering of lowlifes from the Grand Tazi.

Where Florian's money came from, no-one was quite sure. When the sun went down, it was rumoured that he went out to play in the secret corners of the city, notably in the *Jardins de la Koutoubia*, where it was reported boys were brought in to satisfy the lusts of the men who lurked there. It seemed that Florian's activities were rather well documented by the gossip tongues, although evidently it did not stop people from attending his events.

It was whispered that Florian was known to prowl certain nightspots, as predatory as his fluffy white cat Mabouche, whom he loved with a passion matched only by his appetite for the working boys of the city. Maia thought that people were so bored here, they might easily read deeper into a rumour of Florian's supposed penchant for perversions. The expatriate community was so small.

When he finally saw her, Florian's scream made him sound deranged. 'Maria!' he squealed.

'It's Maia.'

'It was made for vice, this place! It could conceal an absolute retinue of concubines in linked rooms.' He was excited by the idea.

Maia looked at the man now standing beside her, and she recognised him as the American, Jacopo, with the Panama hat from whom she had been trying to escape in the souk.

'I've seen you before. What are you doing here? How do you know Florian?'

'I'm an artist. Perhaps we met at the Grand Tazi?' She smiled politely at his abrupt manner.

'An artist! Where did you meet Florian?'

'The only bar I go to here, the Grand Tazi,' Maia said wearily.

'Oh, that old place. I used to go there.'

'What made you stop?'

'A difference of opinion. That fat old guy Mahmoud. I didn't want to give him my money anymore. And he was always pushing drugs on me. I didn't want to get involved.'

'I see.'

'It looks like we have a lot in common. I am an antiques restorer.'

'Why would we have anything in common?'

'You are an expatriate, I'm an expatriate, and we both like art.'

He was staring at her, and Maia returned the look. He had a shock of bright orange hair, and two front teeth. His face was huge and his skin had a waxy pallor. He was monumentally ugly. She decided to make her excuses to leave as he began his story about a decidedly nasty case of hookworm.

Maia passed shadows hunching behind one another, flickering tongues, all-encompassing mouths set in protruding jaws. Cologne reeked strongly, cruelly pinching her nostrils.

As she thought about leaving, Maia's heart sank as she recognised the Bambages approaching. She nodded at them, and Martin Bambage looked away. Since they had last met, Lucy Bambage's skin had blistered and coarsened, her skin nearly crimson. Maia had no idea what to say to the woman, but Florian broke the silence.

'How do you like my riad? I rescued it from ruin!'

'It's fabulous,' said Lucy Bambage. 'The house, the night, the people, the people!' she bellowed hideously, and the insipid moon illuminated her unfortunate face. Lucy Bambage was even more tiresome than Maia remembered.

'Have you met Mabouche?' Florian asked, to no-one in particular, and he began to mumble delightedly to the cat, which jumped out of his arms, looked at him contemptuously, and went off to feed into the night. Maia was filled with a desperate, painful envy for this cat.

The Historian appeared, and without saying anything to Maia, he simply handed her another glass of wine. He seemed to already know the Bambages, for there were no introductions.

Maia walked on into the enormous courtyard and saw the fig trees and the huge hanging brass lanterns under which some guests were sprawled languidly.

She could hear people laughing at her, she felt sure of it. She heard Mahmoud's bellowing voice.

'She has had far too much again. You had better not let her drink any more.'

Maia couldn't reply. She saw them and tried to speak, but was unable. She wondered why he was so concerned about her alcohol levels of all things.

'Nonsense,' came the Historian's voice. Maia made her way over to them, as a tall, imposing man with a huge grey moustache came up behind the Historian and slapped him on the back, grabbing his hand affectionately. 'This is my brother,' said the Historian. Maia was flustered, reminded how little she really knew of the Historian and his former life.

And with that, a woman appeared beside the Historian's brother and linked his arm to hers.

'Noor is a doctor,' said the Historian. The woman smiled proudly, wearing a sleeveless fuchsia dress that on any other woman might have revealed a severe lack of taste. She held out her hand, and Maia was gracious.

'I've heard so much about you,' said the doctor's wife.

Maia ignored her and turned to the doctor.

'What type of medicine do you specialise in?'

'I only work with people who have contracted certain diseases. Sub-Saharan ones, mainly.'

'Do you know much about hookworm infestations?'

The wife sniggered.

'No, no!' Maia said. 'It's not me, I met someone earlier who started to talk about a nasty infestation.'

'Do you really think this is appropriate?' said the wife.

The doctor rubbed his chin. 'I would like to meet this man. I believe I may have once treated him.'

'He was telling me all about it. It sounded very unpleasant. His name is Jacopo. He is an antiques restorer. An American. He was telling me all about it but I walked away.'

'No wonder!' said the wife, who was still staring at her coldly with her brilliant blue eyes.

Maia turned back towards her. 'From who have you heard about me, exactly?'

'From Mihai, of course,' she said. Her voice had an American twang. Maia shrugged her off, turning and heading back into the throng of people lining the marble staircase, and up into the house.

16

Armand was returning from a meeting in Tangier. Having driven for hours, the prospect of the evening ahead filled him with an unusual sense of apprehension. He felt a slight twinge of guilt for testing merchandise on Maia, but she was useless to him now. She was becoming an irritation, more than a minor inconvenience. She would take anything he gave her. Perhaps it was best to leave her to her own devices. He thought of Maia's face. It was utterly unremarkable, and he found her beautiful only in her fear. He hated how her sad eyes followed him around. But the entire duplicity had filled him with a sweet, subtle pleasure; this was how real vice tasted.

The people with whom he had been dealing were particularly difficult. He knew that others were out to get him.

From a wealthy French family of Moroccan origin, Armand had enjoyed oblivion in the past but he had never allowed it to better him. Armand enjoyed control and power far too much for that. Yet Maia was the first woman who had ever tempted him to share the experience. When he watched people taste it for the first time, as he had watched Maia, he squirmed with distaste, not pleasure. He found it obscene, like watching someone else having sex. And although he was the executor of the Historian's wishes, he got as much pleasure from observing the emotions of that pitiful creature as he got from anything. He took part wholeheartedly in the man's misanthropic experiment, just as if it were his own, and in a mere few months they had closed the gap between a curious innocence and the sweet, succulent knowledge of evil. By nurturing her cravings, her inhibitions had waned. It was an amusing process, but she irritated him and she made him need to purge this irritation she caused him. He had led her gradually, with his devious steps, from humiliation to humiliation, and a degradation that he had found delightful, and now the gratification he derived from this cruelty had become a necessity to him. But recently he had sensed a change in her. Surely he was not losing his grip on her?

Armand played his cards close to his chest. He was renowned for his utter inability to trust. He never revealed much about himself because he believed that it would give people ammunition against him. He was always careful of being watched, or of having his calls intercepted, as a suspicious, residential foreigner.

It amused Armand to think that at this event of Florian's, he would be mingling with the officials and elite who were so dependent on men like him and Florian. For both their illegal income which buoyed up the city, and their own wealth, as well as their own private pleasures.

Armand stared blankly at the empty road as Palmeraie rose up ahead of him. Throwing his cigarette out of the window, he thought about Maia. She had got what she had come searching for, and now she was a casualty. What a perfect example of supply and demand.

★　★　★

At that moment, Maia was wandering aimlessly through the party, past the questionable figures and their debauched characters. She blundered through, passing their gargoyle-like faces, the sickly scent of their perfumes. The masque swirled on. Maia caught the eye of a man and he grinned at her, flashing his perfect white teeth, and she looked away. Through tall marble columns, she entered a maze of corridors, which led into rambling, ruined, empty rooms lit by large, white candles. In the centre of a small square stood a statue, a Priapus on a plinth. This Priapus was carved out of marble; it too was perfectly proportioned and grotesque in member. As she looked up, its smile leered down horribly.

At the far end of Florian's vast garden, grass covered the steps going down to the pool, around which strange statues were placed in a bizarre mix of tastelessness. Myriad lights reflected on the shallow water of the pool, so shallow that it was almost empty, and the soft spheres of the lanterns were illuminated as the aroma of oranges lingered delicately in the air. Every so often, the moon vanished behind the clouds.

Maia found herself stuck with Konstantin in a booth. He was moaning about his decrepit lodgings, the general hopelessness of his life. She could no longer stand him, and she stared at the blurred outlines of the passing figures.

'Have you seen the exhibition yet?'

'No, Konstantin, I've been exploring the house. It's huge. It reminds me of a Roman villa.'

Konstantin repeated as if from a textbook, 'The basic riad floor plan is plain and geometrically precise, consisting of rooms surrounding a central courtyard. It is a Roman villa designed to meet African climatic conditions. The riad provides shade and shelter from the African heat and the central courtyard is a peaceful oasis lush with plants and surrounded by fountains and pools.'

'Is that what you tell the tourists, Konstantin?'

'Unfortunately, yes,' he said and began to sob.

Maia felt only irritation. A coldness overtook her. 'What is it now, Konstantin?'

'I love, and I am not loved.'

'Who is it?'

'I hate him!' he said vehemently, clutching his fists together. 'You know who.'

Already she knew who it was. But she said, 'I don't know, Konstantin. Let's look around.'

'He is here! I know it! Don't lie to me. I hate him!'

'Why don't you let him go, Konstantin? You don't hate him.'

'I do, I do!' he cried out, like a child. 'I know he is here with Armand!'

He rounded on her, and hissed, 'Your inability to confront him is inexplicable.'

Maia looked at Konstantin; his face was horribly contorted as if a different man stood before her. She stood, abruptly, and walked along the edge of the pool, heading for the exhibition.

A series of photographs was being shown in

the crumbling garden, each one as similar and as insipid as the last. Maia thought they were rather banal. The feted photographer was Blake Cram, who had been lauded with compliments for his work for several American magazines. He was renowned for his use of light and focus. If this exhibition was the purpose of the party, as Florian had claimed, then why, she wondered, were they being exhibited far away in his underground garden? Blake Cram was nowhere to be seen.

Stands were placed around the periphery of the garden on which photographs were perched. The women in the photos stared blankly back at her, or their eyes were filled with pain. Not one of them exuded joy.

As the Historian approached, Maia looked around for a place, for someone to escape to. But she resolved herself, and her resentment made her cold, hard and angry. 'I saw Konstantin just now.'

'What, here?'

'I am sorry to disappoint you. No. Not here. Outside, into the garden.'

'I must find him,' said the Historian.

'He is very upset with you. What's going on?'

'I knew he would react like this.'

'Like what? You have done something to him too! What have you done?'

He was silent and walked away from her, leaving her rooted to the spot. Only when he had disappeared around the corner did she hear him laugh.

'Like waxworks,' said a low voice in her ear. Maia turned to look at Armand.

'The people, not just the photos.'

'Why is Florian showing them out here, not at the party?'

'Florian told me he likes the subterranean atmosphere for people to view the photographs. What he really means is that he doesn't like to detract attention from Florian.'

'Abracadabra!' A scrawny, sly-faced man jumped out in front of them. 'A beautiful couple!' he shouted, and then there was a bright flash before Maia could cover her face.

'Get him to stop it!' yelled Maia before she realised.

'Don't be so ridiculous.'

The man didn't acknowledge her. 'Your girlfriend is very drunk.'

'Ignore her. I'm Armand.'

'Rodger.' The two men shook hands and Florian rushed over.

'Are you enjoying yourselves? Isn't my house fabulous? Don't you love the photographs?'

'Not really,' Maia interrupted. 'I don't know why you think they are so good.'

'Shut up.' Armand shoved her in the small

of her back and Florian looked down his nose at her, as if staring at some sort of strange curiosity.

'Blake Cram has plenty of other talents as well as photography,' Florian lisped.

'I can't wait to find out what they are.'

'I'm afraid you can't tonight, Maia. He had to fly back to New York for a shoot.'

'Now that is a shame. I would have loved to have met him.'

'Blake Cram has a talent for revealing things as they are, for enlightening us about personal situations.'

Maia looked at a series of photographs of a well-dressed woman washing at a kitchen sink whilst holding a baby. There was nothing original there. Maia drank some more, and the photographs blurred before her eyes.

'The images are not to be taken at face value,' Florian was saying. 'Space creates a gap, a dislocation between how we are meant to view these photographs and what they actually represent.'

The nature of the photographs was ambivalent. Maia resented the fact that the women in the photos were made to look so available for consumption. They should have been lounging as if they were there of their own choice, not only at Blake Cram's demand. Maia did, however, admire how the artist had managed to capture the sky, a hint of freedom, a clear blue with a few whispers of clouds. Through the high windows, the sky filtered open and limitless, and the harsh geometrical tiles on the walls were dappled with sunlight, as if reflecting the fissures and gaps available to those women who might escape.

'Look at these photos!' Florian screeched. 'When we stalk the streets for clientele, the person is conditioned by social class, job, culture and nationality. There are several personas we use to suit different occasions. Yet we adopt a general persona based on our own superior functional type. Don't deny it. We all do it!' People began to look uncomfortable and they began murmuring amongst themselves again.

Maia was curious. 'What do you mean, Florian?'

'It is obvious! These things condition the persona. We can use several different personas to suit our own superior functional type, like thinking — whatever comes easiest to us.'

'But . . . '

'You all know, for example, that the unconscious side of the persona is the soul image, which is represented by the opposite gender of the individual.'

Here, Florian turned and gave her an unwavering stare. Maia strongly suspected that Florian did not much care for the opposite sex. She knew the theory about soul image; how it is an archetype, which can represent the whole of the unconscious, and is modified by one's actual experience of the opposite sex. In her blurry state of mind, she relished the idea of a debate.

'Do you identify with the anima, Florian?' She smiled at him, but he understood her underlying inference, that the complete identification with the anima can lead to effeminate homosexuality.

Florian ignored Maia's question, and continued with his monologue.

'Listen to me, don't you understand? Here we are all the same! Here we can be whatever we wish! The persona is a theatre mask. It is the face we wear for society. It is conditioned by many factors, and we adopt varying personas for different situations . . . '

Now, Florian pointed his finger directly at Maia.

'But note, guests, friends, the danger is identifying totally with the persona, being nothing but the role you play. And what role do you play, Maia? What is your role? I know who all these people are, but I don't know you. Who are you?' His voice was getting louder, until it was almost a scream.

'Calm down, Florian, you're wearing

yourself out,' said Paola, who had wandered over at the sound of raised voices.

'Now, the perfect persona can lead to a one-sided personality. You are alienated, Maia. You are afraid of dropping the mask and being revealed as hollow. You are a mask. A mask!' He reached for her face and flung himself upon her, shrieking, 'I want to rip off your mask, Maia. Let me rip it off!'

Armand grabbed him and tore him away from her. 'Take him away. He's completely out of it.'

'You drop your mask!' For a moment he seemed calm, and then he began shouting again. 'The magic hour is approaching!'

'What the hell is he shouting about now?' asked Armand.

Paola shrugged. 'He's just very exhausted.'

Armand was laughing at his hysterics. 'Like I said, waxworks. Let's get away from them.' Armand took Maia's arm and they walked until they were alone. Her heart beat frantically against her breast. In the corridor they passed Florian's cat, and without thinking she reached out and stroked its soft white coat. But suddenly its paw lashed out, and she realised she'd been scratched.

'Come with me, I'll clean you up.'

Maia looked up at him. 'I don't want to come with you.' Instinctively she shrank away from him. He scared and revolted her at the same time.

Armand ignored her dramatics, and led her through the crowd.

Maia tried to look at Armand properly, but she couldn't focus. 'What do you know about all these people, Armand?'

Armand was silent for a moment. 'You know he was struck off for irregular experiments in Amsterdam?'

'Florian?'

'Yes, of course. Who else? He is completely obsessed by the persona of the soul image, and the face we wear for society. You know he used to be a rent-boy himself? He had a powerful mentor here. And he thinks his cat used to be one too.'

'His cat Mabouche? Florian is completely cracked.'

Armand sat down beside her. 'Oh, he appears so. But he cultivates the image. He is more astute than he wants others to believe. It suits him for people to think he's mad. He is actually quite logical.'

He went to kiss her, but her lips were now set and hard against him and she pushed him away. But he kissed her anyway; he would decide when things started, and when they would end. A rush of sobs choked her, and he looked at her crumpled face.

'Control yourself.'

'What do you want with me? Why won't you leave me alone?'

Armand smirked. 'You never really wanted to be left alone. You really are disappointed, and that is amusing.' He stroked her face. 'You know, you are really quite sweet. But you like the idea of this older eccentric rambling around his renovated riad, showing photographic exhibitions, the bar you can go to every night and hear stories. It is our real life, not just entertainment for you. This ridiculous impression you have of expatriate life here can't be allowed to continue.'

'What impression?'

'That we are all here to amuse you. Characters that you can paint. Your mistaken view of the women here. Your preconceptions. This extended holiday you're having. Go home.'

'I can't. I may never go home.'

'But you must. You cannot stay here.'

'I want to be in peace. I like this life.'

'You will never belong here. Life here will always be impenetrable to you, for however long you stay. You want to be known for your painting. Here you will only achieve obscurity.'

'I don't want that life.'

'You are not in peace here and you never will be.'

'You set me on this path!'

'I never forced you to continue on it.'

'I never had a choice!'

'But you did. You wanted everything we have shown you.'

'I have nothing now to go back to.'

'And how is that our responsibility?'

She looked at the rough face, the powerful body. She took out from her small evening bag a verdant green trinket of a fertile green and held it up to the light. With her slim fingers, she steadily adjusted the tantalising vessel of her craving, and taking a small length of leather from the bag, unwound and tied it neatly around her arm. Taking up the syringe, she thrust it in, and sank back onto the tiles.

★ ★ ★

When Maia awoke several hours later, Armand was long gone. Her head was draped over the toilet seat and her arm was bleeding, her dress was undone. It was all unnaturally familiar to her.

She walked along the corridor until she heard discrete voices muttering through a half-open door.

'I hope Tangier went well. For all our benefit,' she heard the Historian say.

289

'They were difficult, but I brought them round.'

'Very good, my good men. Now, I must get back to this party,' said Mahmoud.

The Historian's voice cut the air. 'You aren't at the Grand Tazi now, Mahmoud. You owe us a share.'

'You do like to make money from the misery of others, don't you, Mihai?' said Armand.

'Do not pretend you don't appreciate my work. You benefit from my profits. It is very interesting,' he continued, stroking his chin, 'that now the girl perceives you as controlling her very survival itself.'

'What has she said to you?' said Armand.

The Historian sighed. 'I wish you had been more careful. She nearly threatened me. But she will not do anything. How can she? Where will she go?' He laughed. 'She cannot travel the way she is now. She is isolated. She is stuck here with you, a man who does not want her. She mistakes any attention from you as kindness, even cruelty. You must tell me how you managed it.'

'Do you hear me complaining about these trivial matters?' Maia saw Mahmoud's fist bang down on the table. 'This is a very good business we have here.'

'Yes, Mihai. Life is cheap,' Armand said.

For a moment Maia wondered if that was a tinge of regret in Armand's voice, but she knew it was impossible.

'Perhaps, if you want power . . . '

'I did not want power, Mihai. That is your field. I wanted the money.'

'And I need the rest of the money for my hotel. Do you really want to see me lose it?' Maia was surprised to hear Mahmoud pleading desperately with the men. 'You could go anywhere, do anything. Go home.'

The Historian laughed; it was a low, tense noise, full of bitterness. 'Do you really imagine, Mahmoud, that I want to go home? Understand this. I do not care about your problems. You concern yourself only with your hotel. Then you expect a huge share of the profits.'

'Please. I have put myself at risk also.'

'I will give you what I owe you. But don't try anything, Mahmoud. I hold just a little too much power here for that now.'

'And you are far, far too wise,' Armand said, mockingly.

'I am on your side, Armand,' the Historian said. 'The girl is irrelevant and you have my support. But do not push me.'

Maia stood at the slit in the door. Only now did the relationships between the men begin to clarify themselves in her mind. She was frightened, but the urge to stay and listen was compelling. It was only Mahmoud who belonged here, and she felt a strange flash of sympathy for him. Despite his huge bulk, he was powerless before the Historian. She wanted him to lighten the mood, to make another of his awful jokes, but he just sat there. Mahmoud and Armand were watching the Historian intently as he wandered about the room muttering to himself. She watched Mahmoud heave his bulk into a low chair, and with a surge of fear, she listened.

'I long to dispatch her,' said the Historian, 'but she is all too visible.'

Maia was sick to the pit of her stomach at the vision of the three men sitting around a table, discussing her corruption. She had allowed herself to be carried along, and could no longer remain dependent upon their whims. Her longing to escape them all struck her with a sudden and elemental force.

17

Maia left the building and walked down through black glades. The land dipped and the garden swept away from her. At the foot of the slope, she reached the shallow, rectangular pool. She observed the different people as they paraded around in front of each other.

'What a shame,' Lucy Bambage was whining. 'The pool isn't filled in properly.'

Maia looked down. It was true, the pool was very shallow.

'I've just had no time this year,' lisped Florian. He was very particular in his manner of speaking, talking in an oddly breathy voice. One had to strain to listen to him, although he often punctured this illusion with his ill-timed shrieks of excitement.

Armand was now in a corner with Paola. The revolting woman was rubbing herself up against Armand like a desperate alley cat.

There was Mahmoud, coming through the great doors towards her, and taking a drink from a waiter's silver tray. Mahmoud was in a discussion with three men; he was recounting a conversation he had had that afternoon with some trouble that had come to visit him at the hotel.

'One of them said to me, 'Are you clever, Mahmoud?' Yes, I am, I told that bald one. I am very clever!'

'Do you think they will bother you again?' asked the thin man with an emphatic moustache.

'No!' Mahmoud shouted. 'I gave them many *dirhams* and some female knickers as a going away present!' He began to chuckle, and turned to Maia. 'Why don't you come to my bar anymore?' he leered.

'I was there just a few nights ago, Mahmoud!'

But he had already fallen back into discussion with the men and chose to ignore her answer.

Lucy Bambage was asking her something. 'Have you been to the souk here?'

Mahmoud had fallen into an animated discussion, flailing his arms around so wildly that they hit a passing female guest on the chin. The men were standing back from him, as to keep his anger at bay.

'*Tout simple!*' yelled Mahmoud, and he strode vigorously from the room. From the corner of her eye, Maia watched him go, but Lucy Bambage continued to twitter.

'I can't blame you for how you behaved

that evening. It all turned out to be very disagreeable. Quite unpleasant. I wouldn't want you to imagine that we think badly of you. Martin was a little shocked, but he can be very uptight. I like to let myself go when we're abroad.'

'Don't worry, Lucy. I don't,' said Maia, wondering if Lucy Bambage really understood what a difficult situation she had rescued them from.

Martin Bambage was staring at her fastidiously. He now seemed fascinated by Maia and her erratic behaviour. She looked at their sumptuous surroundings and wondered why they were filled with such dreadful people. She heard the trickle from the fountain, saw the pine trees stretched up to the sky and quickly made her exit from the present company.

The doctor approached her. 'Where is this Jacopo you spoke of? I have failed to find him anywhere.'

'He was in the garden . . . ' Before she could finish her sentence, she was shocked to see the doctor's leering face drifting far too close.

'I know your type,' he said.

Maia pulled back from him. 'You know nothing.'

She took a sip of her whisky and the man pushed her down against the side of the wall before Maia started to retch. When she looked up, the doctor had left her. Beside the garden wall Paola was watching them, a strange look in her eyes.

Maia realised that she was more intoxicated than she thought. Around her, the faces of the guests whirled. The urge to vomit overtook her and then Armand was standing next to her once again.

'I can't leave you alone for even five minutes, can I?'

'You can leave me alone now.'

'I want you to hear about something, Maia,' Paola said as she simpered over to them. She took Maia by the elbow, and led her towards the exhibition. 'I want you to know that I knew the Historian you work for. A long time ago, I went to his wedding, as a guest of my Uncle Morris.'

'I wasn't aware the Historian had ever been married.'

'Oh, but of course he was. I had Armand too.'

Maia was shocked at her frankness.

Paola was looking at her. 'So he makes you feel that way too, does he? He ruined it all, you know. He was a very secretive man . . . he did things that no-one would ever have expected of him,' she said, completely oblivious to the inner turbulence that Maia was suffering. 'Yes,

I knew him very well. He was very different.'

'How do you mean, exactly?' prompted Maia, hoping she could remember the details in the morning.

But Paola was lost in her reminiscence, and a vague look washed over her face and she murmured something inaudible. Maia repressed an urge to shake her.

'Tell me again,' she said.

But Paola came to her senses. 'Now, if you'll excuse me,' said Paola, and she stumbled off into the darkness.

As she turned, the Historian was standing there, as if waiting for her to notice him. 'I think you are a silly little girl with a great deal to learn. You leave too much to chance.'

Maia was surprised at the sudden confrontation. 'You mean, I trusted too much, and wrongly.'

'When I took you on, I have to admit that I expected rather more.' His fish-eyes swam all around her.

'You are a lonely and disillusioned old man who can never go home,' said Maia, encouraged by the alcohol.

At first Maia believed he had been misunderstood, she felt injustice had been done to him, but he was revealed only as the blandest procurer and collector of human vices.

The Historian looked at her.

'You imagine that everybody wants to know your story. I came here, in awe of working for a famous Historian. But you are mundane. Just like my paintings, according to you. I pity you. In any case, I suppose you can't use and destroy people you have contempt for, Mihai.'

'You do not know the whole truth,' he said.

'People talk about you. They say you are utterly corrupt.'

'I know,' he said, grinning proudly. 'I know what they say. You know, Maia, you do not have a monopoly on suffering.'

'But you have a monopoly on inflicting it. I'll be gone tomorrow,' said Maia, before she realised she had made the decision.

'I will ruin your reputation in the art world. It will not be hard; your talent is weak. It is a mess. Just colour, cloying colour. You are deluding yourself if you believe that you have any chance of success.'

'I trusted you when I came here.'

'Never trust a historian,' he said as he began to chuckle.

'I know you were behind it. I want to leave.'

The Historian bent down towards her, and this time he spoke softly. 'You listen to me now. They gave you excitement, forgetfulness, what you craved when you came here to me. And how do you think you will cope on your own? You need us now. You are in no position to make demands.'

Maia saw how he now wanted to be rid of her. Before, he was able to use her, but now she had become damaging, and she would have to disappear. He was searching for a way to rid himself of her.

'Are we really reducing ourselves to this, Mihai?'

'As I have told you before,' he smiled nastily, 'when you look at a situation from different perspectives, there can be so many varying truths. You never imagined that he truly cared for you, surely?' He gave a hideous laugh. 'I employed him to corrupt you. For him, you have been a means to an end.'

'Look at how you treat your pet,' said Maia, reaching out for one last pathetic stab.

'Konstantin knows where his loyalties lie.'

The music throbbed and excitement was generating as though the evening was heading towards something intangible. Maia looked at the Historian; she recalled him sitting around a table with Mahmoud and her lover Armand, all three men discussing her and her use to them and then her ultimate fate; she surmised each one of their motives and her corruption and at this vision she was sick to her stomach.

'You are the coward, Mihai. You fled.'

'I came here to escape from achievement.'

'And look at you now.'

'I see, and yet look at what has become of you.'

His cold composure infuriated her. But when she spoke to him, he made her so nervous that she knew her face wore a foolish smile.

'What did you want from me? Why did you use me?'

'Must one do everything for a reason? Perhaps I do it merely to amuse. You are an experiment. Not so innocent, but certainly naive.'

'Does the process of corruption amuse you?'

'It does. I am bored, am I not? I have reached success in the world. I have what I need. I am growing old, and now I am becoming ugly. I am excluded from all I once held dear. My old colleagues forget me. A minor scandal, instigated by a jilted student — not even a boy, a student, a man, a man who expected too much, too many favours, then I was gone. They paid me nothing. I was forced out. A man like Konstantin. So you see, if the situation is considered from each perspective, there can be so many truths. Perhaps that is what you hoped to find in your paintings,' said the Historian with a cold and casual cruelty.

'The truth is what I found,' she said sharply, all effects of the drugs and alcohol having worn off.

'Ah, a hint of defiance. Finally, I like you. I get so irritated by weakness.'

Maia looked at the Historian and saw a washed-out, shabby old man. He looked at her with the cold, limp eyes of a fish.

'Do not believe you are indispensable,' he said. 'None of us are. You will never find happiness. Wherever you go.'

A wave of fatigue washed over her; she saw the absolute futility of the conversation. She wanted to leave. She was tired of all their façades, their relationships and their masks. She had reached the end of her period of curiosity with these people, and she no longer cared for the truth about any of them.

Her thoughts were interrupted. She could hear shouting, which grew louder by the minute. There was a shrill and terrible scream, and as she looked up, she saw Mabouche flying through the air. There was a sickening, almost human shriek of pain, and a heavy thud. In a shocking abruptness the cat was lying sprawled on his back.

Members of the crowd looked up, but of course there was nobody there. Florian was screaming like an old woman, and a man she had not seen earlier had his arms around him.

In the ensuing silence she stood frozen, looking down at the dead cat with distaste. Its head appeared to be cracked, and blood seeped onto the tiled floor. Maia was fascinated for a moment by the contrast of scarlet and cream, the creation of the pretty flowing puddles trickling between the tiles. She began to laugh quietly to herself, but in the midst of the horror, nobody paid her any attention.

'How horrifying,' said the Historian, in a diffident tone, and his face was expressionless.

'You should get that cleaned up straight away, Florian. You don't want to stain your beautiful tiles,' said Armand, patting the man's arm. He simply walked past the cat, and looked at Maia, almost apologetically. 'It was certainly swift.'

'It was cruel and pointless,' she replied. She could not understand how she could be so disgusted by a man to whom she had devoted herself. Now Maia knew who she was, and the door of her fantasies slammed shut. Armand shrugged, and stalked off into the night. Behind the door, the noise of Florian's party ebbed away.

Guests began to disperse rapidly, like

spirits. Some guests were still strewn across the floor, their bodies lying crumpled, and their masks discarded. A woman turned and moaned in her sleep as Maia stepped over her. Florian's lauded party had now become the remnants of a nightmare. She felt sick, an overdose of pleasure. For a long time Maia sat savouring the smell of the garden at dawn. As the darkness fell from her eyes, she recoiled as flashes of last night's sordidness came back to her. She tried not to remember, and she focused on the hibiscus opening to the dawn. Maia walked briskly from the house down the long driveway in search of a taxi.

Empty, barricaded properties circled the silent highway. Behind her the house rose up, brutally imposing in the pale light, all its glamour gone. The road was unnervingly exposed, and she hurried on, before suddenly breaking into a fast run. She realised she was no longer wearing shoes, and the smooth tarmac had melted away into rubble and potholes. The stones were cutting into the soft soles of her feet, but she was desperate to escape, and for now, at least, she felt no pain. She didn't care that her feet were being shredded beneath her; she needed to flee.

Evil, the final conclusion of her loathing, pulsated through her veins. Stumbling through the wreckage of abandoned refuse, iron and bricks, she was sharply aware of her own fatigue. Making her way back to the city's centre, she felt exhilarated at the thought of freedom. With each step, the shackles loosened. She was becoming herself again. As far ahead as she could see, the road stretched empty before her. Her anger tempered by fear, she moved on.

18

When Maia awoke to the flush of daylight, vivid images of ghastly clarity filled her mind, and the tears poured down her face. As she hastily packed her few belongings, the house was silent.

She left the house without seeing Ina or the Historian. But as she was getting into her taxi, Konstantin brushed past her in the dust swirling up the street, and he pretended he had not seen her. For a moment, Maia was unable to breathe. She watched Konstantin go. He was wearing his spectacles and a long, black cardigan, his head cocked to the side in a strange angle. She realised that despite her sympathy for him, he was just as suited to life here as the other men she had met, and she let him be, watching him slinking away into the dusk. She fled to Tangier, from where she arranged for her paintings to be sent to London. She wanted to disappear. The weaning process began.

For months she experienced an utter loss of will. Muscle aches, cold flushes and diarrhoea. She locked herself in a hotel room, screaming uselessly.

Maia was desperate to purge herself, to fully return to the old Maia. The nights in particular made her quake. Tormented, she suffered a raging despair. She slept through whole days, and she knew that the nights would soon fill her with their horrific dreams.

Maia dreamt of so many things: nuns who strangled babies and washed them out to sea, and the Coptic Christians of the East. She dreamt of the holy men who prowled the tombs and kidnapped little girls for their pleasures, and the same men of La Koutoubia, who wandered the nearby streets with their bright eyes and flickering tongues. Obscene in the dusk and gruesome in the darkness.

One dream in particular reoccurred each night. Maia was running through a dark, barren forest chased by mysterious creatures. Impeding her was an arrogant angel and his devils, an ogre holding a bellyful of babies and a monster followed by hordes of young men. All of them were foaming at the mouth, and someone was dragging himself laboriously, scraping his body along the parched earth. She was running, turning round constantly for fear that one of them might reach her. They were all shouting incoherent phrases. At a certain point, she stopped paying attention to the obstacles and began shouting back.

She saw the kind face of a man who, taking her by the hand, led her through dark secret paths to the foot of a high tower. He held up a finger and said, 'Ascend the stairs and never turn round. At the top, you will halt and discover what you sought in vain. Now, run, before you meet up with them again,' the man screamed, violently shaking his head.

'But you are my saviour! I don't need to climb the tower, I have already found you!' This time she was shouting joyfully.

'Run!' he repeated. Then his eyes changed, turning red and ravenous, and he ran off, foaming at the mouth.

Always in the background there stood that imposing, grinning Priapus, leering at her hideously. Inside the tower, something flew in and out of the window. A muttering woman in black appeared and a chess box was left on her windowsill. She caught a glimpse of a figure in black, sure that it was Ina scuttling away.

Maia looked at the chess box, scared to touch it. There were Arabic letters carved into the beautiful dark wood. She took a knife and ran it deftly along the rim of the box. Curves of red wax fell onto the floor, and she read the paper inside but understood nothing.

With a start, Maia jumped back, away from the box. Cockroaches fell onto the floor, scuttling away into unknown corners of the room.

A cold horror took hold of her. She began to scream and could not stop. She believed that Armand was shaking her. He looked at the box and took it away. Maia would wake, curled into a small knot, her head aching from screaming, and her body wracked with dry, soundless sobs.

When she thought she felt well enough to leave the room, Maia opened the door into the dark hallway. She anticipated confrontation with the monsters of her dreams. A succubus sat on her chest, a shroud wiped her face, a snake brushed her with its soft scales. Along the hallway ran her memories, and they sucked her backwards. She expected a hand to reach out to grab her, but when she opened the door, there was nothing there, and the sky had already begun to grow light.

Maia suffered delusions and hallucinations, the shudders and the terrors, the freezing and the extreme heat, until one morning, she felt well enough to leave her room. When she had arrived at the hotel in such a panic, she had paid the proprietor in advance. He was a pleasant enough man, with a wide, open face.

'I would like a receipt,' she had said.

'Why, do you not trust me? I have given you the keys.'

'I don't trust anybody,' she replied.

The hotel owner had looked her over. 'Many travellers get into your state,' he said, as he handed her the receipt.

But now, after many months, he seemed pleased to see her. He served her breakfast on the terrace, and handed her a French newspaper, which he held out to her between his sausage-like fingers. Autumn was approaching, and the air was gentle with a slight chill. Although she began to feel better, a nagging feeling still gnawed at her.

She struggled to read the newspaper article, as the small black print squirmed before her eyes. A pornographic scandal had shaken the country. Thirteen people had been arrested, one of them was Armand. His photograph was placed prominently in the centre of the article.

The men were paid only five hundred *dirhams*, and a promise of immigration to France. They were accused of encouraging sexual tourism. This was typical of the men she had left behind. Armand, described as a French national of Moroccan descent, was handed six years in prison, and Maia knew that for the moment, at least, she was safe. Relief swept over her, as she felt the last of their tight grip slip away.

What she found amusing about the

self-righteous, supportive tone of the article was the claim that 'Mahmoud Arouss, an upstanding member of the community and long-time hotelier, was not aware that the rooms of his hotel were being abused for such a pestiferous purpose.' Mahmoud had made a point of cultivating useful acquaintances, and she wondered how she had never suspected. The hotel owner peered over her shoulder as he placed her breakfast on the table, and sniffed.

'Whatever they say about him, he knew. He was no decent man.'

There was no mention of the Historian. He had gone utterly undetected. Maia wondered what Mahmoud, with his corpulence and his convivial façade, would do now. In shock, she nodded; she folded the newspaper carefully, laid it on the table, and went out of the café, blinking into the light.

She entered the modern streets, looking at the women mixing freely; at the people sitting on steps and strolling along. The views from the port were sweeping and it was a beautiful clear day. She watched the men lounging on the front, looking wistfully across the straits, imagining a different life. These were Armand's victims, thought Maia, whilst Mahmoud was his associate, the Historian, his boss. Visible in the distance was Spain, the land of plenty, with employment in bars, driving taxis, sweeping floors, all for the dim possibility of citizenship. In this gateway to Europe, some of these men might pack themselves into small boats to struggle across the nine choppy miles, which might transform their lives of poverty into one of supposed wealth. They might evade men like Armand, or they might submit to the oblivion on offer.

She found herself desperate to leave Tangier. Her affinity with the city was too great; like her, the city was still living under the shadow of its sordid, notorious past.

Maia walked up the Rue d'Angleterre to St Andrews, and the quiet of the church was an antidote to the cacophony outside. She sat for a while in a pew, and then she went into the lemon tree filled garden. The cemetery was deserted, and she passed an hour wandering amongst the graves, thinking about the expatriates who had once lived here, where they had revelled in a place where nothing was truly forbidden and anyone, or anything could be purchased at the right price. Here in the cemetery, where the dry air felt cool, she wandered amongst the white tombs stretched out into the distance like great hunchbacked whales, marooned and forgotten on a foreign shore.

Maia left Tangier by bus, when she was still

in the last struggle of her fight against her cravings. She travelled for a while through the desert wilderness, in the grip of a fiery, vengeful rage.

But when she returned to her own country, she found that her will to fight was replaced with something else. The adventure was over. She experienced a sense of a key turning in a lock, the faint heartburn of the displaced.

In London, she took back her flat and received uplifting news from her agent, who was surprised at her sudden return. A gallery had expressed interest in exhibiting her paintings. Somehow word had got out about her project to portray covered women in a different light, and a few months after she returned from Marrakech she was finally invited to display them.

Maia was filled with excitement at the opportunity to finally show what she had been working on for so long. Her exhibition was full every night for the first week. Commercially, she achieved the success that for so long had eluded her, but the reaction of the audience surprised her. The paintings on which she had laboured for hours, focusing on the women going about their daily tasks, laughing in the private courtyards, playing with their children, and then ignored in the streets, were ultimately ignored in favour of her paintings based on what she had seen in the *hamam*, and from when she had used the disloyal Safira as her model. They called to her mind those long, hot evenings stretched out in the shade of her room. When she looked at them, sensations flitted through her, but it soon changed from a desperate anger to a melancholy sadness. Although the other paintings were lauded as controversial, it was her series of paintings of women in varying poses which were most popular. Individually, or in intertwining groups, they raised their arms, arched their backs, reclining passively in the habitual anatomical distortions of the female nude.

Maia continued to follow the case with interest. Armand was sentenced for many crimes. He had produced pornographic films, incited prostitution, and dealt in illegal drugs. Mahmoud did not go to prison — he had too much influence for that. But to make a show of intolerance, the Grand Tazi was closed down. She had learned in Marrakech that life could be a delicate balance. It was a place of seductive contradictions.

In an interview for an art magazine, Maia told the journalist of her disappointment, her worries that in painting the women she had only served to inflate the whole host of stereotypes about the female. But as she expressed her disenchantment with what she had attempted to do, the journalist, who with his arched, dark eyebrows and dismissive demeanour reminded her of the Historian, was unsympathetic. Barely moving his thin, pursed lips, and gingerly sipping his coffee, he dismissed her anxieties. He made her feel exactly as mundane as she was convinced she had become. He asked her why she had rejected the smooth qualities of painting.

'I do not simply wish to recreate scenes,' she said.

'It seems to me that you have a need to force the spectator to be aware of the physical act of painting, by making every gesture of the brush visible to the eye.'

Maia wondered at the man's hostility. 'I do not think so.'

'Why do you sometimes paint the female figures in red, when we all know perfectly well that they are draped completely in black?'

'Just because something is black does not mean that it should necessarily be painted as black.'

For a moment Maia was silent. She was recalling a party at which strange conversations had taken place, where indistinct characters peopled her memories and her dreams. People drifted towards her, sat with her, rejected her with their refusal to meet her eyes, before drifting away to other people. She was forced to raise her eyes and voice, to be solid and open. But then she would always hear her own voice out loud, as if it was coming from someone else.

'In fact I am consoled,' Maia continued, 'because I have refused to depict the faces of the women in my paintings.' She pointed out the blank, beige faces of the women staring out from the canvas.

'And why is that?' asked the journalist.

'In showing the faces of the nude women, I would open them up to further surveillance. The viewing audience would invade their privacy. In this way, the woman shuns and rejects the overpowering viewer, and retains her mystery, her safety.'

'Is that your concern?'

'To show their features would be to contradict my values.'

'What difference does it make? You have shown them nude in any case.'

In a short space of time she was already taking a rabid dislike to this journalist, but the interview was vital. After so long, finally she was poised on the very edge of success.

'A true artist can paint faces,' the journalist said, trying to rile her. 'Do you perhaps feel that you are not competent to depict them?'

'No, I never said that. I can paint faces; of

course I can paint them!' she protested. In her head she heard the Historian's voice telling her, 'You will betray those ideals of yours.'

Later on in the exhibition, it emerged that it was not the nudes that were the most popular, but another painting that was lauded. It was her favourite work; a painting she had done of Safira, a nude woman holding a mirror to her face. The face in the mirror image was blank, whilst the nude woman on the rooftop was surrounded by veiled women absorbed in their daily tasks, and a café below, crowded with men, staring up at the scene. This painting, Maia considered, was indicative of how strongly she had come to view life, and to depict people with irony. The very limbs, the hands and feet of the men in the café trailed off to convey their listlessness and despair; the despondency she had experienced with the men in the café in the Atlas mountains.

Her agent had named the painting, 'From the Erotic to the Mundane', and people worked themselves into a frenzy attempting to discover what Maia had intended to say when she had painted the scene. The truth was that Maia had not intended to say anything; it was simply a personal memoir to herself. She enjoyed the attention, took the money, and satisfied herself with the fact that she was now recognised as a successful woman in the eyes of her peers, even if she did feel some residual guilt for exploiting her own sex. But this, she comforted herself, was what women always did, and if she did not do it, then another woman certainly would. This, she realised, was not the only truth. Men act, and women appear and watch themselves being looked at. She had been handed the opportunity to freely express her sensuality.

Close to the end of her exhibition, Maia was appalled to receive a letter from the Historian. She read the scrawled handwriting: 'Did you obtain what you wanted? So this is your sacrifice. One does not escape. MF.'

Her success had made her bold; she knew of his private despair, his academic failure, his financial ruin. She no longer had time to mourn for her lost integrity. He could never touch her now.

As time went on, memories of the Historian no longer made her shudder, and she began to find it difficult to even remember his face. Surely, when she failed to recall details about him, forgetfulness was the ultimate revenge. She was free from her cravings, from the Historian, from Armand, from George.

Years later, Maia returned to the city. Everything had shifted; nothing was in its right place. Its air of authenticity and dissoluteness had disappeared. There were more foreigners, greater openness and more openly distasteful behaviour, but there was greater transparency, too. The hotel where she stayed was so bland it might as well have been in London. She wandered the streets, almost hoping to at least catch a glimpse of her former associates.

When Maia looked back upon all the wretched deceivers she knew that summer, amongst all the liars and the false sophisticates desperately hawking their false histories to disbelieving acquaintances, the only character that Maia was able to recall with anything approaching fondness was Konstantin, who maintained his constant vigil in the private bar at the Grand Tazi.

As she sat and looked at the boarded-up building, she forgave herself for the vulnerability that had once made her so attractive. She turned to face the sky. She had spoiled this city for herself.

But an unbearable truth stole up on her, a truth so unpalatable that she could hardly bear to entertain it: the fact that she had been shown her most authentic self. They had shown her who she was.

Sitting outside a café in the clear freshness of a November morning, Maia asked the waiter if he had heard of the Historian and his work.

'Yes. I know he used to live in the medina. Everybody knew him. He was friendly with the owner of this place. Before the scandal.'

The Historian merely aroused a quiet horror in her. Once he had terrified her, but ultimately he had revealed himself as powerless. As Maia listened to the waiter, she considered him and thought how friendly he was, how polite, so different to the men she had once known here.

'What scandal?' she asked sharply, wondering if the Historian's involvement had been discovered. But it was evident that the Historian had friends in high places, for the waiter was referring only to the Historian's death.

'It was a strange time. I was a boy, but I still remember it. A two-headed cow was found wandering the Bab Agnou gate and the streets were in uproar.' The polite waiter was eager to tell her about the rumour of madness that contributed to the Historian's death. 'The owner of the Grand Tazi had disappeared.'

'Mahmoud.'

The waiter was surprised. 'You knew him?'

'We were acquainted. Go on.'

'The police didn't pursue him, he had some friends. But the Historian, this man you

319

talk of, he died insane. He was a recluse, I hear, and after the Grand Tazi went, people left. The foreigners you see here now, they are all new. None of the old lot we used to see. But the appearance of the cow caused a terrible stampede, and this man was caught up in it.'

'And that was how he died?' An image came to Maia of a frail, white Historian, caught in the excited stampede.

'Yes. Horrible, isn't it?'

'You really were there? Surely though, it was just a rumour?'

'Exactly! But people still believed such things happened. They still do. But I never came face to face with the man you talk of,' the waiter said.

'He was a miserable man,' said Maia.

The waiter said nothing, and he just stood there, looking at her as if waiting for her instructions.

'I know the gate. It reads, 'Enter with blessing, serene people'.' Again she imagined the Historian, flailing around desperately in the crowd, crying out and no-one paying attention. His face came to her mind: the knitted eyebrows, his voice, precise and low, his maliciousness. His only gift to her had been a terrifying glimpse of degradation.

'That's the one,' said the waiter.

320

'It was a fitting end for him,' she said, and smiled brightly at the waiter.

The waiter looked down at Maia strangely as he poured the tea into her glass and hurried away. For hours Maia stayed sitting there, sipping her tea, looking down into the glowing street.

We do hope that you have enjoyed reading this large print book.

Did you know that all of our titles are available for purchase?

We publish a wide range of high quality large print books including:
**Romances, Mysteries, Classics
General Fiction
Non Fiction and Westerns**

Special interest titles available in large print are:
**The Little Oxford Dictionary
Music Book
Song Book
Hymn Book
Service Book**

Also available from us courtesy of Oxford University Press:
**Young Readers' Dictionary
(large print edition)
Young Readers' Thesaurus
(large print edition)**

For further information or a free brochure, please contact us at:
**Ulverscroft Large Print Books Ltd.,
The Green, Bradgate Road, Anstey,
Leicester, LE7 7FU, England.
Tel:** (00 44) 0116 236 4325
Fax: (00 44) 0116 234 0205

THE MOON AROUND SARAH

Paul Lederer

Born with the ability to speak, but not the inclination, Sarah lives in silence. She is surrounded by the noise of her bickering family, who are gathered to discuss the selling of the family homestead. There is no room for sentiment and a young selectively mute girl is not a burden any of them wants to shoulder. Escaping from this madness, she befriends a young man who finds her silence eloquent. If they are to understand each other, and escape the shadow of her family, they must learn a deeper form of communication.

THE SKINNING TREE

Srikumar Sen

During the Second World War, nine-year-old Sabby lives in a Calcutta family where sophisticated British habits such as bridge and dinner parties co-exist with Indian values and nationalism. But when he is sent to a boarding school in northern India, that world is soon forgotten; and Sabby is subjected, with his fellow pupils, to the teachers' draconian regime. The boys themselves take on their educators' cruel traits, mindlessly killing animals and hanging their skins on a cactus, before their thoughts turn to even more sinister schemes. Conspiratorial whisperings and plans of revenge spiral into a tragedy engulfing Sabby, in an engrossing novel exploring human nature's darkest facets.

EVERY PROMISE

Andrea Bajani

When Sara leaves him — broken by their inability to conceive — Pietro reverts to a younger self, leaving the dishes unwashed and the bed unmade. Soon after, Sara confesses that she is pregnant from a casual encounter, and comes to rely on Pietro's mother for support. This leaves the three of them in an uncomfortable limbo, unable to move on. Into all of this falls Olmo, an old man haunted by memories of war. When he asks Pietro to travel to Russia on his behalf, to right a wrong from his past, Pietro sees a chance for a new beginning.

ENON

Paul Harding

The Crosbys had lived in modest bliss in the small idyllic town of Enon for generations. But after the tragic loss of his thirteen-year-old daughter, Charlie Crosby finds himself the last living member of his family. Paralyzed by his loss, Charlie allows his relationship with his wife to rapidly disintegrate. His despair spreads like a disease and he finds himself living in squalor with a heavy dependence on pain killers. Unable to lift himself out of his misery, Charlie embarks on a dream-like form of remembering, wandering the forgotten paths of the town, and of his history, in an attempt to make sense of his loss.

A THOUSAND PARDONS

Jonathan Dee

Separated from her husband, Helen and her twelve-year-old daughter Sara leave their family home for Manhattan, where Helen must build a new life for them both. Thrust back into the working world, Helen takes a job in PR — her first in many years — and discovers she has a rare gift: she can convince arrogant men to admit their mistakes, spinning crises into second chances. Faced with the fallout from her own marriage, and her daughter's increasingly distant behaviour, Helen finds that the capacity for forgiveness she nurtures so successfully in her professional life is far harder to apply to her personal one . . .

BEST LAID PLANS

Patricia Fawcett

The pressures of the recession have left the Fletchers' business in trouble and the family in a similar state of disarray. The lack of a bond with her daughter, Amy, has left Christine Fletcher feeling guilty about the amount of time she spends instead with her artistic daughter-in-law, Monique. But Christine's husband and daughter don't believe Monique to be as innocent and uncomplicated as she seems. A family Christmas reveals surprises, and when Monique disappears to her cottage in France and Amy's new relationship runs into trouble, Christine in forced to act to save both her family and the business.